GUILD OF IMMORTAL WOMEN

DAVID ALAN MORRISON AND H. L. MELVIN

BOOK PUBLISHERS NETWORK
Changing the World One Book at a Time

Book Publishers Network
P.O. Box 2256
Bothell • WA • 98041
Ph • 425-483-3040
www.bookpublishersnetwork.com

10 9 8 7 6 5 4 3 2 1

Printed in the United States of America

LCCN   2014947374
ISBN   978-1-940598-44-4

Editor: Barbara Kindness
Cover Designer: Laura Zugzda
Book Designer: Melissa Vail Coffman

*"When one is immortal,
one should keep a low profile."*

—Quote embroidered across the top of each of the fifty wall-size tapestries inside the historic mansion in Montpelier, Vermont, dubbed 'The Bastille' A single family has occupied The Bastille since its construction in 1771.

I N THE WOODS OF MONTPELIER, Vermont, a loud crack cut through
the early morning silence, a flash lit up the dell, and a foot appeared
out of the early morning mist. A muscular, dark-haired Frenchman
uncoiled from the nothingness, stretched for a moment, and then
offered his hand to the empty air. A fleshy, tattoo-covered arm emerged
from the void, reaching out to the handsome Frenchman. He pulled a
plump twenty-four-year-old woman with long, oily red hair and acne
scarred skin onto the soft grass.

"Oh. My God!" the young girl gasped, looking around at the glade.
"It. Worked!"

The man grunted as he wiped his leather boots on the turf and
inspected his sole for animal droppings.

The young redhead squealed, leapt like a child into his arms and
wrapped herself around his neck.

He pulled her body against his and ran his palms down her back,
holding them onto her copious cheeks as she ground her hips against
his. Just as his tongue found her lips, her squirming stopped and she
pulled away. "Oh…I don't…I feel…really. Really icky," she muttered.

Then he felt the young woman wither. Her flaming red hair faded
to gray. Her pimply forehead dried and cracked with age. Her pink
cheeks turned pale and hollow. Her plump body wilted, leaving her
clothes hanging from her flesh-covered skeleton. Her many tattoos
converted to small splotches of black ink on gossamer skin.

With a grunt of disgust he pushed the old woman away. She
stumbled backwards, stared at her hands, looked to him in horror and

mumbled, "Like. What. Went wrong? What…" The last of her words were lost in a violent gasp as she clutched her chest and fell to the ground with a dull thud.

He bent over and lifted the eyelid of this once-nubile young woman. The green of her emerald eyes stared up at him—dead and empty.

"Damn. That was extremely unfortunate." He pulled out a pack of Gauloises, lit up and kicked at the corpse as he sucked on the cigarette. He flipped open his cell phone, pushed the speed dial button, and waited for the Doctor to answer.

ANTHONY GORDON 'MATT' MATHERS, Junior, took one last picture of the dead woman's ankle tattoo, then rocked on his heels while surveying the crime scene. This was definitely a shame. Of all the things that could be associated with the Ladies, why did it have to be a murder? A dead body showing up on their grounds was a hell of a way to pay them back for their generosity. While not quite 'celebrity' status, Eleanor and the Other Women of the Bastille were regional icons. He had seen them countless times at fundraisers, charity events and, of course, the yearly Medieval Faire they hosted on the grounds of their immense estate. Their mass acreage, vast amounts of old family money, and public generosity were renowned throughout New England. He had yet to meet anyone who disliked a single member of the Emerson family for the past hundred years. The joke around town was that they were Vermont's guardian angels, taking on human form at will. Well, with any luck, and Janet Gage's help, he could keep this one off the media radar. He'd be damned to see unnecessary negative publicity reflected on these people.

He sighed and jiggled his keys. The afternoon breeze tickled his thick hair and he caught a whiff of tangy sweetness. Lavender? Honeysuckle? The gardens surrounding the main building were thick with scented flowers. Matt couldn't pinpoint the specific fragrance. Not such a great detective, was he? He should have taken horticulture as one of his electives in college rather than European history.

He stopped rocking and closed his fist around his keys. This corpse didn't make sense: Caucasian, roughly eighty years old, dressed in traditional medieval clothing: light green bodice, long chintz dress, and simple leather shoes. No snaps, no Velcro, and ties in lieu of zippers. The belt around the woman's waist was roughly cut from a larger piece of leather and the holes for the simple buckle were slits of a knife instead of the clean, circular holes punched by a machine. Mathers was not an expert in costumes, but it sure looked authentically medieval.

The scene was full of inconsistencies: a tongue piercing, several earrings adorning the ears, and a brightly colored Mickey Mouse tattoo. He made a note to research the history of Disney—the year Steamboat Willie morphed into Mickey Mouse may be an important fact. While it was unusual for women to get tattoos in the 1950's and 1960's, it did happen. But in 1960, this woman would have been forty years old. What forty-year-old woman in the year 1960 would get a colorful Mickey Mouse tattoo and a tongue piercing? He knew tongue piercing was popular with the younger crowd, but older folks? The waitress from Denny's he dated last year had a pierced tongue. He thought it disgusting at first, but three dates later, he decided tongue piercings were a good thing. He shook his head to erase the images of her. It wasn't his fault she stopped returning his phone calls. Was it? What was it women wanted, anyway?

Mathers toyed with his keys again. Regardless of the oddity of the circumstances, at least tracking the identity of an eighty-year-old woman with a Mickey Mouse tattoo and tongue piercing would be easy. How many could there be?

Meanwhile, Janet finished her stroll around the area and stood making notes on some important-looking forms. He wasn't sure what she did for the Department of Forests and Parks, but she sure looked professional doing it. The two met a few years ago when Mathers replaced Detective Williams on a murder investigation. Several months later, during a manhunt for a suspected terrorist who had fled into the mountains between Vermont and New Hampshire, he made friends with her husband, Sal, and the three of them had become quite close. She proved herself a great guide as well as an all-around smart gal.

Mathers returned his gaze to the body when he heard Gage call out to him. "I've got to call this in, Detective."

"Don't call me that."

"Sure thing, Anthony Gordon." Janet's voice carried the tinge of sarcasm that Mathers found as annoying as endearing.

"If you ever call me that name in public…"

"I don't know why you hate 'Anthony'. It's a great name," Janet said, motioning to the radio.

He nodded for her to call it in. "I'm done here. Anthony was my father's name."

"So?"

"I don't even know who he is."

"And 'Mathers'?"

"Mom's surname."

Janet pointed to the corpse. With a huge sigh, she added, "Why do these things always happen the day AFTER vacation?"

"Luck?"

Janet chuckled and grabbed the handpiece to the radio. Anthony Gordon, aka "Matt" Mathers, was a pleasant chap: tall—about six one, six two maybe—with jet-black hair, closely trimmed beard, and piercing eyes. 'Dashing' was the word she used to describe him to Sal. Janet liked Detective Mathers because not only did he resemble her college professor in the Forestry program, but because Sal and he were such good friends. It struck her odd that her anti-social husband insisted the detective drop by for dinner whenever he was in town. Not that she minded. Sandwiched between two handsome men drinking beers made her feel somehow…wicked.

"Yeah, what?" Alice's gruff voice shot back through the Jeep's speaker. Mathers smiled. He could imagine Alice sitting at her ancient desk, hunched over a pile of folders, thumbing her nose at the NO SMOKING sign with a cigarette dangling from her lips, gray hair a frantic mess upon her head. Did he like her because of that, or because Alice reminded him of his grandmother? Either way, the woman was a bitch-on-wheels and nothing caught his attention more than a strong-willed woman.

"We have a situation, Alice." Janet said into the mic.

"Situation?" the woman mimicked in an all-too-familiar tone. "What kind of situation?"

"We're going to need the Sheriff's office down here."

"Where're you again?" Alice asked. Janet could almost hear the papers on Alice's desk flying as she searched for her work order. "Out at Eleanor's place?"

"Ten-Four," Janet sighed. "The Bastille."

"Jesus F Christ, Janet!" Alice spat, "you're only out there to check the god-damned drainage on their back forty! Pace out the flags, sign the authorization forms for the damned Faire, and get your ass back here. Cooper called in sick this morning and I've got those New York developers on my ass about the building permit. I need some god-damn help here!"

Janet winced. Alice's bark was worse than her bite, but her bark was damn painful. "Alice. I found a body."

Silence.

"Alice?"

"Say again?" The fury had evaporated from her voice and Alice sounded almost stunned.

"Caucasian female. Approximately eighty. Medieval dress."

"If this is your idea of a joke… "

"It's not!" Janet shot back with equal gruffness. Mathers chuckled and Janet silenced him.

"What the hell is an eighty-year-old woman doing in those clothes?" Alice asked.

"Halloween? It's fucking June," Alice snapped. "I'll get the Sheriff's office. You hang on there."

"I hope you won't get reprimanded for this," Mathers said, leaning against the Jeep.

Gage shook her head. "We'll just tell 'em Sal invited you to dinner and we swung by the Bastille on our way so I could issue the permit. Then, oops! A dead body. No problem."

"How's Sal doing?"

"He's fine," Janet smiled broadly, "he's got a new hobby. He's building model cars." Mathers laughed. "Seriously. Like he's ten or something. Well, keeps him out of trouble." She rolled her eyes and continued. "He's on his yearly 'we-have-to-use-the-grill' kick. I think he's torching some chicken for dinner."

"Great. Love barbecue," Mathers said, looking back toward the body. "I'm afraid this incident will be a terrible topic for dinner conversation."

"Nah," Gage laughed, "Sal's a good guy. Anything to help the Ladies."

"No footprints," he said.

"What?"

"No footprints indicating any sign of entry into the glade despite the wet ground. Just...what looks like boot prints...exiting the area. No overhanging limbs, either. Couldn't have dropped down from above. How did she get there?"

Gage scanned the area. Trees surrounded most of this part of the Bastille's property, but the dead woman lay on the grassy patch in the middle of a small ring of trees.

"Well, she had to have gotten there somehow. She didn't just... materialize out of thin air."

"You there, Janet?" Alice's gruff voice bellowed from the radio.

"Yeah, I'm here."

"Sheriff's boys are on their way." Alice coughed a hard, long cough before continuing. "They're putting in a call to Mathers."

The ranger shot a glance at Mathers. "Tell 'em I got Mathers with me."

"What?"

"We were on our way to dinner."

"Convenient," Alice said.

"Yeah."

"So I guess Sal knows you're alone in the middle of the woods with a handsome bachelor man?"

"He's at home grilling us some chicken. I keep him on a tight leash."

"Just wait for the Sheriff," Alice said. "Out."

Janet hung up and settled into the Jeep to await the arrival of the Sheriff. She watched as Mathers wandered towards the body again and stood staring. *Damn, he is handsome.* She sighed and fiddled with the dials on the radio.

"This is private property," Mathers' voice took on that distant quality that told Janet he was analyzing clues. "Private drive. Fenced property. Gated grounds around the house." He turned to her and asked, "Makes one wonder if it's an inside job, doesn't it?"

Janet shook her head. "The Ladies?" She laughed. "They wouldn't harm a fly."

"I heard that younger one…"

"Abbey?"

"Abbey. She's a bit…off." He tapped his temple for emphasis.

Janet shook her head. She respected him; too bad he lived in a world of his own.

ABBEY PANICKED, clawing towards the surface of the water as the weight around her leg pulled her farther into the deep. From beneath her, a dull, rhythmic *THUD THUD THUD* echoed up out of the darkness as she struggled towards air. *THUD THUD THUD*. She could see the sun above her, its rays sending rainbows shooting across the surface of the ocean as she felt herself sinking, her world becoming murkier, smaller and dimmer... *THUD THUD THUD*.

Abbey snapped awake at the pounding on the door. She bolted upright in bed, gasping for breath. Her pajamas stuck like glue to her body.

"Abbey? Edna?" called the voice on the other side of the door. Normally, Abbey felt comforted by the familiarity of that cheery, nasal voice that only spoke in questions. Today it grated on her nerves. "Rise and shine? Are you two up and showered?"

A weight sank onto the bed next to her and Abbey managed to force a smile at her roommate, Edna. The thin octogenarian clutched Abbey's sweaty palm in her bony grip and smiled back, her pink gums standing out against her pale skin. "You dreamed again last night," the feeble woman said, patting Abbey. "I heard you crying in your sleep."

Abbey turned to avoid Edna's eyes. She inhaled deeply, letting Edna's sweet cologne—a mixture of cinnamon and lavender—calm her. "Edna, you need your teeth."

"Bad teeth. They hurt," Edna whispered.

"Edna? You need to come get your meds? The nurse is dispensing them now?" The cheery voice continued its incessant questioning through the closed door.

Abbey forced herself to breathe normally. She closed her eyes to chase the last remnant of the dream back into the recesses of her unconsciousness.

"I'm fine, Edna."

"Abbey? Edna? Am I going to have to walk into your room?"

Edna spun and screamed at the door, "WILL YOU SHUT THE FUCK UP YOU STUPID WHORE!" Then, calmly, she winked at Abbey and whispered, "I stole some Tylenol from the nurse's station if you need one. They're under my pillow."

The voice behind the door tittered shrilly. Abbey sometimes pitied Heather, the woman behind the voice. Heather spoke in question marks and tossed her hair with such force Abbey feared the girl would give herself whiplash. Heather bragged about her daddy paying for the Certified Nursing Assistant training and her mother getting this job for her. Working at this loony bin wasn't a job for Heather; it was a holding pattern.

"Now, now, Edna? Is that bad language I hear?"

"CLOSE YOUR DAMN RAT TRAP, YOU IGNORANT BITCH!" Edna ran her thin fingers through her sparse gray hair and stood up. "Are you hungry, dear? I could bring you coffee from the dining hall. I never drink mine." Abbey shook her head.

"We are fine, Heather. Thank you for your concern," Abbey yelled to the closed door. "We will join everyone at breakfast in a moment."

"Sure?" Abbey could almost feel Heather tossing her hair back. "I'll be waiting for you at the nurse's station, okay? Want your belated birthday cupcake?"

"ABBEY DOESN'T NEED YOUR FUCKING SHITTY BIRTHDAY CUPCAKE !" Edna tenderly kissed Abbey's forehead and whispered in her ear, "I love messing with that girl's mind!" She giggled and shuffled to the door. As she turned the handle, she whispered over her shoulder. "Happy birthday, Abbey. I love you." Abbey nodded.

"Edna, be nice to Heather. She's just doing her job."

Edna nodded and smiled. "If that airhead girl had wings, she'd fly backwards. But you, Abbey, you're an angel." Abbey shrugged. "I'll see you in group?" Abbey nodded. Edna smiled and grabbed the door handle. "BACK AWAY FROM THE DOOR, YOU WHORE, I'M COMING THROUGH!" Edna winked at Abbey before opening the door and exiting.

LYNN SWANSON HIT SAVE ON THE KEYBOARD, leaned back in her chair and toppled a pile of papers with her elbow. Reaching down to pick them up, she farted. *Great.* She sighed in resignation. This whole month had sucked, so why not have gas, too? When she kicked off her fortieth birthday by playing Cribbage with her parents and their seniors group, she should have known the year was going to be a bummer. The day after her birthday, a wasp bit her when she pursued the neighbor's cat into the garden in hopes that the gorgeous, barrel-chested blond would be impressed by her gusto. He was. So was his boyfriend. Yesterday, a cop cited her for both a non-functioning tail light and for not wearing a seatbelt. Normally a uniformed police officer would add a thrill to her catatonic sex life, but he was one of those who wore mirrored sunglasses and swaggered. As he took his place near the driver's door, he stood with his crotch at her eye level and with one look, Lynn realized why he was so angry: he was still waiting for his testicles to drop.

That excitement paled in comparison to last night, when she spent two hours staring at her keys hanging from the ignition while waiting for the automobile club to arrive, which meant she had to be at work by six o'clock this morning to finish paperwork she should have done last night.

She no longer believed that her life sucked worse than anyone else's. She was *positive* of it. Actually her life had skyrocketed out of suckiness, past depressing and shot into "pathetic." And she had only been over the hill for two days.

She looked out her window at the single-story brick building that housed the patients. Another fun, fabulous day had dawned here at 'The Meadows' which, ironically, was hidden deep within thick woods. Most of the patients in the facility were rich people from richer families whose only psychological problem was a mild case of sleep disorder. She did get to treat the occasional addict, anorexic or nervous breakdown, but those patients never stayed. They had the gall to recover and return home, full of chipper glee, with their Mercedes-driving, Gucci-wearing, sympathetic family members.

She sighed and logged off her computer.

All this contemplation didn't change the fact that she was a forty-year-old, unmarried woman with the uncanny ability to attract dorky cops and dust bunnies. Not to mention she worked in a loony bin.

She scooped up the files on her desk, grabbed her plastic travel mug, and headed out of her office. She had just enough time to grab a refill (with any luck, the new C.N.A. —what was her name? Harriet? Heather?—brewed the Starbucks instead of the Folgers), review her case notes, and make it to group with plenty of time to spare.

After triple checking the office door to ensure the lock engaged, she headed left down the hallway of the remodeled manor. Her life could be worse. She could still be in graduate school, scraping up enough cash for tuition by mowing lawns at the wastewater treatment plant. At least here there's no smell of excrement stuck in her nostrils making everything smell like shit. Or she could still be working with the sweet old woman on the hill who turned out to be a glue-sniffing, enema-loving Harpy.

At least at The Meadows (or as the newly hired CEO called it: "Your Home Away from Home" —yeah, right, YOU come live here!), you stood amongst one hundred beautiful acres of Vermont countryside, complete with duck pond, walking trails and ancient folklore. Lynn had snagged the corner office from that presumptuous Ph.D candidate after she creamed the bitch's ass in the now legendary "Ping-Pong Death Challenge." Plus, the therapists' offices were in the same hallway of the main building as the administration staff—a richly decorated, brightly painted Tudor-style English manor that once housed the estate owner's British family. Lynn loved the heavy mahogany staircases and horsehair plaster walls. She loved the slight squeak of the wooden floors under her feet and the doors of the meeting room that slid silently into their pockets in the walls. It sure beat the hell out of the oily garage floor of the wastewater treatment plant.

At the end of the hallway, she paused at the large maple desk with the brass nameplate reading MARTHA MALONE – ADMINISTRATIVE ASSISTANT and, after a quick glance to ensure the short, silver-haired Hitler was nowhere in sight, she snatched the notepad from the desk and scanned it. Martha meticulously notated any phone calls, e-mails, snail mail, visitors, gossip, stray glance, or telepathic alien contact with the merciless detail of an anal-retentive FBI agent on the trail of a serial killer. Lynn learned the hard way to never—and she meant NEVER—touch Martha's book without Martha's permission. Murder may occasionally be justifiable, but touching Martha's schedule book without permission wasn't.

Satisfied nobody had tried to infiltrate the bowels of this facility during her time in the office, Lynn turned and walked through the high archway which separated the manor from the clients' quarters. Just as the manor reflected the tasteful elegance of the era in which it was built, the building that housed those quarters reflected the society of its day. The rectangular brick building was composed of four long corridors running the interior perimeter of the structure, with the apartments opening into these main arteries. The hallways twinkled with brightly colored fabric runners and ornate trim. Delicate sconces lined the upper parts of the walls, spilling their light onto the ceiling for maximum bounce.

These apartments ranked better than her own, thanks to her crappy salary.

The group meeting rooms lay on the opposite side of the symmetrical building. While Lynn strolled down the western hallway, she flipped open the file containing today's assignments. At the top of her 'to do' list, was, of course, group—which was at the top of every day's 'to do' list. Second on the list was Martha's bold, thick, perfectly printed handwriting with the name: EMERSON, ABBEY—DISCHARGE INTERVIEW. Lynn's heart sank.

Lynn knew all about the Social Worker code of ethics, of course, and would refuse to admit it publicly, but Abbey was her favorite patient and she would be terribly melancholy to see her leave The Meadows.

The twenty-five-year-old was brought to the Funny Farm (she must stop saying that. If she let it slip out during a staff meeting, she'd be sacked for sure) by her Aunt Eleanor, a stately woman who, by her own account, must be about eighty, although she didn't look a day over sixty. Eleanor said that Abbey's semi-catatonic state was trauma due to a terrible crash several months ago. While Eleanor had done her best to look after Abbey, the girl needed professional help. She cried when she left Abbey that first night; Abbey herself remained in a near-catatonic state and reacted very sluggishly to any stimulus.

Over the next several days, Abbey steadily improved at a surprising rate and within a month, she appeared to be a normal, social and energetic young woman. Abbey had a mystique about her, a depth, which Lynn could only describe as 'spiritual.' It was as if Abbey didn't communicate with people as much as she peered into their soul.

Abbey was wise beyond her twenty-five years.

During this time, the family visited often. In the beginning, Eleanor was accompanied by another woman, identified as Aunt Ruth. Ruth was so maternal in her actions that Lynn wondered if she wasn't actually Abbey's birth mother, disguising herself as a relative. Then Lynn decided that idea was insane and the logical explanation was the most simple: Eleanor and Ruth were lesbians and the co-parents of Abbey. After Abbey's sudden and unexpected improvement, Eleanor visited with a rotation of other women: Aunt Tommy (now that was a lesbian name if she ever heard one), Aunt Zen, and someone called "Livia." As wonderful as the visitations were, Lynn wondered why Abbey required so many lesbians to raise her.

It was during the time following her lucidity that Abbey's dreams manifested. She reported that her dreams were so vivid that she often awoke unable to discern dream from reality. Lynn addressed this issue during her individual sessions.

"These dreams…are…they feel real," Abbey related, getting up from the overstuffed chair Lynn had bought at a second-hand store because she forgot to submit her furniture request form. "I want to know why I suffer from them."

Lynn said softly, "Did your family ever mention a near-drowning incident or water accident?" Abbey shook her head. "How about fire? Ever burned as a child?"

"I don't believe so." Abbey shrugged. "But remembering *is* my problem, is it not?"

Lynn grimaced. Nice one. She tried a different tactic. "Why don't you tell me what you remember of the dreams."

"The water dream?" Lynn nodded. Abbey took a deep breath. "I feel myself flying. I feel good. It feels like home. Does that sound crazy?"

"No. It sounds wonderful."

Abbey sighed and nodded. "The blue sky calms me. I see sparks of light all around—like diamonds in the sky." Abbey's smile faded. "Then...I do not know why, but I begin to fall. I remember panicking, feeling as if I can no longer control anything around me. Then..." she paused, getting a faraway look in her eyes, "Water grabs me, pulling me under and I can do nothing. I see the sun, but I...keep sinking. Then someone reaches for me. I...I think it's God, but..." Her voice cracked and she turned away from Lynn.

"Is this too much for you?"

Abbey shook her head. "I want to know what happened to me. Why I lost my memory."

"That's very brave," Lynn reassured her.

"These dreams scare me. I do not like feeling scared." Without waiting for an answer, Abbey continued. "There's a man there. Tall. Thin. Each eye a different color."

"Did he scare you?"

Abbey shook her head. "He comforted me. Then he's gone."

"Do you want to see him again?"

Abbey nodded. She cleared her throat and continued. "The fire dream is different. I remember more of that one. Shall I tell you?" Lynn nodded.

"I walk through a crowd. They are angry and scream at me, as if I am a criminal. Hundreds of people crowd around me, but they can't touch me."

"Why?"

"Soldiers surround me. They are my protectors."

"Do you remember where you are?"

Abbey nodded. "A large stone building—like a castle—that has a huge wall all around it. People stand on the walls. They throw things at me." Lynn let Abbey sit in silence for a moment. Then the young woman grabbed the small silver crucifix around her neck and began to speak again. "Then…the flames…"

Lynn debated if she should stop Abbey, but decided against it. After a moment, Abbey began speaking quickly, fondling the crucifix again.

"The flames grow all around me. I feel a burning on my feet and then I can't feel anything below my knees. I scream, but no sound comes out. The crowd screams and points. I look up and see them."

"Who?" Lynn asked, sitting on the edge of her chair.

"…my angels. God has sent me salvation, so I cry out to them. But they do nothing. God's punishment for doing something wrong. Or being wrong. I wish I knew which."

"Then?"

"Then I awake in my room," Abbey said. "And Edna is patting my hand." She looked to Lynn and added pointedly, "Every time. Every time."

"Why don't you just talk to me about the two elements in general terms? Let's begin with the first memory of fire you can recall."

"The first?" Lynn nodded. Abbey wandered aimlessly around the room, gently fingering Lynn's collection of plastic Disney figurines that she either borrowed from the children's ward or stole from her dentist's office.

"I was…oh…I can't remember. Ten? Young." Abbey's voice became soft, "Father—we always called him Father—was standing in front of a huge fire. He threw twigs into it and I stood there watching." Abbey replaced The Little Mermaid and picked up Snow White.

"Did he burn you?" Lynn felt compelled to ask, although she knew the answer.

"No, no he didn't," Abbey replied, her voice sounding small and childlike.

"Why did he make the fire?" Lynn pushed.

"I…" Abbey searched her memories and rubbed Eeyore. "I think we were camping," she said finally. "I remember animals, a big fire and little huts like tents. The next thing I remember is smelling…burning flesh…"

"Ah! Roasted weenies!" Lynn joked.

Abbey dropped the figurine of Mulan.

That was the last time Abbey spoke of her dreams in such concrete terms.

Whenever Lynn brought up the subject, Abbey lacked the ability to be as emotionally vulnerable as she had in their previous meetings, but Lynn noted that the dreams remained consistent in their details, eliminating the possibility of false memory. Lynn empathized with the young woman, but secretly celebrated the breakthrough and sensed that any day Abbey would remember everything about her life before her untimely accident.

Then came the phone call from Aunt Eleanor. Word reached her about Abbey's improved condition while the old woman was away in southern France. She would return to the States immediately, of course, to reclaim her niece. Lynn, aghast, explained that would be contraindicated, as it would benefit Abbey to remain in the treatment center until she fully recovered her memories.

Eleanor would hear none of it and insisted that Abbey return to the family estate at once. No matter how Lynn tried, there was no persuading Eleanor of the benefits of continued treatment. In the end, the family won, of course. Abbey was placed here voluntarily and, therefore, could leave whenever she wished.

Something wasn't quite right with this whole situation and Lynn couldn't put her finger on it. Questions sat in the back of her mind, making her increasingly anxious as the time of Eleanor's arrival drew near. It seemed a bit too...suspicious...that just as Abbey began to regain some of her repressed memories, Eleanor suddenly wanted the girl at home. If she loved Abbey so much, why insist that Abbey leave treatment before the girl recovered? Lynn sensed there was more to this "horrible crash" than the old lesbian wanted to admit.

Mr. Stewart, the resident clown of The Meadows, invaded her personal space and brought her out of her contemplation. Mr. Stewart's only illness was his cheap gold-digging whore of a third wife. What is it with men? Couldn't they figure out that the main attraction between a twenty-eight-year-old model and a sixty-eight-year-old sickly millionaire was a credit line? Then again, Lynn sighed, if I was sixty-eight and dying, I would easily exchange a million dollars for spending the last few months of life boning an underwear model.

To be honest, she admitted to herself, she would exchange a million dollars for spending a few months with any stray erection with a pulse.

"My peter's dead." Mr. Stewart's thick southern drawl poured into Lynn's ears. She looked up and smiled at the innocent, wrinkled face.

"Morning, Mr. Stewart. How did you sleep?"

"My peter's dead," the old man smiled, revealing a set of the most expensive white teeth a wealthy New England family could buy. "He was just standing up, and now, the darn thing fell over."

"Really?"

"It's a fact." Mr. Stewart nodded.

"Well, we can tell the story in group, Mr. Stewart," Lynn muttered, continuing down the hallway.

"Will you give my peter mouth-to-mouth?"

"Very funny, Mr. Stewart. See you in group."

THE HANDSOME, DARK-HAIRED FRENCHMAN waited in the back seat of the limo wondering when he would succumb to temptation and kill the chauffeur.

"YOU CAN'T ALWAYS GET WHAT YOU WANT...YOU CAN'T ALWAYS GET WHAT YOU WANT..." the young, lithe man in the driver's seat bopped his head in time with the music while drumming the steering wheel.

The Frenchman set his glass of cognac on the side table and rapped on the glass partition.

"Yeah, man?" the mocha-colored chauffeur asked as the barrier descended. The beat of the music was pounding against the Frenchman's chest.

"Joshua, the music."

"Too loud, boss?"

"Yes. And don't call me boss."

"Sure thing, Robert." Joshua leaned over and turned the music down. "You know that's the Stones, right?"

"Please do not refer to me as 'Robert'. And, no, I did not know."

The young man's eyebrows furrowed. "Um...well, then 'Sir'?"

Robert sighed. "Mr. de Baudricourt will suffice."

"How do you pronounce that again? I'm not very good with Italian."

"French."

"That neither."

"Of course," Robert muttered. "When the Doctor hired you, he did not instruct you as to the pronunciation of my name. How thoughtful of him."

"Ah, the Doc is okay. He's here."

"Who?"

The knock on the glass answered his question. Robert looked to the rear passenger window and motioned for the thin, clean-shaven bald man to enter. The Doctor jiggled the limo's handle to signal that it was locked.

"Want me to let him in, Rob—uh, Sir?"

"Yes, Joshua, please do so." As the Doctor climbed in, Robert motioned for Joshua to close the window and Joshua nodded. "Oh, and Joshua," he sneered, "please return the Stonies to their prior volume." He sipped his cognac.

"Stones."

"Yes, of course."

After the window closed, Robert glared at the Doctor. "Must you always complicate my life by hiring idiots?" He spat as the car began to quiver to the sounds of "Satisfaction."

The Doctor shrugged and took one of Robert's Gauloises. "What happened?"

"The girl died."

"So you said. Explain."

Robert described the scene in the woods the night before. The Doctor nodded and jotted down notes. "Your calculations were wrong. The lineage was incorrect. Are you certain you can trust your sources?"

The Doctor shrugged. "Doesn't matter." Robert eyed the man suspiciously. "About an hour ago, my associate at The Meadows called to tell me our girl is being released." Robert smiled. "Her 'Aunt Eleanor' will fetch her."

"Splendid." The Doctor nodded in agreement.

"I assume you will intervene?" asked Robert.

"No." The Doctor shook his head. "You will."

"Me?"

The Doctor nodded. "I have a plan. It begins this afternoon before The Meadows' visiting hours expire."

"Fortunately, I am free this afternoon."

The Doctor tossed his cigarette butt into Robert's cognac, settled into his seat and spoke.

Robert listened, becoming more irritated by the moment. By the time the Doctor finished outlining his plan, Robert wasn't sure which he hated more: the Doctor, his plan, or the Stones.

6

"M R. CHOW?" Heather's chipper voice filtered into Lynn's consciousness, "Put your penis back in your pants, okay?"

"Damn bitch!" Mr. Chow muttered.

Lynn turned from the group and found herself staring into the face of Mr. Chow, a short, balding, wrinkled man of uncertain Asian descent. He flipped Heather the bird and grabbed his crotch.

"The boys need air."

Heather sighed. "Please? Come on?"

Lynn forced her eyes to remain on Mr. Chow's face. What genetic mutation caused the males of the species to be so enamored with their dicks? Women didn't spend half this much time talking about their vaginas.

Unlike Mr. Stewart who liked to *talk* about his dick, Mr. Chow's favorite pastime was showing his, wandering the halls with his fly open *sans* underwear. His family 'suggested' a stay at The Meadows a year ago after a particularly embarrassing encounter with the local Red Hat Ladies. They didn't care if Lynn discovered why Mr. Chow was so obsessed with airing out his balls; their only goal was to avoid any more attention caused by the public indecency. Theirs was old, old money and old, old money knows how to keep things quiet.

When she was first hired, Lynn spent the first few weeks writing incident reports on Mr. Chow and the boys until Martha barked at her one afternoon, "Mr. Chow's wang does not require any more documentation."

"But…but I thought…"

"Mr. Chow's boys are quite legendary here at The Meadows," Martha snapped. "I will read no more about them. Understand?" That was the last time she, or Martha, ever talked about Mr. Chow's private parts.

"Mr. Chow! Good morning!" Lynn said meeting his icy gaze. "Is that your I.Q or your sperm count?" she asked, indicating his middle finger.

Mr. Chow lowered his hand. "That's an old, stupid joke."

Lynn nodded. "Yeah, I guess it was." She looked at his flaccid penis and wrinkled testicles. "How are the boys today?"

"Okay."

"Well, I tell you what," Lynn said calmly. "How about you send the boys home and join me in group."

"I can do anything I want," he sneered. "If my family didn't own half this county…"

"If your family didn't own half this county," Lynn sneered back, "you'd be in jail showing your boys to some inmates who call you 'bitch.' Now, it's time for group."

The withered man turned and plopped himself into a vacant chair.

Lynn grabbed the remote and switched the TV off. Despite the grumbling, the patients slowly began moving to their places. Lynn scanned the room for Abbey, but the girl was absent.

The obese black woman seated to Lynn's left said loudly, "I gotta problem."

"You always gotta problem!" Mr. Stewart snapped.

"Do not!"

"Do too!"

"Mr. Stewart, Mrs. Bailey, please stop bickering." Lynn tried to sound patient. It was only nine o'clock in the morning for god's sake! Can't they put a sock in it until at least ten? By ten she'd be on her sixth cup of coffee and wouldn't care.

"I gotta tell ya," the fat woman said, "that Fung Shi doesn't like it here this morning." She looked into her cupped hand and began petting her imaginary creature.

"Oh?" Lynn asked, "Why not?"

"Fung Shi doesn't like Mr. Chow's cock."

"You look very nice today, Mr. Rix," Lynn said to the young man wearing the long black wig, red stilettos, and skin-tight dress.

"Cher," he replied. "You may address me as Cher. Everyone does."

"Of course." Lynn smiled. "You look very nice today, Cher."

"Thank you."

"FAGGOT!" screamed Mr. Chow, his hands placed strategically over his crotch. "You…" Suddenly, he fell silent and turned to stare at the space behind Lynn.

Standing in the doorway of the day room was Abbey, dressed handsomely in dark, pleated slacks with so much starch that the crease could cut a glacier. She wore a billowing lace shirt and boots which were better suited to medieval times rather than twenty-first century group therapy. Abbey had pulled her hair back and tucked it up on the nape of her neck, giving her an androgynous quality that Lynn found fascinating.

She commanded silence with her glance. Once all eyes were upon her, she strode purposefully into the room and took her seat beside a lanky black man wearing a beret.

Lynn said, "As you know, Abbey will be leaving us soon." The room erupted into a cacophony of voices. When she finally regained quiet, she turned to Abbey. "Would you like to say anything?"

Abbey remained mute. Her eyes moved from one person to the next until she made contact with Lynn. "Yes, I would." She waited. The group held its breath. "Thank you, everyone. You shall all be fine." She then sat down.

"Why does she get to leave?" Mrs. Bailey squealed. "She heard fucking voices!"

"You calling Abbey a freak?" Cher said, snapping her fingers.

"I'm just sayin'…"

"She hears angels," the black man sitting next to Abbey whispered.

"What, Mr. Graves?" Lynn asked.

"She hears angels. Not voices. Angels are a good thing to hear."

Then Lynn asked, sitting on the edge of her seat. "Do you hear angels, Mr. Graves?"

"No," he muttered. "I wish I did, though."

"I wanna go home, too!" Mrs. Bailey screamed.

"I need to piss!" Mr. Chow spat.

"I am so over this," Cher exclaimed.

The rest of the circle erupted in chaos. Lynn sighed and laid her head down in her lap.

Across the room, out of sight of Lynn's resigned sighs, Mr. Graves clutched Abbey's hand in his. "I know you can't say about the voices," he said, "or they say you crazy. But I know about 'em. The voices be good, right?"

Abbey smiled and squeezed his hand.

"YOU'RE GOING TO DIE."

"Edna." Abbey sat down on the bed next to the old woman and hugged her. "I am not going to die."

"You're leaving me and never coming back. It's the same thing."

A knock on the door interrupted their moment. "Edna? Abbey? Do you need help?" Heather's voice scratched their ears.

"WE DON'T NEED YOUR DAMNED HELP, YOU SMELLY WENCH!" Edna wiped her eyes and held Abbey's hand. "You aren't supposed to leave me until tomorrow."

Abbey shrugged. "My aunt is...unpredictable."

"I need more time with you. I need you, Abbey."

"You don't," Abbey smiled, "you have Lynn, and Mr. Stewart."

"He likes me, I think."

"I think so, too."

"Abbey, it's time to go, right? Lynn's waiting, isn't she?" Heather's voice lilted through the door.

"WE HEAR YOU! WE'RE NOT DEAF YOU STUPID PUNK!" Then, to Abbey, "I guess your Aunt Eleanor needs you too." Abbey shrugged. "Yes, she does. I can tell. She loves you, Abbey." Edna squeezed Abbey's shoulder. "We all need you."

"I'll be back to visit, Edna."

"No, you won't." Edna said, tears rolling down her cheeks. "But it's okay. They need you more."

"Edna, you help Abbey get her things together?"

"I *AM* HELPING HER, YOU MOTHER-FUCKER!" Edna pulled Abbey close one last time. "You're our guardian angel."

Abbey winked at the old woman. "No, but thank you for the kind thoughts."

Edna became serious and gripped the young woman tightly. "Protect us, Abbey. Help us." Abbey stared at the old woman, mystified by her strength. Another knock broke the silence.

"Abbey? Edna?"

"Edna. Promise me you'll be nice to Heather."

Edna nodded. "I will." Without another word, the old woman shuffled to the door and opened it. "WILL YOU GIVE ABBEY SOME TIME ALONE, YOU INCONSIDERATE TWERP?" She turned, shrugged at Abbey, and closed the door behind her as she left.

Abbey threw the last articles of clothing into her duffle bag, sat down on the bed, and wondered if she could escape Aunt Eleanor and the Aunts. Surely, she, herself, had some power in the final decision to stay at The Meadows, did she not? For the past six months, this facility was the only part of her life that she could vividly remember and the idea of leaving the familiar setting unnerved her. Not only would she be leaving her home, but also the possibility of connecting the dots of what her life before the accident looked like. The frustration of sifting through the fragments of memory that floated around her mind was almost more than she could bear. While she appreciated all the help her aunts gave her, the old photos, family heirlooms and handwritten letters they brought her had not jump started her mind to recall who she was before The Meadows. Right now, the need to unravel the mystery of her past was stronger than the need to reconnect with family.

The closest she came to any substantial cohesion of her life before the accident was in therapy with Lynn. There was a hard edge to the therapist that struck Abbey as both sturdy and fragile. Abbey sensed a gutsy facet to the social worker's personality that belied the kind, professional exterior. She respected the woman and her motives. If anyone could help her, it would be Lynn.

Abbey lay down on her bed and fiddled with her necklace. She felt guilty about lying to Lynn during her recent session, but despite the social worker's efforts to build a solid rapport, Abbey knew that keeping mute on the details of her dreams was the right decision. These last two weeks brought dreams that were fiercer and more vivid than she let on. In the latest version of the dream, she was not flying under her own power, as she told Lynn, but inside the cockpit of a small prop airplane. She remembered the plane lurching and then plummeting into the sea. She remembered knowing—in that deep-seated way that only dreams can know things—that her fall into the water was a terrible miscalculation of some kind. She remembered clawing at the water, digging her way to the surface while both fearing the water's depth and welcoming its embrace. She remembered feeling that someone was supposed to rescue her and that 'someone' abandoned her.

Three nights ago, she had her most startling dream to date; this one not about fire or water, but Aunt Eleanor. She dreamed that she and Aunt Eleanor walked the halls of a huge building—like a castle, but more modern—and Aunt Eleanor wanted her to do something. In the dream, they sat together in a beautiful sprawling garden drinking bitter coffee and watching the sunrise. The flowers bloomed and bees buzzed through the air amongst the brilliant reds, whites and yellows. Then, Aunt Eleanor turned to her and faded away, leaving Abbey alone amongst the birches, firs and pines. As Abbey sat watching ladybugs inch along the stems of the flowers, a fire sparked under her and spread throughout the garden. Soon, she was sitting in the middle of a ring of fire and Aunt Eleanor stood outside the circle watching her die.

There were other parts of the dream as well, such as—Damn! The vision was gone. Just when the memories started to flow back to her, they jammed again, like a pile-up on the freeway, leaving the wreckage of disjointed mental pictures. Abbey leapt off the bed and kicked her duffle bag, sending it flying across the room. Damn! Why could she remember some things so clearly and others not? She could remember going to church. She remembered the kindly priest sitting with her on hard, wooden pews discussing angels.

She stopped herself from hyperventilating by collapsing to her knees. Automatically, she folded her hands in prayer and bowed her head. Praying always gave her a sense of calm. Was she always this way? So many questions flooded through her she found it hard to concentrate on the Lord's Prayer. All she knew for sure was that she didn't like feeling angry. The anger quickly took control of her and made her violent. She didn't want violence in her life. She didn't want to fight. Had she always been a fighter?

No. She had no desire to fight. Her problem was fear. The idea of going back home with the two women who knew more about her than she knew about herself terrified her.

Besides, what kind of people name their home 'The Bastille'?

A curt knocking on the door and Heather's melodic voice penetrating the silence. "Abbey? Abbey, your aunt is here? Okay? Let's go meet her?"

"Hey!" Mr. Stewart bellowed as she followed Heather down the hallway towards the administration wing, "Remember to piss before you leave. Can't pull over you know. Better go now."

Abbey smiled warmly. "Thank you, Mr. Stewart. Good advice."

The old man scowled at her for a moment and grunted. He then continued shuffling his way down the hall.

"Girl, you look great!" Cher said, dabbing her tears with a tissue. "Here."

Abbey held out her hand and Cher laid a handmade necklace of multicolored plastic beads in it. "How sweet," she said, donning the ostentatious craft. "You made this for me?"

The sobbing head nodded violently. "That awful crafts class. A girl can never have too much color, you know." Cher held out her hand and Abbey took it, gave it a quick kiss and looked into the mascara-strewn eyes. "Be safe, sister Abbey."

Abbey nodded. "You, too. And dear," she pulled the thin body close to her and whispered, "God has a reason to place you on Earth."

Cher yanked her hand back and opened her mouth to say something, thought better of it, and silently turned away.

Abbey almost made it out the door when Mrs. Bailey's booming voice flooded the hallway. "Hey! You!" Abbey stopped mid-step and turned. The bulky woman stood in the center of the hallway, only one strap of her bib overalls fastened over her shoulder. The other strap dangled uselessly around her leg. Mrs. Bailey's immense left breast lay trapped within her flimsy T-shirt, while her right breast hung down to her waist where the rotund woman had it tucked neatly inside the overalls.

"This is for you!" the woman screamed maniac-like. In a flash, she had unclasped the strap of her overalls, yanked the bib down and whipped off her T-shirt. Both of her huge breasts sagged and bounced against her flabby ball of belly. She smiled broadly as she offered the T-shirt to Abbey.

"Mrs. Bailey?" Heather scolded. "You're undressing again? Stop it, okay?"

Abbey smiled and took the shirt.

"Thank you, Mrs. Bailey." Mrs. Bailey was, perhaps, the only woman Abbey knew who had no body image issues.

As Heather ushered Abbey through the door into the executive wing, Abbey spied Mr. Graves leaning against the wall. He gave a tiny wave to Abbey. She waved back as Heather secured the fire door behind her.

W HEN ABBEY WALKED INTO LYNN'S OFFICE, the smell hit her like a fist—lilacs with a hint of cinnamon. From somewhere in the back of her mind, another orb of memory floated into consciousness. This was the smell of the kitchen at the Bastille. This was a comfortable smell, sent to comfort her. She had smelled this scent ever since…damn! The orb faded again, leaving her standing in the doorway feeling cheated out of one more piece to her life's puzzle.

Inside Lynn's cramped office, Aunt Eleanor sat in the ratty overstuffed chair opposite Lynn's huge office window while Aunt Ruth rearranged the chocolate chip cookies on the dime store platter. Eleanor's hands clutched the Louis Vuitton bag and worried the zipper. Her forest green Chanel dress was of simple design, yet flattered her body, still quite curvy after all these years. Upon her head sat a tasteful matching hat with only one telltale sign of tackiness: a diamond studded broach incorporating the letters G. I. and W. By contrast, Aunt Ruth wore a simple brown shift that hung off her shoulders like a gunny sack, worn Birkenstocks, and a tattered brown pill hat clung to her frizzy hair as if hanging on for dear life. The only sign of her wealth was the silver Star of David hanging around her neck and an identical diamond stickpin with the initials G.I.W. She bent over the cookies, restacking them with frenetic, nervous movements as she muttered incoherently to herself.

"My dear!" Eleanor said, rising. She opened her arms widely, motioning for Abbey to embrace her.

Abbey stood frozen then felt a gentle nudge from Lynn. Abbey dropped her duffle bag on the floor and stepped into the woman's embrace. Eleanor smelled slightly of lilac and jasmine—a floral design rather than floral assault.

"Abbey, I think we should talk about your plans for the future," Lynn said, taking her place behind the desk.

"Future!" Eleanor gasped. "Why, her future lies within the fold of her family."

Lynn smiled. "Of course, Mrs…"

"Eleanor. I have requested you not to refer to me as 'Mrs.' several times now, I believe."

"Yes, Eleanor, you have."

"Then, pray tell, why do you not do so?" Her eyes bore into Lynn. Lynn squirmed slightly.

"Well…" she began lamely.

"Cookie?" Ruth asked, holding the plate to Lynn's face. "I made them for you. You have been so kind and gentle with our girl! Have a cookie."

"Oh," Lynn muttered. "Thank you."

"They have cinnamon," Ruth smiled broadly, handing the platter to Lynn. As Lynn gingerly took one, Ruth giggled. "They're for you. Good heavens, yes. Natural ingredients."

"Oh…thank you."

"Keep the platter."

"We shall speak no more of Abbey," Eleanor interjected as if Ruth did not exist. "Abbey has suffered through a series of life-altering, extremely traumatic events, would you not say?" Lynn nodded. "And now the painful repercussions of these incidents are retreating into a place within her which allows Abbey to begin leading a full and happy life, would you not also say?" Lynn's smile twitched. How could this woman make her feel so idiotic?

"I feel it's important to discuss how Abbey will transition from The Meadows into her daily routine with you and her…aunts."

"She will transition beautifully." Eleanor's face carried no hint of sarcasm and Lynn faltered in her response.

"I have no doubt," Lynn managed to say. "But sudden changes can be disconcerting to people transitioning into the home environment again."

"Sudden changes?"

"Yes." Lynn searched for words that wouldn't belie her annoyance. "For example, you were scheduled to collect Abbey tomorrow afternoon, not today."

"Is that a problem, doctor?" Eleanor snapped.

"I'm not a doctor."

"Correct." Eleanor smirked. "You are not."

"Abbey's well-being and recovery are my main concern."

"We shall bake!" Ruth said with a giggle. "Do you remember, Eleanor, how Abbey loves to bake?" Ruth shuffled to the young woman and took Abbey's face in her hands. "Do you remember, dear? Bundt cake?"

"See?" Eleanor hissed, "she will have Ruth, her aunts, me AND Bundt cake."

"Eleanor, I can't stress strongly enough how crucial it is to continue our intensive therapy sessions. In a short time, Abbey has remembered so much…"

"What?" both women shot back simultaneously. The speed of their response amazed and surprised Lynn.

"I am remembering…much," Abbey whispered.

"That is wonderful, darling!" Ruth said, kissing the girl's cheek. She started humming a lively song and grabbed Abbey's hands.

"Not now, Ruth, we've a function at the Bastille," Eleanor snapped. Ruth dropped her hands. Eleanor turned her attention to Lynn.

"I am certain you have done wonders for her." Eleanor descended upon Lynn in sharp, quick steps, stopping only when she reached Lynn's desk. "I am confident the support and love of her family will continue to heal her."

"We still have discharge paperwork to complete. And, there's the treatment plan I outlined…"

Eleanor cut her off as she adjusted her hat upon her head. "Of course, my dear. And you shall do an outstanding job of describing the exact details of those plans." She slid the gloves onto her hands. "In addition, I am of the understanding that when you work out the exact dates of your visits, you shall notify us in advance. Of that, I am grateful."

She turned to Abbey and gestured to the duffle bag. "Take your things, dear."

"No," Abbey answered.

"What did you say, dear?"

"No," she repeated. "I want to remember. I need to know who I am."

Eleanor stepped closer to Abbey, turning her back slightly on Lynn and Ruth. With a deft movement, she dug something out of her purse and held it out to Abbey. It was a small, brass, toy prop airplane about four inches long and two inches tall. Abbey took it, stared at it a moment, and held the small trinket closer. On the right side of the plane, beneath where the pilot would sit, were four words:

FOR ABBEY

LOVE ELEANOR

Abbey turned the plane around to the other side of the fuselage and read the four words etched into the side of the toy:

AND YOUR

G.I.W. FAMILY

Eleanor leaned into Abbey's ear and spoke in barely a whisper, "I know who you are." She pulled back and locked eyes with Abbey. "Do you want to know?" She snatched the brass bobble from Abbey's hand and shoved it back into her purse.

"Abbey?" Lynn spoke up.

"I shall be fine," Abbey managed to say, her face still blank. "May I call you if I have difficulty?"

Lynn nodded. "Yes. And we can conduct an impromptu therapy session, if you'd like, during my home visits." She glanced at Eleanor. "Remember? We discussed that on the phone."

Eleanor nodded. "You also mentioned faxing several documents."

"Yes. The work I'd like Abbey to continue. Her journaling, some writing exercises to stimulate her memory." Ruth laughed uproariously.

"Oh! What a delightfully clever idea!" Ruth said through guffaws. Eleanor shushed the woman and grabbed Abbey's bag.

"No," Lynn said, standing up, "we have someone who will do that."

"No bother," Eleanor said. "You shall find that our estate is a bastion of self-supporting women. We come from healthy stock." She turned to Abbey. "Come along, dear. I have taken the liberty to call for our limo to meet us around back." She turned and focused her gaze upon Lynn. "Thank you for all you have done. The aunts and I shall take it from here."

"I'll be in touch." Lynn held Eleanor's gaze.

Ruth hugged Lynn. "You are such a dear. Tell me, do you like maple bars?" Lynn nodded. "Good. So do I. Bye." She hurried out the door.

By the time Lynn looked up, Abbey had gone.

"CAUSE OF DEATH, OLD AGE."

"Old age? Is that a medical condition?" Mathers asked, jiggling his keys and scratching his nose. The stench of antiseptic burned the insides of his nostrils. Damn! Why didn't he carry a handkerchief?

"If I start rattling off terms like 'obstructive pulmonary disease,' 'hepatic system failure,' and other medical jargon, would you understand any of it?" The young woman spoke from behind plastic frames with lenses as thick as bottles. Mathers shook his head. "Then please don't waste my time," she continued.

Mathers assessed the woman. Dr. Helen Zyback couldn't be more than twenty-five, but she certainly knew her job. He arrived at the medical examiner's office shortly after the corpse of the old woman arrived; he was sure he'd wait for hours while the usual process of examining the body dragged on. To his surprise, the young woman with stringy hair and protruding overbite was already elbow-deep in the procedure. As he entered and stood reeling from the thick air of formaldehyde, she glared at him with disapproval and motioned for him to leave. He wandered out through the hallway trying to clear his head when he noticed the worn door on his left with the freshly painted words: MEDICAL EXAMINER: HELEN ZYBACK and realized he had just met the new county employee. He made a mental note to ask Janet where her predecessor, Henry, had gone.

"So you are certain this woman died of natural causes?" Mathers asked, studying the corpse of the old lady that lay on the exam table.

Helen's response had a crisp vibrato, the vocal equivalent to the snapping of a whip. "It's quite a stretch, but I'm willing to bet my two-hundred-thousand-dollar medical school loans on the odds that this woman died of old age." She glared at him and unblinkingly asked, "What's your guess, Detective?"

"I'll trust your judgment."

"Good boy." She sighed and shook her head. "The one medical condition we can never counter—death. Eventually, we all must die...pay taxes...get the flu..."

"I don't."

"You don't pay taxes?"

He shook his head. "Get the flu. Never have. I just don't get sick."

"Then I guess you won't die of old age, either?"

Mathers smirked at her not-so-subtle condescension. This was a game he was good at. Growing up with a mother and two sisters taught him a few things about women.

"I trust your judgment," he said.

"Goody for me. Are we done?"

Mathers lowered his head so she wouldn't see his smile. God, how he loved ballsy women! "I do have a few questions."

"Imagine. A detective with questions." She peeled off her latex gloves and turned on the water in the sink. "Learn that from *Law and Order* or are you naturally curious?"

"I assume she's eighty-ish. Agree?"

"More emphasis on the 'ish,' but yes."

"Why would her heart just...stop?"

Helen pulled at the paper towel and dried her hands. "That's what happens when you're old."

"A heart attack is usually associated with a sudden shock, isn't it?"

Helen sat down at the small table and logged into her computer. "People die. Old people die because their hearts are old and arteries get clogged with junk food. Remember that the next time you shove a donut in your mouth." She spun her head and shot him another icy glance. "Want me to reel off the medical descriptions of organ failure?"

"Please don't."

"Then ask me smart questions." Helen began typing up her report while Mathers walked around the body.

"Any sign of trauma?"

"No. Next."

"Any sign of foul play?"

Helen sighed loudly. "Again, NO. I would have told you that. While we're at it, 'no' on any sign of sexual violation, 'no' on any sign of struggle, 'no' on naturally developing distinguishing marks such as moles, birth marks or discoloration and 'no' on toxicology." She stared at him for a moment before continuing in a voice rich with sarcasm. "I am ready for your smart questions. Will you be asking them anytime soon?"

"How old is that tattoo? The one of Mickey Mouse."

"Why?"

"I'm a detective. I'm curious." He shrugged. "Okay...I confess...I saw it on an episode of *Law and Order*."

Mathers thought he saw her smile. "I'd estimate fifty years or so. Next question."

"How many eighty-year-old women have you seen with a tattoo of Mickey Mouse?"

"One. Our Jane Doe. Next."

"Don't you find that strange?"

"What I find stranger," Helen stared at him unblinking, "is why an eighty-year-old woman had her tongue and labia pierced." Mathers froze. "Did you hear me?" He nodded at her. She sighed and continued. "You DO know what a labia is, I assume. Or...I apologize. Perhaps labias don't interest you."

"I'm intimately familiar with labias," Mathers said.

"Okay." She turned back to her report. "Not that I care one way or the other. Live and let live I always say."

"So we have an eighty-year-old that has Mickey Mouse tattoos, pierced labia..."

"...pierced tongue," Helen added. "And an MP-3 player inside her skirt."

"Does this make sense to you?"

"Detective, I graduated as the valedictorian from medical school and was forced to accept a job in Backwoods, Vermont, because my parents' health deteriorated unexpectedly. I passed up a job in Los Angeles as ship's doctor with Carnival Cruise lines, AND an enticing offer from an oil company. NOTHING makes sense to me." She turned and began typing.

Mathers looked at the dead woman's face peering out at him over the top of the thin sheet. Under these bright lights, he saw the high cheekbones, pug nose and broad forehead that he hadn't noticed in the field behind the Bastille. The face looked familiar to him. Had he met her before? He couldn't remember meeting any elderly people since his parents died, so what was it about this woman that struck him as familiar?

"Detective?" Helen's voice replaced the clicking of the computer keys. He looked over at her. "Anything else? I'm busy."

He shook his head. "I need to go talk to the women at the Bastille and question them regarding Jane Doe."

"When you get there, send me a postcard. Bye-bye now," Helen shot back.

"The reason I'm telling you this," Mathers explained, "is that if any possibility of foul play exists, I'm going to…"

"There is no foul play. Go check the old folks' homes for Alzheimer's patients who may have wandered off."

"I did. Everyone is accounted for." He checked his notebook before continuing, "and there have only been two missing persons reports in the past few months."

"Congratulations," she said. "Detective, I speak three languages, so if you'd prefer I can tell you the same thing in French or German, but I prefer my native tongue, so please listen," Helen muttered from her computer screen. "She's old. She died. She probably wandered onto the property chasing pretty butterflies." Helen entered a few more notes, then without looking up, said, "Go tell the ladies to continue with the Faire."

"How do you know about that?"

"It's a small town. That Faire brings in lots of money." She hit 'save' and pushed away from the computer. "Bye-bye now."

With that, Helen dismissed Detective Mathers.

"**M**R. RIX?" Heather whined at the thin figure wearing the sequined dress striking a pose in the day room. Huge chunks of costume jewelry sparkled in the sunlight, making the trim body look like a thrift store mannequin.

"Liza," Mr. Rix snapped, smoothing her blazer.

"Liza, will you please sit down?"

"Fucker can't!" the grizzled voice shot from the back of the room.

"Mr. Stewart? Language?" Heather sighed, handing a folder to Lynn.

"You gonna walk me home?" Mr. Stewart asked.

"No," both Heather and Lynn responded in unison.

The desk phone gave a shrill ring. "Want me to get that?" Heather asked.

"It's your desk." Lynn shrugged.

"Station?"

"Station. Desk. Whatever." Lynn spun back to Mr. Stewart. "I would really like it if you read that book I gave you."

"'bout women?" he spat.

"About relating to women."

"I know 'bout women," the old man laughed. "I've been bangin' 'em for years!"

"You're disgusting!" Liza quipped, as she spun and shot a double jazz hand at him from the window seat of the day room.

"Goodbye, everyone," Lynn said, winking at Heather. "Have a good weekend."

"Wait?" Heather motioned to Lynn to step closer. She covered the phone and whispered, "It's Martha? She says she doesn't have your progress notes? They're due?"

"Not until tomorrow. At FIVE." Why was she explaining this to Heather? "Never mind. I'll go tell her myself." She spun away from Heather, who was now nodding her head at the receiver, eyes wide and growing paler by the second.

"You leavin', Miss Lynn?" a voice cried from the corner.

"Yes, I am, Mrs. Bailey. Is everything okay?"

"No, it ain't!" the heavy woman said, rocking gently. "Fung Shi is scared."

Lynn motioned to Heather to get the girl's attention, but the C.N.A. was engrossed in her conversation. Lynn turned her attention back to Mrs. Bailey. She didn't care what the official research stated—people's behavior changed on full moons.

"Why is Fung Shi scared?" Lynn asked, moving closer to the hefty woman who rocked herself and clung to the imaginary creature. As she approached, the sting of stale urine overwhelmed her. "I smell urine."

"He heard something last night. In the yard. It scared him."

"Heard something? That's what made him pee? Maybe it was a fox."

"No," Mrs. Bailey whispered, "it wasn't any animal."

"What do you think it was, then?"

"Something bad. Real bad."

Before Lynn could respond, the woman's head shot up and stared directly over Lynn's shoulder. "You take that thing out, I'm cutting it off and feeding it to Fung Shi!"

Lynn turned just as Mr. Chow pulled out his penis and flashed it at Mrs. Bailey. Before Lynn knew it, the fat woman jumped up, shoved her aside and dashed at the small man. "I'M GONNA SNIP OFF THAT WANG, BOY!"

Pandemonium broke out. Liza launched into a chorus of "Come On, Get Happy!" and tap danced her way across the day room. Mr. Chow, screaming in fear, raced down the hallway with Mrs. Bailey hot on his heels. Mr. Stewart lifted his fist and shouted, 'GO, GIRL!' and from somewhere a woman's scream pierced the air. Heather slammed her fist against the red panic button and a pleasant mechanical voice announced, "Code Red, Day Room." Heather chased after Mrs. Bailey, leaving Lynn squatting alone as a chunky, pink-faced young man rounded the corner, Snickers bar in his hand.

"Kenny, give me the Snickers." The boy handed it to her and Lynn removed the wrapper. Kenny had a penchant for eating Snickers bars, wrapper and all. "Did you steal this from the nurse's station?" Lynn asked. The boy gave a shy nod, snatched the candy from her, and shoved the chocolate into his already-stained face.

On her way past the chaos to the administration building, Lynn noticed Mr. Graves standing motionless, staring out the window.

"Mr. Graves?" When he didn't answer, she strolled up to his side and followed his stare out over the manicured lawn that separated this wing from the visitor parking lot, a sliver of which was visible past the trees.

"What is it?" she asked. "You miss Abbey?" As an answer the man lifted one arm and pointed. Lynn followed his gesture, but saw nothing.

"He was here last night. He scared Fung Shi."

"Who?" Lynn asked again.

"The angel of death."

Lynn sighed. Mr. Graves hadn't had the Grim Reaper vision in such a long time that this was a disappointing setback. "Mr. Graves, I'm sure he's not coming for you or anyone else here."

"No. He wants Abbey."

Lynn felt the hairs on her arm tingle. "But Abbey left a couple of hours ago, remember?"

"Check on her." With a gentleness that belied his bulk, he took her hand in his. "Please."

She nodded. He smiled and wiped the tear from his cheek. This was going to be a long night for the third shift. She didn't envy them at all.

WE DO NOT YIELD TO THREATS OR INTIMIDATION," the voice slid like a glacier through the air. "If you would prefer, I can summon the police to talk to you. If that does not fulfill your dreams, I would be more than happy to hail the SWAT team."

Well, Martha's on a roll, Lynn thought, taking pity on whomever it was who pissed her off. Lynn loved watching the little Nazi spar with a rude visitor. She turned the corner into the entrance foyer and saw Martha leaning toward a tall figure, her face crimson with rage.

The figure turned toward her and smiled. Standing at least six feet tall, he sported a mane of thick black hair that hung in curly ringlets to his broad shoulders. He had a strong, well-defined jaw line and a nose that fit his face perfectly. His olive skin showed no blemish, no mark, and no imperfection of any kind. A woolen trench coat hung lazily across his shoulders and a finely tailored suit traced his muscular body. Diamond cufflinks held together the ends of the light blue shirt peeking out from beneath the suit coat. He leaned heavily upon a thick wooden walking stick bejeweled with sparkling gemstones.

Lynn knew immediately that this man was God's representative on Earth. He must be listened to, respected, revered. There was nothing in his life in which this man did not excel.

He winked at her and smiled, displaying a set of movie star perfect teeth. "Good day, Mademoiselle," he said in a heavy French accent, bowing slightly.

The man bowed. He spoke French. He is God. He must be obeyed.

"Can I help you?" she managed to mutter.

"NO, YOU CAN'T!" Martha snapped. "I've got Mr. Fancy Pants all wrapped up."

"I wish you no trouble, Madame," Mr. Fancy Pants said in a voice as smooth and sweet as Vermont maple syrup. "I merely wish to have my questions answered."

"I know what you wish and I'm telling you No," Martha snapped back.

Lynn stepped closer to the god. Martha was as immune to his divine aura as she was to human emotions such as politeness, sensitivity and love. Martha was insane. This Frenchman wouldn't hurt anyone. Unless asked.

"Martha…"

"Don't 'Martha' me. We don't release information on our patients, period!" Martha snapped.

"Of course you do not, my fine lady," the man said calmly. "Nor would I wish you to break any law. I merely asked if I may speak to the professional dealing with my niece Abbey."

"Abbey?" Lynn asked quickly, before Martha could say anything further.

"Yes, Abbey," the man said, moving away from the nasty Nazi Martha and closer to Lynn. He smelled of lilacs. Lynn loved lilacs. Lilacs were her favorite flower. "I wish to see her as, alas, I have been out of the country for some time. I wish only to discuss her progress and ensure she is well." He smiled. Was it her imagination, or did sunlight sparkle off his perfect teeth?

"IF she's your niece," Martha spat with disgust, "you'd know who her doctor is!"

"I'm sorry," Lynn said, "but we can't disperse any information about patients."

"Yes," he said, bowing to her slightly. Lynn could see the tanned scalp underneath the thick black follicles of his hair. "That is as this woman," he gestured toward Martha, "has told me. The Hippo law."

"HIPPA," Martha sighed.

"Besides," Lynn said, staring into his eyes and deciding that these eyes held nothing but sweetness, "we have no information regarding discharged patients."

Martha hissed an intake of air.

For a second, Lynn thought she saw a dark cloud of anger flash across his face and his smile falter. But she must have hallucinated, for he instantly took her hand and with a quick kiss, brushed it across his lips.

"Many thank yous, milady," he crooned. Then with a flurry, he set his bowler atop his head and hobbled out the door, his cane grasped in his perfectly manicured hand.

"You're going to hell," Martha spat after Mr. Most Wonderful Eyes closed the door behind him. "I think you just broke three HIPPA regulations."

Lynn ignored her. She was sure telling that a patient had been discharged was not a violation of HIPPA regulations. Then a sad thought came to her.

"He never told me his name," she sighed.

"Robert," Martha snapped, "Robert Something—French-sounding."

"Ah!" Lynn smiled, "He *is* French."

"Yeah," Martha grunted, "big whoop-dee-doo."

Lynn smiled at Martha and headed down the carpeted hallway towards her office. The sunlight streaming through the windows cast a warm, welcoming glow on the austere mansion, providing a much-needed air of comfort. Robert. Bob. Robbie. Rob. All of these contractions seemed to dull the otherwise royal aura of the regal name and Lynn found herself wondering why any man would ever allow such a proper name to be shortened into something so...simplistic.

She grabbed the handle of her office door and pushed and smacked headlong into the heavy wood. Of course she locked it, what was she thinking? She always locked her door. She smiled to herself and fished her keys out of her back pocket, wondering all the while if the Frenchman would like her decor.

ROBERT STOOD AT THE EDGE of The Meadows' parking lot and flagged down his driver. It irritated him that the fool would park so far away from the front door when he gave precise instructions where to await his return. Didn't the dolt realize that Robert would emerge from this forlorn structure at its main entrance and not hundreds of yards away? Robert sighed in disgust and shifted his weight from leg to leg, broadcasting his disappointment and wondering where the man's sense had gone.

Servants were so hard to train that he often wondered why he bothered to try and educate them on his unique needs. Perhaps he should learn how to do these menial tasks himself rather than rely on the Doctor to choose his support staff. This practice of hiring locals to work for him may be useful in avoiding direct contact with authorities, but it required much effort and patience on his part.

And patience was a precious commodity these days.

As the black sedan rolled steadily towards him, Robert analyzed his plan once more, scouring it for flaws and risks. He knew Abbey would be at the Bastille by now. Where else would those harpies take her? Leave it to Eleanor, the witch, to gather the girl into the fold of the Guild earlier than expected. Eleanor was clever. Damn her. Perhaps he should forget this ill-fated game of Cloak and Dagger and merely saunter to the front door of the Bastille and demand the shrews take him to see Abbey. Does he not have the right to see her? Does he not have the right to access the Tapestry? He has the same rights as the Guild of Women, just like every other Immortal. But, no, he dare not do this because of Abbey. Because of what Abbey may have told the witches about him; because of what she may have remembered.

He shifted his weight again and rubbed his scalp vigorously. Damn her! If only he knew what the silly girl did or did not remember; if only he knew what she did or did not tell the witches; if only he knew what she did or did not reveal to the Guild! This one unanswered question, this one tiny doubt, is all that kept him from storming onto the grounds of the mansion, taking the girl and disappearing into the Tapestry. What to do now? Abbey must be his or die. Simple enough. He'd killed thousands of people before Abbey; what's one more? God knows he had enough reasons to kill any of the damned witches of the Guild. Eleanor could be defeated. Did she think the Bastille was impenetrable? Did the witch really believe the fortress's defenses would stop him from getting to the girl or the Tapestry? Had Eleanor become so confounded by age, power or wealth that she no longer realized how fragile her life was? The women of the Guild could die; he proved that time and time again by murdering the witches himself.

The limo floated along the curb until the back door came to rest a good meter to his right. Couldn't the sod see where Robert stood? Why must he always make adjustments for another's incompetence? Joshua lowered the volume of "HEY, YOU, GET OFF OF MY CLOUD." Robert closed his eyes and controlled his anger. He could not kill this young man. Yet. He waited until the oaf got out of the car and began walking towards the rear of the vehicle before yanking the rear door open. He threw himself into the back, dispensed with the useless cane— not even the 'cripple' façade had solicited sympathy from that ice queen of a secretary—and slammed the door closed just as the fool reached for it.

"Where to, boss?" Joshua asked after climbing into the driver's seat.

Robert sighed. If he drove past the Bastille tonight, he risked tipping his hand before the time was right. But if he waited, it was likely the wenches would conceive some plan to whisk Abbey away before Robert could get to her. Which would it be? Damn. If only he had arrived at The Meadows earlier today, he might have been able to get to the girl before the women. He should have known Eleanor would...

"Boss?" the voice floated from the front seat.

"I have asked you repeatedly not to refer to me by that moniker," Robert snapped.

The young man flashed a smile into the rear view mirror, his perfectly straight white teeth glimmering in the fading light. He winked, nodded and shoved the dark glasses over his eyes. He flicked a button on the CD and music boomed from the speakers. "I WAS BORN…"

Robert shook his head and ground his teeth together. "To the penthouse, please," he muttered.

"Right-e-o, boss!" the driver chirped and pressed a button on the dashboard.

As the dark glass partition slid between the driver and himself, Robert sighed. Yes, he would definitely kill this man. Eventually.

13

"**I** BELIEVE THERE IS A WOMAN RUNNING ALONGSIDE THE CAR," Abbey said, staring out the window of the limo.

"That would be Boo," Ruth smiled, as her hands flitted over her needlepoint.

"She's blue," Abbey said.

Ruth laughed loudly. "Boo does have a fondness for blue!"

"And she's naked."

"Abbey, dear, your Aunt Boo has a few…idiosyncrasies," Eleanor muttered from beneath closed eyelids. "One learns to adapt."

Less than an hour ago, the trio had loaded themselves into the limo and sat in uncomfortable silence as the car meandered around the curves of the road leading away from The Meadows and towards the Bastille. Ruth chatted nonstop about the weather, gluten-free snacks, cloud formations, and the benefits of baking with honey; through it all, Abbey nodded patiently. She desperately wanted to talk to Eleanor about the brass toy airplane and the cryptic message written on its side, but felt it rude to change the topic. After spending only minutes on the freeway, the limo exited onto a side road that paralleled the river.

Turning off the road onto a smaller drive, the limo cruised through thickly wooded countryside on a smooth, freshly paved road with PRIVATE DRIVE signs every few hundred feet. It was then that Abbey turned to look out the opposite side of the car and noticed the naked blue figure running alongside. As the limo passed her, the blue woman locked eyes with Abbey. The look lasted only a moment before the woman turned and disappeared into the woods.

"I know this place," Abbey declared, gazing at the countryside.

"Yes!" Ruth squealed. "Yes. What do you remember?"

Try as she might, Abbey caught only pieces of the mental visions: walking along the water, laughing at the sky, a long, straight stretch of road. She shook her head.

"Let me know when you remember something more substantial," Ruth cooed and returned to her needlepoint.

"Ah! We have arrived," Eleanor said, pulling herself upright in the seat. The limo sat in front of two huge iron gates and mounted inside were the largest stone pylons Abbey had ever seen. Behind the gates, Abbey saw turrets standing high above the treetops.

The driver punched a code into the keypad and the gates opened, allowing the limo onto a wide stone driveway flanked by a high, sturdy-looking fence to the left of the vehicle. To the right was a huge rectangular stone building with eight turrets spaced along its outside walls. The land around the structure was perfectly manicured, with stone pathways, patches of flowers, and small iron benches under large shade trees. Abbey turned her attention to the immediate right and stared at a drawbridge that doubled as a front walkway leading to two enormous wooden doors.

"Welcome to the Bastille," said Eleanor.

"Not the REAL Bastille," Ruth laughed. "That's in France."

Eleanor looked to Abbey. "How much of this do you remember, dear?" Abbey shook her head. "The construction of our Bastille took over two years, and has been in the Emerson family since its completion in the 1700's.

"The Bastille sits on five of our one thousand acres. The five acres of the grounds are protected by the fence you see as well as an assortment of monitoring devices."

"Why the security?" Abbey asked, gawking at the flags posted on top of the turrets: USA, France, Canada, Ireland, England, one she did not recognize.

"We live in dangerous times, do we not?" Eleanor answered.

"You live here, my love," Ruth added, patting Abbey's hand. "You will remember. I'm sure of it."

The limo pulled to a stop in front of the drawbridge. In a flash, hands opened the car doors and Eleanor stepped out, followed by Ruth.

Abbey followed the two aunts while a thin man appeared out of nowhere to haul her bag from the trunk. His dark hair was parted in the middle and lay expertly to either side of the part. His long, thin face ended with a pointed chin and his ears were too small for his head. As he passed the three women with the bag, Eleanor turned to Abbey.

"You remember Fred, my dear?" Eleanor said, nudging Abbey towards the man.

"Good evening, Abbey." His crisp pronunciation crept over his perfectly aligned white teeth that appeared whiter against his tanned skin.

"Hello," she responded, staring into eyes that sparkled in the afternoon sun. A faint air of recognition fluttered through her. She knew him, she was sure of it, but for the life of her, she couldn't remember. Suddenly, it struck her that he had one brown eye and one blue.

"Good afternoon, Fred," Ruth cooed. "How fares the Bastille?"

Fred grinned. "Tomyris has left the dogs to their own devices in the east wing," he said calmly. "They seem to have discovered the joys of… how shall I say? They discovered the joys of dirty lingerie."

"Wonderful," Eleanor's sarcasm seeped into the air. "Just what I wanted to see—Tomyris' worn panties. Goodness knows where they've been."

"Perhaps they raided the panty drawer in order to rinse the delicates," Ruth smiled.

"If only the dogs were that useful." Eleanor turned to Fred. "Is it safe to assume the garments in question are still lying about?"

Fred laughed. "The way I see it, there are some things a man doesn't need to acquaint himself with."

"Unless, of course, he had a hand in their disposal?" Eleanor grinned.

"This way, dear," Ruth muttered, grabbing Abbey by the elbow and guiding her into the mansion. "There's something you must see."

Abbey turned and waved to Fred as she followed Aunt Ruth, her gut churning. This man was with her when she sank beneath the waves and the darkness dragged her into the depths. As she watched, he waved to her, nodded and disappeared from view as Ruth pulled her into the Bastille.

The foyer of the mansion spread out before her with dazzling brilliance. A huge chandelier hung from the ceiling, spilling its colorful arcs across a floor of white Italian tile. The sparsely decorated walls held a huge mirror framed in gold above a table opposite the double door entrance. To her left, a fire crackled in a stone fireplace along the wall of the sitting room filled with vintage Victorian furniture. To her right, a dark mahogany door sporting a brass knocker in the shape of a gargoyle took up half the wall. In front of her, next to the mirror, an arched doorway led to the remainder of the mansion.

"Ah, you are all here," Eleanor said as several women rushed into the foyer.

"Of course!" sighed the thin black woman wearing a brightly colored, flowing robe and several gold necklaces.

"Boo is out," barked the olive-skinned woman with chiseled features, dark, penetrating eyes and full, sensuous lips. Abbey guessed her to be Italian. "Imagine—Boo stalking the woods. Perhaps she'll return with something she's strangled with her bare hands."

"Oh, dear, I hope not." Ruth shook her head. "I have no other recipes for crow. Although I suppose I could mix the bird into a stuffing."

"Yes, I know all about Boo," Eleanor muttered under her breath. "She will be along momentarily."

"Abbey, you must be dead-tired after your trek from town." The third one in the group, a middle-eastern woman, with smooth, dark skin, wore a tank top that revealed muscled arms decorated with primitive tattoos. Woven throughout her long black hair were ostrich feathers and colored beads. Peeking out from her hip pocket was an iPod. Four Salukis sat at her heels, looking to her with anticipation. "Would you like something to eat? Ruth can whip you up something. Cornish hen? A cake? Baked Alaskan?"

"Oatmeal bars!" Ruth piped up enthusiastically. "With figs!"

"Abbey, do you remember any names, or do we have the Mickey Mouse roll call again?" the middle-eastern woman asked, ignoring the oatmeal bars Ruth held out.

Abbey nodded, "Of course, Aunt Tom." She hugged the petite woman fiercely as the dogs groaned in disapproval. She nodded to the ebony-skinned woman in the bright colors, "Aunt Zen, and Aunt Liv." She smiled to the Italian woman with the chiseled features. "It is only my distant memories that fail me."

Aunt Liv smiled broadly and her arms swallowed Abbey. It felt more than an embrace, tender, solid and welcoming. Abbey resisted the touch at first, then slowly she sensed the love emanating from her arms and smooth skin. She melted into the olive-skinned beauty. Soon, all the aunts surrounded her, giggling, while the dogs paced the floor. Ruth reached into her purse and retrieved several small cookies which the animals gobbled down.

"Please don't feed them, Ruth," Aunt Tom groaned.

"I would suppose the poor things are starving!"

"Please," Liv ordered, holding out a hand to both the women. "This reunion is about Abbey and how much she remembers us."

"She has seen you *all* at The Meadows," Eleanor snapped. "She's suffered amnesia, not mental retardation."

Abbey ignored Eleanor and wrapped her arms around the three aunts. "I remember everything." The aunts' smiles faltered and they shot a fervent look to Eleanor. Abbey, oblivious to the glances, continued. "Aunt Tom, you are from Iran and you used to lecture me on the finer points of democracy versus totalitarianism."

She turned her attention to Zen. "You worked at the museum in London. Your specialty is ancient Egypt." To Liv, "You teach ancient history at the university. You speak fluent Italian, English, Greek and French."

"Yes!" Ruth screamed and began jumping up and down.

"Ladies," Eleanor's voice dripped with impatience. "There is much to do and little time to do it."

Eleanor pulled Abbey away from the aunts. "Abbey, come with me. I'll show you to your room." She guided Abbey out of the foyer gently as the four women stood watching breathlessly.

14

"POWERFUL?" ABBEY ASKED, walking alongside Eleanor.

"What?" Eleanor broke out of her reverie to look at her.

"Oh! Heavens! I do get carried away when I speak of ancestors, don't I?" She laughed and hugged Abbey tightly. "I think all the women in our family were powerful. Despite the general feeling to the contrary, not all families are patriarchal."

Eleanor guided Abbey down the stone corridor that lined the perimeter of the Bastille. "Take your time examining the family's Tapestry, Abbey. All these embroidered scenes"—she motioned to the tapestry that lined the long walls of the corridor—"depict a story, sometimes several, from the lives of women who came before us."

"A medieval scrapbook," Abbey muttered. Just moments ago, Eleanor had guided her through the archway of the main foyer, around a corner and into the residential wing of the mansion. They walked down a long hallway whose walls were constructed from huge blocks of stone while the floor was made of a smooth marble. Torch-shaped sconces lined the wall to her right, which also contained several heavy wooden doors, all of which led to a room that Abbey could only assume were guest rooms. The wall to her left was the one that fascinated her. This exterior wall contained thick glass windows spaced several yards apart overlooking the immense woods of the Bastille. Between each window, hanging from the ceiling to the floor, was a huge tapestry made of woven linen material. This was 'the Tapestry' which Eleanor was explaining.

The fabric felt heavy between her fingers, at least an inch thick of soft, strong fibers. Embroidered into the dark fabric were hundreds of smaller panels, each containing a picturesque scene, ranging in size from three or four inches square to almost a square foot. Although sewn with hundreds of colors, Abbey noticed the threads used for the scenarios had a commonality—they sparkled as if the thread was made of mirrors. Even in the flickering, dim light of the cavernous stone hallway the illustrations shimmered with an eerie life-like quality.

"The tapestry runs the entire exterior wall?" Abbey asked.

"Yes. And more," Eleanor said from the doorway opposite the young woman. "Two sets of parallel hallways create a central square. The Great Tapestry hangs from floor to ceiling in fifty sections along all four of these hallways."

"Just like The Meadows," Abbey murmured.

"What, dear?"

"The building is constructed exactly like The Meadows. Hallways surrounding a central arena."

Eleanor giggled. "Thus the name 'The Bastille.' Before it was a prison, it was a French stronghold."

"A prison. Just like The Meadows."

"Really?"

"They are exactly alike." Abbey fixed her gaze upon Eleanor.

"How unusual."

"Yes."

"Yes!" Eleanor broke the gaze first, "you are quite right in your description of the Tapestry! A medieval scrapbook!" She giggled childishly. "Pictures before the camera was invented! Come look into these pictures and know that at some point, human hands embroidered every one of them."

"Unbelievable," Abbey said, eyeing the image of two boys playing under a tree while a watchful mother played a harp.

Eleanor laughed. "Yes," she said simply.

Abbey spotted another, smaller image. This one of a woman sleeping under the night sky as two large stars shone onto her. She stepped closer to the Tapestry and looked more closely at the woman sleeping. She shifted to a different angle, but couldn't see the face of the young woman any clearer. Was it the dark threads that made this small figure look like herself? Why would a likeness of her be inside the Tapestry?

"The handiwork…they look alive, do they not? Almost like magic."

"Almost."

The sound of dogs barking erupted from within the mansion and Abbey rolled her eyes. Why couldn't any of these ladies take a fancy to songbirds?

15

ABBEY AWOKE TO THE SOUND OF HORSES' HOOVES on stone and immediately registered two things: She was naked and someone was watching her. She pulled her matted hair from her face and scanned the room as her feet searched the bottom of the bed for her nightshirt.

The full moon illuminated the room through the French doors, casting gray shadows on the marble floor. Abbey's panic faded as she recognized the familiar furnishings of her bedroom in the Bastille; the heavy mahogany canopy bed consumed only a fraction of the huge turret room. In addition to the king-size bed and the cedar chest at its foot, her quarters held the Louis XIV desk, the clothing armoire, a vintage dressing table, and a variety of sitting chairs. A monstrous fireplace ran the length of the wall opposite her bed, with two suits of armor acting as bookends. After such meager furnishings at The Meadows, the ostentatious made Abbey feel decadent.

Her toe found the nightshirt and she slipped it on, all the while her eyes darting around the room for signs of an intruder. She saw nothing. This didn't stop the hairs on the back of her neck from standing on end and gooseflesh from erupting along her arms. She knew someone was watching her; she could feel it. From outside her door, the sound that awoke her repeated itself. Abbey froze, listening intently. She could have sworn that the sharp, heavy clopping was a horse's hoof hitting the stone floor of the hallway.

The sound came again, this time closer to her door. A slight pause and then another clump on the stone rang out. Another, faster now, as if the animal was speeding up. No doubt about it—a horse was inside the mansion.

Abbey flew out of bed, the cool night air pinching her sweat-soaked skin. She grabbed for her robe, shoving her arms through the sleeves as she grabbed for the door.

It stood ajar. She froze. She had closed the door tightly before she retired, she was sure of it. Someone had opened it while she slept. As she stood with her hand inches from the handle, the faint sound of a horse's neigh floated through the air. She whipped open the door. The cool stone bit the soles of her feet, but she barely noticed as she ran into the middle of the wide hallway. A flash of color to her left drew her attention and she turned toward the sight. The tapestry fluttered against the wall, as if it was a giant flag caught in the wind. Waves fluttered down the length of the hallway like ripples on water. Abbey's eyes followed the rippling fabric until she caught the slightest glimpse of flowing red hair disappearing around the corner. Aunt Boo? What was she doing up so late? Why did she bring a horse into the house?

Abbey dashed down the hallway, took a sharp left turn as she headed back to the main foyer. As she rounded the corner, she ran headlong into a wall.

"Abbey! Dear! What are you doing?"

She hadn't run into a wall. She had run into Aunt Boo. Abbey looked up at the red-headed naked Amazon and noticed that Boo stood next to Aunt Zen (looking quite spiffy in a tri-colored muumuu) and Aunt Ruth. All three held shovels.

"I…heard…" Abbey managed to say before blurting out, "Aunt Boo, why are you naked?" Suddenly, the pungent smell of horse manure assaulted her. She looked down. A huge pile of steaming horse droppings lay at the feet of the three women.

"Couldn't sleep?" Aunt Ruth laughed. She wore a tattered, brown terry-cloth robe, which she held tightly closed around her neck. Her feet sported thin leather sandals, the kind normally worn in the desert. She looked like a biblical refugee.

"What's that?" Abbey asked, pointing to the horse droppings. "Why are you all awake?"

The aunts looked to each other in silence.

"Could you not sleep, child?" Ruth asked Abbey again.

"Uh...no, I slept fine," Abbey said, shaking the remnants of sleep from her head. "Did you hear..."

"Heard something?" Ruth asked, taking Abbey's frozen hands in hers. "What? Did the telephone ring again? That sound! It's so...harsh on one's ears."

"It sounded like a horse."

"Oh, my word!" Ruth laughed, her serious countenance melting under her smile, "of course! The horses from the stable!" Then, with a dramatic tone continued softly, "Your Aunt Eleanor loves those damn beasts!" Zen and Ruth broke out in loud laughter. Boo shook her head in disgust.

Zen smiled broadly, leaning on her small spade. "That must have been what you heard, my dear. Horses from the stables. One of the steeds must be wandering around and awakened you from your sleep."

"Oh, you poor dear," Ruth continued. "It must be *ages* since you've heard horses' hooves, hasn't it?" She pulled Abbey close and hugged her.

Abbey nodded and Ruth pulled back to look into her face. "Come, child," Ruth ordered, taking Abbey's hand firmly. "I spent the day making ginger treats. You must have one with me. Come." The small woman tugged at Abbey.

"But Aunt Ruth," Abbey began, "the droppings." She pointed behind her toward the pile of dung.

Ruth lowered her head to Abbey's ear and spoke softly. "Honestly, don't you find horses the most unclean animal?" Then, with a chipper giggle, she added, "I have ginger snaps—three kinds of ginger: gingerbread (that's Tom's favorite!), ginger pudding, and a delightful recipe I pulled from a magazine." Turning to yell over her shoulder, she addressed Zen. "Go get the others, girls! COOKIE TIME!"

Abbey let Ruth's voice drone on. As Ruth tugged her arm, Abbey's focus shifted from the aunts to the tapestry. The corner of the twenty-five by twenty-five section nearest the women fluttered again as if caught up in a breeze. Abbey noticed something lying on the stone floor almost hidden by the tapestry's bottom edge. She stared at it so long, that she barely noticed the stone floor giving way to the imported woven runner lining the floor of the foyer and stumbled when Ruth pulled her around the corner, heading for the kitchen.

Only then did Abbey take her eyes off the half-eaten apple.

"A WHAT?" ABBEY ASKED, with the ginger chocolate chip cookie poised halfway to her mouth.

"A Faire," Aunt Eleanor answered, pouring more Sevigne Blanc into her crystal goblet.

"Actually," Ruth giggled, "a Medieval Faire!" She slid another cookie onto Abbey's plate and patted the girl's head. "It is *such* fun!" she exclaimed, clapping her hands together.

"You *do* know what a Medieval Faire is, don't you?" Boo's voice reverberated so loudly that Abbey felt as if an earthquake rumbled under the house. "It is a re-creation of a period in history. Reminiscent of a living museum. Very real." She punctuated the last word by slicing an apple in half with one fierce stroke.

"Where do you host it?" Abbey asked as she gobbled the rest of her cookie.

"Here," Aunt Tom responded firmly. "More precisely, *there*," she added, pointing out the kitchen window toward the woods.

"On the grounds of the Bastille?" Abbey questioned. The aunts nodded. "Why?"

"Well, dear, it is a family ritual," Ruth reassured her, patting Abbey's arm lightly.

"Ritual," Boo echoed, nodding her head.

"Yes," Eleanor concurred, "for the past several…"

"Six," Boo interjected.

"Eight," Tom corrected.

"Ten?" Zen chimed in.

"Years, the Bastille has opened our lands to the glories of history," Eleanor finished. "Pass me the cookies, won't you please, Ruth?"

"We find it relaxing!" Ruth chuckled, clapping furiously.

"Fun," Zen said, nibbling an apple.

Tomyris agreed, rolling her eyes. "If you're a loser geek. I'd rather stay in my room and play Wii."

"Thank you for that outpouring of support." Eleanor drained the last of her drink.

Abbey chewed on the cookie as Ruth placed the now-empty cookie jar into the sink.

The immense kitchen rivaled any restaurant, easily taking up over a quarter of the first floor. An entire wall of the room sported a marble counter, barely visible under the platters of cookies, plates of pies, cakes and brownies, all handmade by Ruth's tireless devotion to all things culinary. In the center of the space sat an island where a wide assortment of pots, pans, colanders and other cooking utensils hung sparkling in the light. Ruth moved the platters of cookies onto the sideboard and fished a huge mixing bowl from beneath the counter. She smiled at Abbey as she measured flour into it and began humming as she folded in a tablespoon of baking soda.

"The yearly event brings the townspeople and the Bastille closer together."

"We tried hedonistic acts reminiscent of ancient Rome, but Eleanor put the kibosh on the orgies and the vomitorium." Tomyris' voice carried a distinct air of disgust.

"I have never been a part of one before," said Abbey.

"Yes, you have," Zen whispered, laying her hand over Abbey's.

"Oh, dear! It's after midnight!" Ruth gasped. "Off to bed! All of you!" She tossed the remaining half-eaten cookies to the dogs sniffing around Tom's feet and began shooing the women out of the kitchen.

"I wish you wouldn't feed them treats." Tomyris snatched a cookie from Ruth.

"The poor things are starving."

"You always say that."

"Good. It's settled," Boo bellowed over the squabbling and headed out of the room. "I'll give Abbey a list of chores by morning."

"It *is* morning, dear," Eleanor snapped.

"Yes, dear, I know," Boo's icy tone cut the air. Abbey nodded to Boo as the aunt disappeared down the hallway.

"Chores?" Tomyris asked, walking through the kitchen on her toes. "Good for the calves," she explained to Abbey.

"I have a question," said Abbey, as Tom settled her feet onto the floor and began her pelvic thrusts. "Can I visit the horses?"

"Horses?" Tomyris shot a sideward glance to Eleanor.

"Of course you may," Eleanor said, holding out her hand. "But now, bedtime, young lady."

As Abbey turned the corner towards the residential wing, she heard Tom whispering something to Ruth and Eleanor, but by the time she turned back to the three women they had stopped talking and were munching on shortbread. Where did Ruth find time to bake all the sweets? Abbey made it as far as the corridor outside her room before she sensed someone watching her again. She glanced over her shoulder and her eyes landed on the Tapestry. She wandered closer to it, imagining that seeing every one of the embroidered scenes would be impossible—there were simply too many of them. As she searched the Tapestry for the woman sleeping under the stars, the tiny figure in the upper corner of the third panel on the right caught her attention. The figure was a peasant woman, dressed from the medieval period. The woman stood on her toes with her arms outstretched reaching into the air. From her vantage point, it seemed to Abbey that the woman was reaching into the corner of the fabric itself, as if trying to escape the confines of her woven prison. All alone in the far-flung corners of the art, Abbey felt a sense of connection to the embroidered woman. She, too, was lost, alone and reaching for something out of sight.

And the tiny woven woman looked just like her.

17

MICK JAGGER BELTED OUT "DOWN HOME GIRL" as the Lincoln cut through the morning mist and glided to a stop on the shoulder of the road running perpendicular to the Bastille's private drive. Robert pressed the electric windows and the tinted glass slid silently down into the car door as he placed the binoculars to his eyes.

"Want me to cut the music, boss?" Joshua asked, obviously trying to sneak a peek into the rear compartment.

"No," Robert answered as he surveyed the manicured lawn across the strip of pavement. "And don't call me 'Boss.'"

Robert saw no activity at all, which surprised him. Surely someone—even several people—would be moving about the grounds at this hour. Eleanor hadn't been able to keep herself inactive for more than five minutes since the Crusades. Ruth, the useless, addle-pated fool, with her endless tinkering and flower gathering, would garden during the apocalypse. Boudicca was…well…Boudicca. That woman was a few bricks short of a load anyway. This hyperkinetic activity is what he was counting on if his plan was to be a success.

Zenobia, of course, was not an issue.

The only woman he had to worry about was Tomyris. The girl was unpredictable and reckless, two characteristics that would work against him. If she teamed up with Boudicca to challenge him, he could be thwarted. Boudicca's insanity and Tomyris' cunning could prove formidable.

Then there was Abbey—the wild card.

It distressed him that he couldn't discover how much Abbey had remembered before the witches got her. He had seen many an Immortal recover from near death within hours. He hated this waiting. Robert was a man of action, not patience, and his insides itched to do something besides sit and watch the witches of the Tapestry.

"Want a drink?" Joshua asked. "I could pour you a drink."

"No," Robert snapped.

Suddenly a car approached from behind and Robert lowered the binoculars to his lap. The car passed the limo, its left turn signal flashing brilliantly. It turned into the private drive of the Bastille and paused as the driver reached out and pressed the intercom button.

A sheriff's police car. What could this mean? Had the women spoken to Abbey and called the authorities? Unlikely. The women of the Guild rarely asked for help and when they did, assistance arrived from other Guild members, not the local police. He wrinkled his brow as he played out the various reasons the police would be at the Bastille. Suddenly, a thought crossed his mind and his blood ran cold.

The Guild must have found one of the bodies.

No. It could not have been the Guild. If they had, they would bury the corpse before questions surfaced. If the Witches of the Guild uncovered the body, they would recognize the signs of the Tapestry's Spell and come after him. Someone other than the Guild must have discovered a corpse. Who else had access to the Bastille's land?

This would not do. It would not do at all.

The private gate of the Bastille opened and the police car disappeared around a bend, leaving Robert's car alone on the deserted road once more.

"What do you want to do, boss?"

"Drive."

"Where?"

"Back to the hotel, my thick young man," Robert snapped, although he didn't care. He needed to think. He needed to talk to the Doctor about a new plan regarding what to do with Abbey.

WHEN SHE FELT READY TO PRY HERSELF from the warmth of her bed, Abbey threw on yesterday's clothes. Luckily they were not soiled and would suffice for a quick trip to the horse barn. She shoved her feet into a pair of woolen socks Eleanor had left for her and slipped on her shoes. If she was to take up riding, she would have to buy boots.

As she left her room, she shot a quick glance toward the Tapestry to check up on the embroidered woman standing with outstretched arms. Abbey froze mid-step. The embroidered woman was gone.

Abbey's first thought was that she had glanced at the wrong panel; in the confusion of her first night home she must have forgotten on which corner the panel was located. She inched closer to the panel. The picture was the same, no doubt about it: the tree standing in the green glade, the mustard-colored sun, and the muted colors of the grass in the glen. The woman in the picture had disappeared.

Was she losing her mind? She often frightened the other patients at The Meadows with her auditory hallucinations, but she never suffered from visual hallucinations. Had her mind slipped this much? Had her amnesia somehow deteriorated into full-blown psychosis?

"Dear?" The voice startled Abbey. "I'm sorry, honey, I didn't mean to startle you."

"No," Abbey croaked, trying to smile, "it's okay, Aunt Eleanor. I...I didn't hear you, that's all."

"Do you still wish to see the stables?" Abbey nodded. "Then come along, dear. We shall meet Aunt Boo on the lawn, no doubt. Target practice," she added, rolling her eyes.

Abbey forced a smile and followed Aunt Eleanor down the corridor, her eyes still fixed upon the Tapestry and the empty space where the tiny woman should be.

19

"If I remember correctly, and I do remember correctly," Martha sniffed, "the policy clearly states that all comp-time will be approved at least one week in advance."

Lynn maintained her composure, struggling to keep a façade of professional politeness. What she really wanted to do was grab Martha's matching silver pen and pencil set and shove them into the bitch's eyes.

She'd been on the run ever since her cell phone woke her at 5:30 AM. The night shift, mostly grad students doing their internships, discovered Mrs. Bailey being intimate with Fung Shi. Mrs. Bailey started screaming about the violation of her pet's rights, which awoke Mr. Stewart who wanted to come watch Mrs. Bailey make love to the imaginary creature. Mr. Rix felt so inspired, he channeled Barbra Streisand and sang "Evergreen." Within minutes, the whole wing descended into chaos.

Ergo, her phone rang before dawn.

During the last six hours she had met with the entire population, coaxing everyone to calm down. Everyone except Mr. Graves who seemed unaffected by the whirlwind of activity. Mr. Graves was not a reactionary person by nature, so this fact didn't surprise her. What did surprise her was what he said during their previous session. She knocked lightly on his door and listened to hear his whispered permission of entry. He stood on a chair gazing out of the tiny window near the ceiling.

"Good morning, Mr. Graves."

"Abbey?" His voice barely carried across the silent room.

"Abbey's with her family."

"Did you see her?"

"Uh…no. No, I haven't." The shift from his usual pleasant countenance threw her. "She…"

"You need to tell her about him. About Robert."

Lynn froze. Robert? The strikingly handsome, dark-haired Adonis?

"Excuse me?" she managed to ask.

"You desire him," Mr. Graves stated.

She cleared her throat, feeling like she had just been caught having sex in her parents' bed. Was her attraction to the stranger so obvious that even the clients could notice? If so, did that make her ineffectual? Stupid? Horny? She hustled back to her office and flopped into her chair and spun herself in small circles. How in the world did Mr. Graves know about Robert? She sat alone in the room, spinning slowly for what felt like just a few minutes, but in reality must have been more like twenty, for when she answered the phone, Martha sounded more irritable than usual.

"I do not see the summary of your time breakdown," she said haughtily, "so I know they must be misplaced. Do you remember where you left them?"

Lynn sighed. She had forgotten all about the end-of-the-month reporting. Martha knew this, of course, because Martha was good at her job. Why didn't the nosy woman go into a profession where she got paid more for snooping on her coworkers?

"I'll print you out another copy," Lynn said politely, spinning to her computer. It took her barely an hour to complete her report and she hit the PRINT button without proofreading. Screw the typos. Let Martha suffer through the bad spelling. As Lynn walked down the hallway, summary report in hand, an idea hit her.

Lynn put on her best shit-eating grin and said to Martha as calmly as she could muster, "I can't get into the Bastille to see Abbey next week. It must be today or tomorrow. I'll use some of my comp time for it."

"And the reason you cannot schedule a meeting in advance and prepare the proper comp time leave forms would be…?" Martha let the question hang in the air.

"Because Abbey is busy next week," Lynn lied.

"Next week is out because…?" Martha sniffed and grabbed a tissue from the hand-painted china tissue holder.

"Because Abbey is busy." Lynn's smile faltered. She could always bypass the writing implements and bash Martha with the phone. "The Faire, remember? Eleanor told me Abbey is participating in the celebration." This wasn't a lie, exactly. Eleanor *did* mention that Abbey would help.

"I must remind you that the usual turnaround for this kind of leave is forty-eight to seventy-two hours," Martha droned.

"And I appreciate your keeping track of that." Lynn smiled at her while wondering if putting sugar in the bitch's tank would be considered pathological. "This is quite nice of you, really. It's going to help me out so much."

Martha gave her one last glance before turning her back on Lynn and flipping on the computer.

"Thank you," Lynn said, as she headed back to her office. It was not quite one o'clock yet. She would have the entire afternoon off. She could easily drive to the Bastille, do a follow-up on Abbey and be home before *The Golden Girls*. And, what the heck, she may as well swing by Dairy Queen for a hot fudge sundae. There's no day so bad that a hot fudge sundae couldn't make it a whole lot better.

If she happened to mention Robert while she was chatting with Aunt Eleanor and Abbey, what harm would it do? Maybe she'd find out more about the handsome stranger and his relationship to the Ladies of the Bastille.

20

"**S**ORRY TO DISTURB YOU, ELEANOR." Mathers heard Janet's voice soften. "I wouldn't bother you if it wasn't important."

"Of course not, Officer Gage." Mathers watched as Eleanor extended her hand, palm down, like royalty.

"Just Janet, please. I'm not an officer."

"Janet," Eleanor smiled, shooting a sidewards glance to Mathers. "And you would be...?"

"Detective Mathers," Matt said. He glanced at the woman in her form-fitting suit, silk blouse and pearls and suddenly felt underdressed. He flashed his identification and Eleanor barely glanced at it.

"Guests?" a cheery voice floated into the foyer as Mathers and Janet entered. An elderly woman turned the corner and stopped in the doorway, her dress belying the wealth she possessed; a plain brown cotton shift with Birkenstocks. Her grey hair spilled out of the bun upon her head and a single band of gold hung around her neck, a dainty Star of David dangling from its center. This woman reeked of prudish elegance.

"Janet, you remember my elder sister, Ruth," Eleanor said.

"Yes, of course," Janet replied, "good to see you again, Ruth."

"This is Detective Mathers." Matt noticed Eleanor's eyes scrutinizing him.

"Cookies!" Ruth screamed and bounced out of the foyer.

"Forgive her," Eleanor sighed, "she does love entertaining so." She ushered Janet and Mathers into the elegant sitting room, where a roaring fire snapped within the confines of the immense fireplace. Mathers took a seat in the overstuffed chair opposite Eleanor and next to Janet Gage.

"I'll get right to the point, Eleanor," Janet said. "Yesterday, I went on your property to set the posts for the Bastille's festival."

"Ah, yes!" Eleanor interrupted, "one of those city ordinances which, I fear, I forget about every year."

"That's all right," Janet said sheepishly. "Livia fills the forms out for the party. That's not the problem." Janet paused a moment and Mathers thought he saw her blush. "The problem is we can't use the northern part of the woods as the front gate this year. With all the rain and runoff we've had, the area is practically a bog."

"Not a party, Janet," Eleanor interrupted, her voice polite but fierce. "A Faire. A re-creation of history—from the best part of history in my opinion—the dawning of the age of enlightenment."

Janet nodded. "Of course. My point is, all of our boundary markers had to be redone for this year's par-" she caught herself, "Faire. You know, making sure the land for the parking was not water heavy, the trees are wide enough to accommodate porta-potties, and the like."

"A great favor to us." Eleanor smiled without passion. "My! We have this down to a science, do we not?"

"Yeah. I'd hate for you to call Tony's Garage every time one of your guests got stuck in the mud." She paused for Eleanor to chuckle. Eleanor didn't. "Well, I was pacing out the distance from the state lands to a dry spot on the Bastille grounds and...I...we, actually, Mathers was with me..."

"*Was* he now?" Eleanor's eyes shot in Mathers' direction. "How did one of Montpelier's finest get down here?" Mathers was caught off-guard and shot Eleanor a suspicious look. "Your police identification," Eleanor explained.

"Uh..." Janet intercepted the question, "grilling out, actually. Sal invited him."

"So, Detective, you are...friendly...with Janet, or her husband?"

"Both," Mathers shot back. "We're old friends."

"Anyway," Janet continued quickly, "we found something." Janet paused. Eleanor waited. "A body."

"Body?" Eleanor repeated.

"Yes." Janet avoided her gaze. "A body. Caucasian woman. Looks to be about eighty or so."

"Well…" Now it was Eleanor's turn to be taken by surprise. "That is quite unexpected."

"Cookies!" Ruth's voice screeched across the room. With a flurry, the woman entered with a huge silver platter. "Enjoy!"

Mathers looked down and saw at least four kinds of cookies, several brownie squares, and what appeared to be a small waffle.

"Ruth, dear, Officer Gage…" she stopped herself and smiled, "Ranger Gage and Detective Mathers found a dead body on our property."

"Body?" Ruth asked. Eleanor nodded. "Dead?" Eleanor nodded again. "Dead body?"

Eleanor snapped, "Would you please ask our sisters to come here?"

"Yes," Ruth muttered. "I will. Dear…dear…dear…" she muttered as she left the room. She dodged back in to say, "Eat. Plenty of cookies." She ran out again.

"What kind of attention can we expect?" Eleanor's voice took a sharper, harsher tone that Mathers picked up on instantly.

"I think I can keep it under wraps for a while," Janet said with a flourish, "but I'm not sure how long before the *Times Argus* finds out. Maybe a day?" She looked to Mathers, but he sat studying Eleanor. Janet continued, "WPTZ and WCAX are bound to get wind of it."

Eleanor nodded. "Can we expect an investigation?"

Janet nodded. "But since Mathers was with me, he'll probably get the case."

"Can you do that, Detective Mathers?" Eleanor looked in his direction. "Isn't the Bastille out of your jurisdiction?"

Mathers smiled. "I believe our working relationship with local authorities is solid enough that I can arrange something."

"How fortunate, then, that you…happened…to be present."

"Yes."

"Tell me about the investigation."

"I'm sure it won't be too invasive." Mathers locked eyes with the woman. "I'm sure you have no idea where the body came from?"

"Has the investigation already begun?" she shot back.

"Investigation? What investigation?" a hoarse voice asked.

Mathers spun around to see four women standing alongside Ruth, who nervously wrung her hands. One was black, with colorful clothing and striking facial features; one was dressed in a business suit and looked Italian; one was a huge woman with broad shoulders and flaming red hair, wearing leather pants; and the fourth was a thin, dark-skinned woman with feathers and bells in her hair. She had an iPod in one hand and a leash attached to four of the ugliest dogs he had ever seen in her other hand. Individually, they were imposing. In a group, they were frightening.

"Janet, you remember my other sisters."

"Sisters?" Mathers asked.

"Yes," Eleanor responded icily. "Some by birth, others by marriage." As if the explanation was unimportant. "Detective Mathers, this is Boo, Livia, Zenobia and Tomyris."

With no further expansion of which sister belonged to which name, Mathers simply nodded.

"Investigation?" the red-haired one said again. "What investigation?"

"Of the dead body, Boo." Eleanor's voice remained flat. "Which was found on the grounds of the Bastille yesterday as the lines were drawn for the Faire's new boundaries."

"I had to set the posts for your party," Janet said.

"Faire," Eleanor corrected.

"Faire," Janet said.

"This is unacceptable!" Boo grunted and fled the room.

"Forgive Boo. She has a tendency for overdramatic entrances and exits."

"Officer Gage," the Italian-looking woman in the business suit said, "where?"

"The southwest corner. Near the guest entrance to the Faire site. And I'm not an officer."

Livia nodded and followed Boo out of the room.

"I would like to know more," the black-skinned woman said briskly.

"Yes, Ms.—?" Mathers began.

"Zen. Zenobia, if you prefer." The woman smiled broadly. "What do you know?"

Mathers flipped open his notebook. "The body appears to be approximately eighty. Caucasian female. Tattoo. Mickey Mouse. On her ankle." He paused for a reaction from the women. Seeing none, he continued. "Actually there were several inconsistencies. Such as a pierced—" he paused. He couldn't bring himself to say 'labia' in front of these women. "Tongue ... as well. She was dressed in medieval clothing, however, if that has any importance."

"Tattoo?" Zen asked. "An eighty-year-old woman with a Mickey Mouse tattoo?"

"That is what I would like to know," Mathers said looking at her. "Along with why she was wearing clothing from a few centuries ago?"

"Any clue is a clue of importance, is it not?" Eleanor snapped. Mathers nodded.

"Is there anything more you can tell me?"

"It seems you do not know much to begin with," Zenobia said with a smile.

Mathers smiled back. Twice he prodded for information and twice the Ladies sidestepped providing anything. The plot keeps thickening here at the Bastille. "No, I'm afraid I don't. Not yet."

This delighted Zenobia. "Well, that is your job, isn't it?"

"Well, then, when you formulate a hypothesis, you must pay us another visit," Eleanor said, standing up.

Mathers stood as well. This discussion was obviously over.

"Like I said, Eleanor, I'll do what I can to keep it quiet, but there's bound to be some questions." Janet sounded apologetic.

"I appreciate anything you can do. The Bastille has been a part of this community for over two hundred years. I would like to avoid tarnishing our reputation."

"Of course," Janet said. "Now, once the authorities get this case, you'll see more police I'm afraid. It's all part of the system."

Zenobia bowed slightly. "If you'll excuse me, I must make a call."

Eleanor nodded back. "You can use the one in the den. We shall meet in there in a moment anyway." Zenobia waved her off. "I have my cell."

Eleanor sighed and nodded toward Janet. Janet nodded in return, put her hat back on her head and Mathers fell into step behind. As Eleanor reached the door, a young woman dashed into the foyer from the hallway. Mathers guessed her age to be about twenty-five. She had short blonde hair and an athletic build. As she stood gaping at him, there was something…odd about her. A familiarity that he couldn't put his finger on, but nagged at him. He felt like he was standing in a grocery store trying to remember what was on his shopping list.

"Oh, Abbey," Eleanor said. "I'm afraid I won't be able to accompany you to the stables."

"Aunt Boo said something about a dead body?" the young woman asked.

"Boo jumps to many a conclusion, my dear. It's a trait you shall come to tolerate." Eleanor turned back to the visitors and continued, "My niece Abbey."

"Abbey, this is Ranger Gage and Detective Mathers."

"Detective?" Abbey asked, her focus shifting from him.

"Yes," Mathers began. He scanned the young woman. This must be the one who just left The Meadows. She looked healthy and her eyes were white; no sign of drug use. But the way her glance bounced around the room, she was hiding something. He'd been on this job long enough to read most people like a book. The guilty always reveal themselves. The question was, what was she feeling guilty about?

Eleanor cleared her throat. "From Montpelier. He…happened…to be with Ranger Gage when the body was found."

Abbey nodded and smiled weakly, her eyes coming to rest on his shoulder. Suddenly Eleanor was standing before him, cutting off his view of Abbey. "Please call again when you—or the authorities—wish more information."

Janet smiled, grabbed Mathers by the elbow and he barely nodded before she yanked him out of the house. He could feel Eleanor dissecting him all the way, stopping only when the heavy wooden door closed behind them.

21

LESS THAN THIRTY MINUTES LATER, Eleanor found herself sitting behind her ancient desk gazing at the women as they paced the huge room that functioned as the office for The Bastille.

"Yes," Eleanor said quietly spinning in her chair, "the time is approaching when we can no longer wait for Abbey's memory to return."

"What are we going to do?" Ruth said timidly, wringing her hands. "If she is unable to participate in the Ritual again…"

"We must not assume anything," Eleanor snapped, then, as Ruth shrank from her, wished she could take it back. She had no time to apologize, as Boo pushed past Tomyris, leaned over Eleanor's massive desk, and stared into her face.

"You know Robert murdered that girl."

"We know no such thing," Eleanor locked eyes with the fiery redhead. "As I said to Ruth, we cannot assume anything."

"I have warned you about him and the Doctor for years!" Boo hissed. "You ignored me in London and look what happened to those women!"

"Let me remind you, my dear Boudicca," Eleanor rose to meet Boo's expression, "we cannot control the Immortals. They have every right to blunder, hate and make poor decisions just as much as any human. And we cannot kill all the male Immortals, either. As much as you would like to do so."

"Typically democratic of you, Eleanor," Boudicca hissed. "Perhaps that epitaph should be chiseled onto the dead women's gravestones."

"Great!" Tomyris sighed, falling onto the couch. "Another pissing match."

"Please!" Ruth shouted, covering her ears with a dishcloth, "we shall speak no more of evil and dead things!" She threw the dishtowel against the wall. "We shall need more Mondel bread. And milk. Milk is good for the bones," she said, as she jogged out of the office and into the kitchen.

Neither Eleanor nor Boudicca broke their stare. "Brownies sound delicious, do they not, Boo?" She leaned into the woman. "It would be a shame to hurt Ruth's feelings, would it not?" Boo nodded and pulled away, slinking to the far wall and sitting against it. Eleanor turned back to address all the women. "I would like an investigation of that area."

Zen smiled broadly, revealing a row of sparkling white teeth among the darkness of her features. "I am on my way." She grabbed a light cotton sweater and threw it over her bare shoulders. "It has been far too long since I tracked something besides Tomyris' dogs."

"Zenobia," Eleanor said as the thin woman reached for the doorknob, "we do not need any more attention than we have already."

"I am never seen unless I wish to be," Zen replied, smiling.

"I shall tell the gatekeeper of the situation," Tomyris said through a yawn. "Perhaps he has advice to offer, or at least something else to do besides bitch." She didn't wait for an answer. "Try to have fun without me," she shot back over her shoulder.

"Tom!" Eleanor yelled, "Please take Abbey to the stables first. Perhaps seeing the complex will spur something."

Tomyris spun and rolled her eyes at Eleanor. "El, don't you think that maybe Boo is right?"

"Right about what?"

Tomyris sighed. "Endless walks around the garden here at the Bastille, therapy at The Meadows…Christ! Even Fred was here pretending to be the butler! Face it, El… she's too far gone. That little swim she took when the plane went down…"

Eleanor was across the room in a flash. She grabbed Tomyris' wrist and squeezed. "Abbey is not a lost cause!"

Tomyris glanced at Eleanor's grip and cleared her throat. "I have killed hundreds of men, El. Your lily-white hand merely annoys me. Let go." Eleanor did. "I'm just saying that I think Boo has a point."

"And I am telling you that Abbey—our Abbey—is slumbering within a mental fog. If we puncture that fog, it will release her mind from its numb state and she will remember. She will remember everything."

"That is why you concentrate on those two lives?" Boo crossed to Eleanor. "Abbey has lived many lives, Eleanor, all of them memorable."

"Those were the two most memorable," Eleanor countered. "If anything can wake her from her amnesia, it will be her memories of Joan of Arc or Amelia Earhart. Trust me."

"Whatever," Tomyris yawned. "You're in charge, El. Just let me know what to do."

"Take her to the stables. Show her the Frisians and the plane. Ask probing questions. Use those tools to prod her into remembering who she is."

Tomyris shrugged, shoved the earphones into her ears, and whistled for the dogs as she disappeared into the mansion.

"He has become too dangerous to ignore," Boudicca said sharply, pulling herself to her full height. "It is time he is dealt with."

"I know," Eleanor said. Of all the women in the Bastille, Boo had forgotten the least and whose memory should be most trusted because of that fact. There could be no denying that Boo had reason to be angry, all the women did, but Boo's addiction to her past tragedies was one trait Eleanor had hoped the woman would outgrow. Sadly, the lines around Boo's face bore no sign of joy, only the deeply cut lines of pain and rage. Eleanor sighed. If there was ever a woman who deserved some shred of happiness, Boudicca was that woman. Life had taught Eleanor many things over the years and one of the most poignant lessons was that emotional scars opened more easily than physical ones; and when they did, the memories flowed thicker and faster than blood.

"If you know," Boo snapped, "then it is time to do something about it."

"Would you have me kill him, Boudicca?"

"Yes."

"Of course you would," Eleanor laughed. "You would have me break one law to justify another."

"They are monsters."

"They are our kin."

Boudicca recoiled. "Robert de Beaudricourt is no kin of mine!"

"Yes, dear," Eleanor said, "he is. He is like the uncle who repeatedly embarrasses us, tests our patience, and threatens to snap our minds." Eleanor sighed. "Yet let a stranger take arms against him and the entire clan rushes to his defense."

"The two of you condemn both Robert and the Doctor without benefit of testimony or proof!" Zenobia said. Eleanor jumped. She had forgotten that the small woman remained. "The Doctor killed those women, Zenobia," Boo shot back.

"And you killed those men, Boudicca." Zen said.

"We should defend a murderer?" Boudicca asked Eleanor.

"Yes," Eleanor said.

"You have lost your anger against him."

"Yes."

"You are a fool," Boo hissed.

"I am tired, Boo. Tired of fighting, tired of politics, and tired of leading leaders."

"Then it is time you stepped down, Eleanor."

"Perhaps." Eleanor looked into Boo's eyes and smiled again, weaker this time. "You wish to carry the torch in my place? You wish to be the Caller when it is time to open the Tapestry? You wish to be in charge of the Guild?

"If you do, Boo, you may do so. Only remember this," Eleanor lost her softness as she pulled the tall woman into a fierce embrace and whispered in her ear, "the battles of today are fought not with swords and fire, but with cleverness and patience. You are so filled with anger; where does your patience live, my love?"

Boo pulled away. Without a word, she turned and walked to the doorway of the office turret. "Robert de Baudricourt will die, Eleanor. By my hand." She disappeared through the door and into the mansion beyond.

"Perhaps we should warn him?" Zenobia asked.

Eleanor shook her head. Another corpse found on the Bastille grounds was not a thought she cherished. Wouldn't that be a terrible way to begin the Ritual?

"WHAT'S THAT?" ABBEY ASKED, pushing past the last of the trees that separated the Bastille's lawn and the horse barn. The huge oval corral extended off the rectangular brick stable and was joined to four horse stalls by an iron trellis. A manicured lawn of thirty or forty yards square lay between the barn and an airplane hanger. Abbey stood with her back to the stables, gazing onto the long, flat ribbon of aging asphalt which extended from the hanger door towards the northern woods.

Sitting on the ribbon of asphalt was a polished, shiny Electra.

Aunt Tomyris followed Abbey's gaze. "That's the plane," she said, taking the stick from one of the dogs and throwing it far into the woods.

"This family has a plane?"

Aunt Tomyris laughed. "Two. That Electra and the jet Eleanor purchased several years ago. Her previous husband, along with Boo's ex and..." Tomyris paused slightly before continuing, "and several nieces... are pilots. Some people take to flying like other people take to animals." Aunt Tom stepped to Abbey's side.

"That runway was constructed long before city ordinances and air traffic regulations inhibited the movement of small planes."

"So we can use this airstrip?" Abbey asked, amazed. "Some bureaucrat hasn't banned small aircraft usage?"

Aunt Tom laughed and to Abbey the sound reminded her of chimes in the breeze. "I have no doubt someone has tried. But your Aunt Eleanor can be...persuasive."

Abbey heard the sarcasm and smiled. "She's quite a woman, isn't she?"

"Magical," Aunt Tom whispered, tossing a stick for one of the dogs.

The two women stood side by side in silence. It was only when the horses and the dogs started bickering that the two turned and went into the stable.

The structure resembled any other stable: a center walkway with loading doors at either end and bordered by eight stalls. However, the center walkway was composed of thick inlaid tile rather than the usual poured concrete and the walls were freshly painted a cheery yellow. It was immaculately clean.

"The floor is set atop a heating system to keep the tiles the same temperature year round," Aunt Tom explained as she showed Abbey the tack room, also immaculately clean and orderly. "We have an expertly trained staff of two women whose only job is to care for the steeds and stable."

"And the hanger as well?" Abbey asked, running her fingers over a western saddle still slick with oil.

Aunt Tom hesitated. "I fear the hanger and airstrip…they have not been cared for with such delicacy in quite a long time." She tossed the ball and the four dogs ran after it in hot pursuit.

Abbey wandered over to the stalls. Six horses' heads peeked out from within the stalls: two Arabians, an ancient Palomino, a Saddleback, and two immense black Frisians. Their manes and tails were freshly washed and brushed. Abbey approached the first stall with the big block letters reading FIRE. She paused, her hand halfway to the Frisian's face. Fire? Why in the world would someone name a horse fire? She looked into the eyes of the horse. The gaze of the Frisian consumed her, and she felt a finger of heat stab into her chest. This horse hated her and she knew it. She stepped away from the creature.

"Good morning, you handsome devil," Aunt Tom said, pushing past Abbey. The horse welcomed Tom's invitation and stepped into Tom's outstretched hand. Abbey stepped backwards another few feet and stood watching the scene: elegant, dark-skinned Tom with the flowing black hair, powerful hands and stern expression, covered by the immense horse's neck as Fire laid her head on Tom's shoulder.

Abbey felt a shove on the back of her head. She spun and found herself looking into the eyes of a younger Frisian, this one with bright eyes, restless feet, and a streak of brown through his black mane. Abbey laid her hand on his head. The horse felt hot and its skin tingled. As she laid her head onto the horse's neck, she glanced down to see his name: Water.

Suddenly, Abbey heard the rushing of the surf and felt waves tug at her feet, threatening to drag her into the darkness.

"Abbey?" the voice filtered through the darkness.

"I...feel a bit queasy," Abbey said, letting herself press up against Water. He pressed back.

"Seriously? What is it?" Tomyris snapped and the dogs stepped away from Abbey.

"Water...in therapy I used to see these...flashes...of water. Something that happened to me...now I ... there's one of fire, too."

"Maybe you should get back to the house," Aunt Tom said, wrapping a thin, yet strong arm around Abbey and motioning for the dogs to follow.

As Aunt Tom led her away, Abbey never looked back to see Fire emerge from his stable, walk to the end of the corral, and watch her until she disappeared into the woods.

"**W**HAT ARE WE DOING HERE?**"** Janet asked as she pulled onto the shoulder.

"Following a hunch," Mathers muttered.

The moment the vehicle stopped, Mathers leapt out and plowed through the grass into the woods, with Janet trotting behind him.

"Want to let me in on the hunch?" Janet shot back.

"They know something," Mathers said.

"Something?"

"Yes." He inched through the thin line of trees. "Did you hear the timbre in their voices? They were concerned about what we knew about the dead woman—not the fact that we found a dead body to begin with."

"Hello! Dead woman! I'd be curious, too."

"But that's just it," Mathers said, "they weren't curious. They had no questions about the crime, just about our knowledge of the victim. They didn't ask about the clothing, the tattoos, the piercing…"

"Matt, you have finally lost it."

"I told you, a hunch."

Janet rolled her eyes. "Have I ever told you I really hate cops?" Mathers nodded. "What do you need me to do?"

"Find some evidence we've overlooked."

"Anything particular or just the neon sign flashing the word EVI-DENCE with a huge arrow?" Mathers sighed.

He scoured the dirt under his shoes. It wasn't unusual for these old, monied families to have a few skeletons in their closets. He worked a case in Maine when he first moved to New England where a family refused to allow the remains of three individuals to be taken from the crawl space.

"These poor creatures are a part of our family heritage," a squat, fat lady with ill-fitting dentures sputtered. "Our great-grandfather killed those men."

"You know about the dead bodies?" Mathers asked her.

"Great-grandfather raped their sister," the woman said proudly. "They came here like a lynch mob wanting to kill him." She sighed and shook her head. "He got beat-up pretty good, our great-grandfather did. Those men beat him up before grandpa could kill them."

"So you are fighting to keep the remains of three men who were trying to kill your great-grandfather." The woman nodded and coughed into her fist.

"These bodies are proof that our family has a long history of overcoming insurmountable odds." She brushed an eyelash from her face and smiled.

"But he was a rapist."

She shrugged. "Nobody's perfect." Then she shut the door in his face.

Although Eleanor hadn't slammed the door in his face, she had been in a hurry to get them out of her house. The stirring in his stomach told him the woman knew about the corpse. Besides, he'd behave the same way if he had a dead body in his woods.

His toe poked at the area surrounding the yellow KEEP OUT tape. As Janet said, this past winter and mud season had taken its toll on the lakeside area. Much of the topsoil had shifted. He wished he knew what in the hell he was looking for.

"Matt!"

Mathers spun around and saw Janet about forty feet from him kneeling on the ground.

"Find something?"

"Oh, yeah," she said. "You better go get your Sherlock Holmes camera and notepad. You'll love this one."

ABBEY STOOD STARING AT THE TAPESTRY for the second time this morning, wondering what happened to the Roman army. She stood in this exact spot when the commotion from Detective Mathers and Ranger Gage distracted her. She knew this was the exact spot, because she noted her location before leaving: third panel on the left, two feet from the section's corner, three hands up from the bottom. Less than fifteen minutes ago, this area she examined held a scene of the Roman army at war with a throng of Celts. The threads were tightly woven and thicker than those of the newer embroidered scenes, yet the older colors that comprised the Roman soldiers had a sheen to them, giving the illusion that dried blood caked their shields. A team of chariots dominated the scene, each one holding an angry driver and muscular Frisian horses. Abbey could see the determination in the faces of the warriors and feel the bloodlust of the steeds.

Now, the scene was a field after a battle; dead Romans lay strewn about the blood-soaked grass, their swords lying useless at their sides. The Celts' faces glowed with celebratory glee. Suddenly the sound of fabric ripping filled the air. As she spun around, her eyes landed on a panel of Tapestry near the end of the hall, where this long section of wall met the perpendicular hallway to her right.

The Tapestry was…bubbling. Huge ripples radiated through the section of wall as if the material were water boiling. A giant tear emerged in the center of the panel and Abbey saw light erupt from behind the multicolored threads. Something behind the panel wanted out.

As she watched, a horse's head materialized from the Tapestry, followed by the neck, legs and body. Frozen, Abbey watched as a huge gray horse stepped out of the wall and stood a few feet away staring at her. Atop the steed sat a thin, frail-looking man with unkempt shoulder-length hair and grubby clothing. He carried a huge broadsword.

The man looked around, took in his surroundings and saw her. He smirked.

"Ah, so we meet again."

He steered the horse in her direction. "I should have killed you last time," he bellowed and pulled back for the blow when several things happened at once. From behind the gray horse, a huge black Frisian leapt out of the Tapestry. From nowhere and everywhere, monotone chanting began—a low, resonating rhythm that echoed off the stone walls. From behind Abbey, a primal scream erupted and Abbey felt the air pulled from her lungs as her legs collapsed from under her and she dropped to the floor. Aunt Boo, naked and painted blue, rushed headlong at the man on horseback, a broadsword swinging over her head. Boo jumped at the man, their swords clashing, sparks dancing in the air of the dimly lit hallway. The ethereal chanting became louder, taking on a deep vibrato that Abbey felt like electric shocks. The Frisian pressed against the grey horse, nudging it backwards towards the Tapestry, as the rider dealt blow upon blow to Aunt Boo, who deflected them with ease.

Boo sidestepped a thrust of the man's sword and deftly cut off his hand at the wrist. The rider's sword clattered to the stone floor, the man screamed in pain as the horse reared. The chanting reached its crescendo with an ear-splitting screech and the gray horse and its rider fell backwards into the wall, merging into the fabric. With a loud BOOM, a flash of light lit up the corridor and Abbey turned away. When she turned back, there was no rider, no horse and Aunt Boo stood with the severed hand in her grasp, the Frisian nudging her shoulder.

"You may need this!" she yelled, tossing the hand into the Tapestry, where it disappeared into the fabric.

A hand clamped down on Abbey's shoulder and she jumped.

"Sorry to startle you, dear," Aunt Ruth cooed. "You look terrible. Would you like a slice of lemonseed cake?"

"We would, Ruth," Eleanor said, holding out her hand to Abbey. "And I suspect Abbey may wish some tea with her snack."

R OBERT GRABBED HIS CHEST as the pain cut through his heart. He sank to his knees, knocking over the bottle of one-hundred-year-old brandy.

"Wow, boss," Josh shook his head. "You totally just screwed yourself on the booze."

"Josh," the Doctor said, sucking on his cigar, "would you please mix me another gin and tonic?" He held out his glass to the young man who stared at Robert.

"Uh...Mr. Doc," Josh stuttered. "Is he, like, going to be okay or something?"

"Or something."

"Dude. You can't die on me. I have a semester of school left."

"Your concern for Robert warms my heart."

"Thanks," Josh smirked. "Phys Ed. Didn't get a scholarship, though." He inspected the brandy seeping into the carpet of the penthouse. "Waste of good booze."

"Joshua," the Doctor's voice took a stern, menacing tone, "my gin and tonic?"

As Joshua mixed the drink, the Doctor glared down at the man on the floor. "Don't worry," the Doctor chuckled, "it shall pass."

Robert struggled to his feet, sweat breaking out along his face and soaking his underarms. "I...felt..."

"Yes, I know. I, as well."

"Doc, your drink."

"Thank you, Joshua. That will be all."

"I'll just clean this up," Joshua said, snatching the near-empty bottle of one-hundred-year-old brandy. "I'll...totally dump the bottle for you." He refused to look at the two men in the eyes as he dashed out of the penthouse scrutinizing the remaining brandy coating the bottom of the bottle.

"Hurts, doesn't it?" the Doctor smirked as Robert nodded. "It lessens with time. The longer you stay on this side of the Tapestry, the less the pain's intensity when Immortals attempt an illegal crossover."

Robert grunted as he lifted himself off the floor. "That sensation...I have never felt it before."

"Neither have I. This pain is different from what I have experienced in the past."

Robert flopped into the chair and closed his eyes. "Why?"

"I have a hypothesis. Purely speculation."

"Enlighten me."

The Doctor nodded and let the smoke snake out of his nostrils. "Abbey's prolonged absence from the annual Ritual caused the witches' spell around the Tapestry to weaken. The fabric has been slowly unraveling. Many years have gone by without a sixth warden, causing the Tapestry to disintegrate at an accelerated rate and the passageway between worlds became less...crisp. Threads of the magic holding it together now tie us to the Mother Tapestry at the Bastille."

"If we succeed, can we repair the Tapestry?"

The Doctor nodded. "Yes, I believe we can. Once we have amassed our own six wardens and killed the damned witches."

"Good." Robert sighed. "I do not wish to endure this pain every time there is a breakout."

"Nor I." The Doctor extinguished the cigar and leaned toward Robert. "The irony is this: The witches could have prevented the Tapestry's disintegration themselves had they replaced Abbey with an alternate sixth warden." Robert raised his eyebrows. "I say 'why should *we* do all the work?' Now that Abbey is reunited with the bitches, let the women mend the tears in the Tapestry during the Ritual. Once that is done, we have only to kill them and maintain the gateway."

Robert nodded. "Do we want Abbey to rejoin the coven? The very fact that she could not be a part of the Ritual for over seventy years is what weakened the Tapestry enough for us to remain here."

"She's no danger once we kill the rest of the witches."

"Do not underestimate Abbey," Robert snapped. "I trained her myself."

"You think so highly of your own skill," the Doctor laughed. "But once she delivers your child, we can kill her, too, if necessary."

"A child needs its mother," Robert sneered.

The Doctor reprimanded, "We shall find a wet nurse. You going soft?"

Robert shook his head. The Doctor nodded and continued. "I don't wish to try the experiment again on another mortal woman. They have a habit of dying. Just make sure you impregnate Abbey this time."

"Oh," Robert laughed, "I plan on it."

26

I N THE END LYNN DECIDED that she needed the double chocolate fudge brownie sundae much more than she needed the peanut buster parfait. Besides, the peanut buster parfait had peanuts in it, and peanuts had nutritional value. That would not do at all.

She steered her tired Ford Focus around the corner just as the red MAINTENANCE REQUIRED light flashed on. Shit. It was probably one of those factory-installed alerts intended to force unsuspecting car owners into the nearest dealership where they would be fleeced for cash, but how could she be sure it wasn't serious? She steered with her knees so she could slurp the ice cream while weighing her options: ignore the light until the car exploded, or take it into the shop and fork over the cash. As she licked the fudge off the spoon she decided to wait until the car exploded. At least that way, she could justify the purchase of a new car.

She spotted the stone wall surrounding the Bastille to her left and chugged the rest of the melted ice cream from the plastic cup. She would be approaching the gates to the private drive soon. The 'aunts' (*why wouldn't they just come out, for god's sake? It's not like the whole town didn't know they were some kind of lesbian commune*) left most of the Bastille's acreage open for public use, only fencing in a portion of the land for themselves. She really should make it a priority to enjoy the Faire this year, as last year's excursion with that guy—what was his name?—turned out to be a disaster. He'd be a jerk with two testicles, but with only one, he was both a jerk and angry.

A thought hit her with such force she gasped. Why hadn't she thought of this before? The Faire! She'd take the clients! The new state regulations required community involvement, so maybe she could arrange for them to be on garbage detail, or cleanup crew. Hell, with her menagerie, she could have *them* perform. Mrs. Bailey could do erotic dancing with Feng Shi, Mr. Rix is a dynamite drag queen, and Mr. Stewart could paint his wang and make it do tricks, like those guys in that show who manipulate their dicks on stage. What a perfect opportunity to spend the day having fun, get out of the office, and fulfill a state requirement all at the same time.

A flash of yellow caught the corner of her eye as she inched down the private road looking for the gated drive of the Bastille. She slammed on the brakes and backed up—POLICE DO NOT CROSS glared at her from the yellow tape strung across the area near the road. Two marked police cars sat side by side on the level plot of land between this access road and the tree line. In addition, Lynn spotted a van with the words CORONER, a green SUV bearing the emblem of VERMONT DEPARTMENT OF FOREST & PARKS, and a couple of unmarked vehicles. As she watched the flurry of activity, she spotted a face she recognized.

"Hey, Janet!" she yelled. Several yards off, Janet Gage turned, waved and began walking towards her car. Lynn threw her car into Park, turned off the ignition, and prayed while the thing shuddered and ping-ed.

"Hey!" Janet yelled as she approached her car. Lynn noticed a man watching them. Although she couldn't see him clearly, he looked rather handsome, with dark hair and athletic build. She waved. He waved back.

"This town hasn't seen this much action since…well, ever," Lynn said, pulling her gaze away from the mystery man.

"And it had to be on the night Sal is making barbecue."

"Someone hit a moose?" Lynn asked.

Janet shook her head. "Found a body. Two, actually." She gestured toward the woods. "That's the investigation unit."

"No shit? Just like on TV?"

"Don't get excited. They were both old."

"Old? Like 'senior citizen who got tainted food from Denny's' old?"

"Funny." Janet kneeled down to look Lynn in the eye. "Like 'dead and buried a long time ago' old."

"Welcome to New England."

Janet nodded. "If I had a nickel for every corpse uncovered in an unmarked grave, I'd move Sal to Tahiti." She looked at Lynn's briefcase sitting on the passenger seat. "Where you going?"

"Guess." Lynn pointed down the road toward the castle-like structure.

"What for?"

"Work. Home visit."

"Oh! That's right!" Janet nodded furiously. "That young woman… what's her name? Abbey? She just got out of the funny farm."

"Please. We prefer to call it 'Your Home Away From Home.'"

"What asshole thought of that?" Lynn shrugged and rolled her eyes.

"Well," Lynn sighed, "you're not supposed to know about Abbey anyway."

"It's a small town. Word travels fast."

Just then the mysterious dark-haired man yelled something inaudible and Janet waved him over. When he arrived, Janet made the introductions. "Detective Matt Mathers, Lynn Swanson. Matt's a detective from Montpelier. Lynn's a social worker at the funny…" she caught herself and shook her head before continuing, "at The Meadows."

Lynn shook his hand. He was more handsome up close. He had piercing eyes that never blinked, a clean complexion and soft skin. "You're the new guy. Took over last year, right?"

"How did you know?" he asked in a voice that should be reserved for phone sex workers. "Let me guess—small town."

"I know most of the cops in the area. Part of my job."

He nodded and gave Lynn a wide smile. *Did she imagine it, or did he just check her out?* "You have ice cream on your...uh..."

Sure enough, a streak of vanilla ice cream had dribbled down her breast. *Great. He wasn't checking her out, he was gauging her mental capacity.*

He glanced at her passenger seat and nodded at the briefcase. "Going to the Bastille?"

"I should just wear a sign."

"I'm a cop. We notice things." He held his gaze just a tad longer than normal and Lynn's heart pounded. First, Uncle Robert and now Mr. Detective-with-the-Look. Maybe her luck with men is getting better. One of the uniformed officers behind Mathers called his name. "Got to go. Janet?"

Janet nodded and patted the hood of the car. "Call me. We'll go to dinner."

"Who's 'we' and what are 'we' having?" Lynn started the car, discouraged that the MAINTENANCE REQUIRED light still blared.

"Anything Sal can grill. And any single guy we can find for you."

"Don't bother." Lynn sighed. "I already investigated and deemed them wanting."

To Lynn's surprise, Mathers chuckled. Was he single, too? With her luck he was either married or gay. Janet waved and turned away, talking with Mathers under her breath.

Lynn pulled the car back on the access road and continued looking for the private drive to the Bastille. Two dead bodies found on the grounds? This wouldn't bode well for the ladies. Hopefully this wouldn't interfere with the Faire. She really wanted to see the town's reaction to Mrs. Bailey screwing an imaginary animal.

27

"OH, NO DEAR, IT IS NOT CONFUSING AT ALL," Ruth said, patting Abbey's hand. "You just need time to adjust. Have another ginger snap."

Abbey did, although she was not hungry. "Thank you."

"Perhaps it is a stroke of luck, however, as time is of the essence," Eleanor said softly.

"Eleven days." Ruth's eyes grew wide and her voice weakened, "We have only until the Summer Solstice."

"Ruth, dear," Eleanor said, patting her hand, "let us not scare the poor girl any more."

"Of course," Ruth smiled broadly. "Tea?" She offered the cup to Abbey.

"This hallway smells of horse dung," Boo scoffed, turning her back to the three.

"Then set about cleaning it, dear," Eleanor retorted before returning her attention to Abbey. "This was not how I planned, nor imagined, your return to the Bastille. I had hoped your re-education would have been more…gentle."

Boo snorted. "We have no time for this, Eleanor. Tell her and be done."

"Boo, your naked body is enough to contend with, let alone your naked emotions." Boo knelt and grabbed Abbey by the shoulders, thrusting her blue face against Abbey's. "It is time you face your past, girl, and rejoin the Guild before you kill us all."

"Enough!" Eleanor's voice cut through the hallway. "You will leave us, Boo."

"Then who will she learn from?" Boo snapped, leaping to her feet. She crossed to the Tapestry and grabbed the nearest panel. "Do you see this?" she asked, pointing to the tear several inches from the top left corner. "This is your fault."

"I do not understand," Abbey whispered. "I have never seen this Tapestry before."

"You are destroying it," Boo insisted.

"I always preferred learning things from the beginning," Ruth chimed in.

"Then let us do so," Eleanor agreed. "My hypothesis is simple, yet plausible," Eleanor stated, as she massaged Abbey's injured foot. "When this piece of the Great Tapestry was stolen," she pointed to the upper right corner of the last panel on the wall, "it must have disrupted the energy that holds the prisoners inside their cells.

"Over the past seventy-plus years, without a full coven for the Ritual, the Tapestry has weakened." She pointed to the outer hems of the panel, where Abbey could see gaps in the weave. "Fissures and small rips have begun to emerge in every panel of the Tapestry. They grow bigger daily."

"And more of them, too." Ruth grimaced as she wrapped Abbey's ankle in a towel that smelled to Abbey like a mixture of vomit and rotten eggs. "It is so hard to keep up with the repairs." Abbey winced when the towel touched her tender ankle. "This will speed the healing."

Abbey looked at the old woman with confusion and Eleanor hugged her. "We repair the tears in the fabric. We are the wardens of its energy.

"Permitting those who are allowed free access into and out of their embroidered memories," Eleanor continued, fondly touching an embroidered scene of a tree and a lake. "And barring those who are experiencing periods of...internment."

"*Supposed* to be." Abbey caught the disdain in Boo's voice.

"Excuse me, Eleanor." The four women spun toward Fred, who either didn't see Boo's nakedness or ignored it. "Abbey has a visitor. Ms. Lynn Swanson. She's in the sitting room."

Eleanor nodded to the man. "Thank you, Fred."

Fred smiled and winked at Abbey. Abbey felt a flutter in her chest as the man's kind eyes took in her injury and frowned. "Are you okay?"

She nodded. His gaze continued to bore into her and she realized she liked it. This was a man she could trust. She didn't know why she could, but she could. It must be something about the different-colored eyes.

"Abbey!" Eleanor brought Abbey out of her reverie.

"Dear, we are in such a hurry!" Ruth began to sob as she stepped behind Eleanor. "Less than two weeks until Solstice!" The frail woman collapsed against Eleanor.

Abbey nodded as Fred reached for her. He grasped her arm tightly and Abbey pulled on him. His arm wrapped around her waist and Abbey felt his strong arm muscles lifting her as if she were weightless. They turned and slowly made their way towards the front of the house. This was the third time Aunt Ruth mentioned the solstice. *What happens at the Summer Solstice?*

28

JUST UNDER THIRTY MINUTES AGO, Lynn had pulled up to the entry kiosk and poked buttons randomly, causing a voice to erupt from the speaker asking her name, business, and if she had an appointment. She must have answered with the magic word, for the gate swung open and she inched onto the Bastille's property. As she crawled down the tree-lined driveway, Lynn found herself mesmerized by the castle-like abode and acres of flowers. Still enticed by the fragrances, she pulled up to the mini-drawbridge and saw a slim man wearing a tux point toward a parking spot marked VISITORS. She managed to avoid falling on her face as she followed the butler over the decorative bridge, through a foyer that was bigger than her apartment, and into a vast room loaded with finely crafted cherry wood furniture. Now, here she was, inside the fabled 'Bastille.' She wandered around the sitting room, marveling at the porcelain dolls, collection of antique nutcrackers and furnishings, which must have amounted to five years of her salary. Apparently, joining a lesbian commune was lucrative.

"Lynn."

She turned toward the voice, but she was alone in the immense room. Then her eyes fell upon the wooden chest in the corner. The hairs on her neck stood up as gooseflesh spread over her arms. Shit! It felt like the thing was staring at her. She glanced around the room, making sure she was alone before tiptoeing over to the ornately carved trunk. The metal hinges and the intricate designs practically screamed Louis XIV. She reached out and fondled the latch. It felt smooth and polished under her fingertips and she had to stifle a giggle as she reached out to heave open the lid. She didn't know what she expected to see, but torture devices were definitely not on the list.

Her undergrad degree was a double major in Art History and Medieval History and in all her studies she had never seen a collection like this. Her sense of curiosity about the Women of the Bastille kicked up a notch. These devices were priceless. Damn! She always regretted getting into Social Work. She only did so because that asshole guy she dated—what's his name?—convinced her that there would always be a future in working with crazy people. She felt an odd sense of giddy smuttiness when her fingers touched the thumb screws. The ethics committee would call this a 'violation of privacy,' but they didn't know how little self-control she had. As she caressed the manacles, she noticed something that made her skin crawl. All the pieces were polished and oiled. They looked new. Jesus Christ! A lesbian commune of sado-masochists right here in Vermont! Who would have thought? A commotion arose from the opposite end of the foyer and she heard hushed voices whispering in a heated exchange. She carefully closed the lid of the chest and scurried to the couch.

Eleanor led the pack of women, followed by Abbey leaning on the handsome butler, Ruth, and a woman wearing blue. She did a double take. The woman wasn't *wearing* blue, she was *painted* blue. She was also naked.

"Ah, sorry to keep you waiting, my dear." Eleanor's voice sounded rushed and lacked the crispness of their previous meetings. Her eyes darted around the room nervously as she tapped her fingertips on the arm of the couch.

"It's…it's all right. No problem." Lynn hoped her voice didn't belie her sense of unease. Lynn watched as a single bead of sweat rolled down Eleanor's usually perfect forehead. Something was wrong. "Abbey, how are you doing? You look injured."

Abbey stared at her blankly before responding in a distant voice. "It is nothing."

Lynn noted this disconnection and the red flags in the back of her mind unfurled.

"Thank you, Fred," Eleanor said with a dismissive tone. "If you would help Abbey onto the couch, you may be excused."

Lynn noticed Abbey's eyes followed the man as he walked. Obviously something was brewing between those two. She turned her attention back to Aunt Eleanor. "How is everything?"

Eleanor uttered a forced, high-pitched squeal. "Delightful!" Her eyes fell upon Boo. "Boo, dear, please dress."

Without a word, Boo spun on her heels and stormed out.

"Abbey, how are your dreams?" Lynn scrutinized Abbey's face.

"What? Oh. Not as vivid."

"Nor as often," Ruth piped up with a voice that was too cheery.

Lynn glanced at the eager faces of the women and took a different tactic. "Abbey, why don't you show me your room?"

"Great idea!" Ruth said, clapping.

"Well, if you don't mind, I'd like to spend time with Abbey alone."

The women's faces faltered for a brief second, but Lynn registered their disappointment. What didn't they want her to know?

Abbey stood up with the energy of a zombie and shuffled out of the room. Lynn made a mental note: dirty clothes, irregular step, and a slight limp. Hell! This visit was not going to be a cakewalk.

STABBING? DECAPITATION? Robert pondered how he would murder Joshua.

"Are you okay, boss?" Joshua's voice filtered through the door of the bedroom, as Robert contended with the horrendous noise the lad called music. It sounded to Robert as if a suffering voice screamed, "Hey, you, get off of my clod." What was a 'clod' and why did the suffering voice want someone off of it?

"I am well," he said to the closed door. "Go away."

"Damn, that boy is irritating." The Doctor laughed. "I must remember that trick."

"What trick? I should think you knew how to irritate me."

"No," the Doctor answered as he searched the drawers of the dresser. "Hiring irritating assistants. They are so much more fun to kill." Finding nothing of interest, the Doctor moved onto the armoire.

"Decapitation, I think." Robert stormed to the closet and threw open the doors. He motioned for the Doctor to join him. "The Summer Solstice is almost upon us and with it the women's gathering at the Bastille for the Ritual."

"Thirteen days. Do you have any brandy in there?"

"No. It seeped into the carpet of the sitting room."

"What a waste."

"We have thirteen days to apprehend Abbey, impregnate her, and kill the witches."

The Doctor nodded. "Good times lie ahead, eh, my friend?"

The blaring music from the other side of the door faded. "Hey, boss!" Joshua said through the closed door. "I'm leaving for the store. I changed the music for you, boss. You said you didn't like the Stones."

The Doctor chuckled quietly. "I see you arranged for privacy."

"I always have a plan." Robert winked. "Thank you, Joshua. That will be all."

Robert gestured to the closet. Several suits hung inside plastic dry-cleaning bags. Next to these hung several uniforms, a variety of sports jerseys, trench coats, a simple brown woven dress, a long black cloak, and several polished broadswords. "You asked how I managed to steal the piece of the Tapestry?"

The Doctor eyed the collection. "Ah, yes, your penchant for disguises." He clapped Robert on the back and squeezed his shoulder. "Good to know some things never change."

"It truly amazes me how gullible the plebeians remain after six hundred years."

"That is why killing mortals never kept me awake at night." The Doctor lit another cigar. "Immortals are naturally smarter than Humans. It is our nature."

The music crescendo from the other room silenced them. The two listened for a moment, trying to decipher the words. The Doctor blew a huge cloud of smoke into the room before shrugging in resignation.

"Joshua calls this one 'Billie Jean.' It is by a singer of ambiguous gender and race."

"Sounds to me as if it's singing, 'Billy G fucked my dog.'"

30

BY THE TIME SHE AND ABBEY FINISHED TALKING, Lynn knew she had a major problem on her hands. Throughout the afternoon, Abbey became increasingly disoriented and distracted. The domineering, regal aura she displayed in The Meadows had vanished, leaving in its place a weak, confused young woman. When asked about her nutrition, Abbey replied that what she ate most of the time was baked sweets. Lynn had never heard of a baking fetish, but she could easily conceive of the sweet, mild-mannered 'Aunt Ruth' feeding brownies to the thin Abbey, then forcing the girl to vomit. Who would have guessed the Bastille harbored a sado-masochistic, lesbian co-op with a baking fetish?

Desperate to linger a bit more with Abbey, Lynn wandered over to the Tapestry on her way out of Abbey's room. "What are these?"

"Embroidered scenes from my family's past."

Lynn thought she saw movement out of the corner of her eye. At the far end of the hallway, the Tapestry billowed. Someone was watching them.

"This looks like you." Lynn scrutinized the scene. "It looks like you tied to that pole." Was that a fire beneath the figure? Could this be the germ of Abbey's torturous nightmares? A simple embroidered picture on an enormous wall hanging? If she had walked by an embroidered picture of herself burning at the stake every day, it would be enough to send her over the edge.

Just then, a low, guttural scream echoed through the hallway. A rhythmic monotone chanting began somewhere to Lynn's left, deep in the heart of the mansion.

Abbey clutched Lynn's arm, "We must go now." Abbey practically dragged Lynn down the corridor, heading for the sitting room. As they maneuvered the sharp turn into the foyer, Lynn gazed back over her shoulder and saw 'Aunt Boo,' still naked and still painted blue, rushing at the Tapestry and brandishing a huge broadsword over her head.

"Thanks for visiting, dear, good-bye." Ruth nodded as she rushed past Lynn and down the hallway towards Aunt Boo. "GRAB SOME BAGELS ON YOUR WAY OUT!"

31

"OH GOODY, YOU'RE BACK."

"How did you know it was me?" Mathers asked.

"Your cologne," Helen whined over her shoulder. Mathers noticed she was playing solitaire. "Smells like dog shit. What is it?"

"Doesn't matter. I won't buy it anymore."

"Good idea." Helen lost her game and swore under her breath. She spun her chair around to face him and sighed. "Let me guess. The recent find on the back forty of the Bastille." When Mathers shrugged, Helen continued. "The CSI team was quick to respond. Not much excitement around this town, I suppose." Helen fumbled through a chart and extracted a report. "Where do you want me to start?"

"At the beginning." Mathers said, opening his notepad.

She sighed again. "No wonder you're single." She took a deep breath. "The dental work on the bicuspids in the mandible is incongruent with the time period that the rest of the skeletal remains...what?" She rolled her eyes at Mathers' raised hand.

"English translation, please?"

"Old age."

"Again?" Mathers raised his eyebrow. "How about...what?"

"May I finish?" He nodded. "No evidence of foul play. No evidence of trauma of any kind. Once again, No on any sign of sexual violation, struggle, No on naturally developing distinguishing marks such as bone discoloration or toxicology. No blunt traumas, broken bones, crushed bones, or tattered bones. Perfect specimen of an elderly person who happens to be dead." She looked up at him and smiled. "Want to hear the really interesting part?"

"There is an interesting part?"

She nodded. "Initial scan of the clothing and artifacts found on and around the body. Bodice, jewelry and various paraphernalia look medieval in orientation."

"That's the same M.O. as our first Jane Doe."

"From initial scans, yes. I've already requested further investigation."

"Let me get this straight," Mathers said, playing with the keys in his pocket, "two dead bodies in one week. Both female. Both old. Both died of natural causes. Both dressed in medieval garb."

"Don't forget: both with incongruities." Helen shuffled through her papers. "In Jane Doe Number One, we had the tattoos and, lest we forget…"

"…the pierced labia."

"Exactly. On Jane Doe Number Two, we have something strange with her teeth and bones."

I thought you said the bones were…what now?"

Helen glared at him. "Can I finish, Detective?" Mathers stood still and folded his arms. "I said strange. What I think is strange is this: if the bones were hundreds of years old, there would be more evidence of malnutrition, vitamin deficiency, and other physical problems people had back then."

"Thank you for the plain English."

"No problem, Detective. But if she died in the 1940's, why was she dressed in medieval garb? Renaissance Faires, King Richard's Faires, and other period festivals weren't popular until…what? 1970?"

"What makes you think she was from the '40s?"

"I'm not an expert…" She caught Mathers' smirk and added quickly, "…in the *dental* field, but I'm sure her dental work is not contemporary. It looks to be the mouth of a woman from pre-1950. I've called in our forensic dentist. In addition, judging by the decay, I would say they've been parked in that spot for about sixty years."

"So you suspect the skeletal remains are from the '40s."

Helen nodded. "Want me to call in DNA people? We can investigate further into the clothing and bits of hair and nails we have from Jane

Doe Number Two and compare them to what we have for Jane Doe Number One."

Mathers didn't answer. He walked in small circles clutching and releasing his keys. Helen watched him for a few moments before he stopped and looked at her. "Let us assume both women died of old age. Playing that hypothesis, doesn't it seem an unlikely coincidence that both females died of old age, both were found in medieval garb, both were found on the land owned by a group of elderly women who host a medieval party every year?"

"I thought they called it a 'faire.'"

"Whatever," Mathers waved her off. "And the only person under the age of forty on those grounds is a young woman who just spent an awful long time in a mental hospital due to amnesia."

Helen whistled. "You're screwed. She's...what? Twenty-five? How in the hell would she do it? You think Abbey knows who did kill these women?"

"Jealous husbands?"

"They're lesbians."

"Jealous lovers, then." Mathers began pacing again. After a few moments of silence, he stopped. "Let me know when the DNA specialists finish their investigation. Also the dental expert. While we're at it, how about getting a confirmed fix on the date of the clothing and other artifacts found on the bodies. Would hair samples help?" Helen rolled her eyes and nodded. "I'll see what I can do. You going back to the Bastille?"

Mathers' response dripped with sarcasm. "I have a strange feeling that 'poor, confused Abbey' is not quite as 'poor' or 'confused' as she seems. My gut is telling me that she's mixed up in something damn serious and the aunts are making sure family skeletons remain in the closet."

"So to speak."

"So to speak." Mathers grinned.

32

LYNN FUMBLED, accidentally slid the Focus into third, and stalled in the middle of the intersection. As the Ford shuddered to a stop, she breathed a sigh of relief that she was alone on the private road. "Damn the fucking, shitting, pissing piss!" she screamed.

Why was she such an idiot for letting Abbey go back? The distant look in Abbey's eyes, the injured foot, her resistance to answering questions, were only compounded by the strange way those women had of following Abbey around. They couldn't bear to leave her alone for a single minute.

Damn, she thought, as a new vision erupted in her head: She was going to be hacked to death by the red-headed blue naked woman. The cops would probably find pieces of her strewn from here to Montpelier. Then, that adorable detective would have another murder to solve. Just her luck, the one time in a year that a handsome man sees her naked and she'll be shark chum.

In a flash of insight, the pieces of the puzzle clicked in place. During some violent, sick game involving medieval torture devices (probably sexual games. Aren't all games involving sex and torture linked to sex? Maybe she was reading too much into it, though. Damn! She had to get laid), one of the aunts murdered those two women, whose corpses Detective Adorable-Eyes had found. Abbey, no doubt strapped to a wall, witnessed the murders and went over the deep end. In a desperate attempt to conceal their behavior, the aunts shoved Abbey into a loony bin to shut her up and make anything she said look like the rantings of a nut-case. Now, Abbey is remembering the aunts' murderous carnage and now the women want her dead. Shit. They were going to kill Abbey. She needed to do something.

She needed proof. What kind of evidence would convince the authorities that one of the oldest and most altruistic families in New England were crazed lesbian pastry-baking psycho-killers? How would she get such proof? Detective Adorable-Eyes! He was on the case, right? Two dead bodies, both found on the grounds of the Bastille, and Mathers was down from the city to check them out. If she could convince Mathers that the aunts were worth investigating, he would surely come to the same conclusion she did. He's a cop and that's what they do—suspect everyone of doing something illegal. It's not their fault, really, it's probably genetic. She couldn't very well walk up to him and tell him the details of Abbey's case, though. She'd be fired for sure.

She started up the Focus and headed towards Dairy Queen. So this would be two visits in one day, but fuck it. She needed another double fudge sundae if she was going to figure this one out.

33

"**U**NTIL THE TWENTY-FIRST," Robert said, slipping on the bra. "The witches have until the twenty-first to plan the Faire, organize their Ritual, get Abbey to full strength, and arrange for the annual crossover." Robert wiggled down into the girdle and held out his hand to the Doctor.

"I suspect the tight time frame will not hinder them," said the Doctor, fastening the black felt cloak around Robert's neck. He handed Robert the rubber breasts.

"Thus the disguise," Robert said, shoving the breasts into the bra. "My wig, please."

"You seem to enjoy women's clothing a bit too much, my friend."

"This is the disguise that saved me many hours and countless confrontations with that damnable Boudicca." He tucked his hair beneath the wig and pulled the curls down over his eyes. "How do you think I managed to slip by the witches so often?"

The Doctor eyed the figure standing before him. A disheveled, broad-shouldered, hunchbacked woman with large breasts and hair resembling dirty straw leaned unsteadily on a walking stick. The woman's complexion lay hidden in the shadows of the unkempt mop of hair, her eyes sunken and dark. While the figure hurt his eyes with its ugliness, it was, nonetheless, a woman. He smiled. "I should have thought of this myself."

"That, my friend, is why you will never reach your potential." Robert smiled broadly. "You do not push the limits of your own creative juices."

"Perhaps. But I shall never cross swords with Boudicca, either."

Robert laughed heartily and clapped the Doctor on the back. "Come. Let us get that simpleton to drive to the Bastille. I would like to see what I can learn of Abbey."

"The chances of you catching her away from the women is, perhaps, one in a hundred."

"One is all I need," Robert winked. "It is all I need."

34

ELEANOR PUT DOWN HER ACCOUNTING as Boo burst through the door of the den brandishing her broadsword.

"We must talk. Now."

Eleanor turned to Zen sitting at the rolltop desk and shot her a questioning look. Zen picked up on the signal for help. "Boo, can it not wait? The accounting has yet to be done for the month."

"No!" Boo shot back, slamming her hands onto the desk before Eleanor. "We must act and act now."

"About what, dear?" Eleanor asked, knowing full well what Boo's response would be.

"About Abbey."

"I feel she is coming along very well," Zen said, placing the thick pile of bank statements onto the sideboard. "Since her amazing breakthrough at The Meadows."

"You know that's not what I meant."

"What I know is that you interrupted me. That is unacceptable." Zen flung herself against Boo so quickly, Eleanor barely saw the woman move. "If you wish to treat the others with such disregard, that is their concern. But when you address me you will do so with the respect I deserve. Do I speak a language you understand, Queen Boudicca?" Boo studied her for a moment before relaxing her stance and stepping away from the thin woman. "Yes, Queen Zenobia."

Zen nodded and broke out into a smile. She grabbed Boudicca by the shoulders and guided her to a chair opposite Eleanor. "Come, love. Let us sit and discuss this in a civil fashion."

"Ring for the others." Eleanor put the papers aside and sat back, smiling. "I adore watching the two of you interact. How much you remind me of myself and Henry."

"Henry was a pig," Boo retorted.

"A worthy opponent. I miss his sparring," Zenobia smirked as she picked up the phone. An intercom system magnified her voice and Eleanor heard it echoing throughout the mansion.

"Did you love him?" Zen asked.

"More than you could understand," Eleanor laughed. "More than even I understand. There will never be another man like Henry."

"Why do we waste time babbling about men?" Boo demanded.

"Idle chatter." Eleanor's voice maintained the quiet softness despite herself. "We shall wait for the others. As we always have done."

"We spoke briefly of you taking a respite," Boo crooned. "Perhaps that respite is now due?"

"You will take control from Eleanor if and when the Guild elects you as her successor," Zen said. "If you wish to do so before a valid vote of all the women, I will stop you, Boudicca." She leaned closely to Boudicca and winked. "And I may be the only one in this mansion who can."

Boo grinned and held Zen's hand. "You may certainly try." The two locked eyes for a moment and Eleanor thought she saw something like love reflected in Boo's face. After a moment, it was gone. "But not today."

"A party? I received no invite. Thank the gods."

Eleanor waved, "Come in, Livia."

"Lady Livia," Zenobia smiled at Boo, who winked in return, much to Eleanor's surprise.

"Lady?" Livia said, gliding into the room. "Are we to be reliving the Roman senate meetings then? Those damned things bore me to death."

"Close enough," Eleanor. "Although without the male of the species, I dare say the entertainment value will be diminished."

"I sent Ruth with Abbey," said Tomyris, with boredom oozing out of her as she lumbered to the leather couch while chewing on a cookie. She wore her usual half-shirt, only today her belly button held a red jewel. She had replaced the eagle feathers with peacock and as she walked, they spun in circles like rainbow-colored propellers. "By now, I'm sure Ruth's baked the girl a batch of unleavened bread, a slew of bagels, and is currently slicing lox." She flopped herself down onto the couch and stretched out, her dogs lying obediently next to her.

"Is she not to be referred to as 'Queen Tomyris,' or do the formalities end with me?" Lady Livia asked.

"Oh, no," Tomyris moaned, "not a fucking 'formalities' meeting again." She picked up a stray magazine, rolled it into a tube, and began swatting randomly.

"Then continue to spar with the fleas and flies," Eleanor said, looking to Boudicca. "I believe Boudicca requested this meeting?"

All eyes turned toward the Celt. She set her jaw and spoke. "We have no more time. Abbey must renew her affiliation with the Guild."

"She has, hasn't she?" Livia said, thumbing through the latest issue of *Vogue*. "Or is that her identical twin sister I see in the hallways?"

"Do not joke with me!" Boudicca yelled.

Livia cleared her throat and continued thumbing through the magazine. "Do not irritate me, Boudicca. While I lack your expertise on the field of battle, Livia Drusilla surpasses you in poisoning, assassinating, and ensuring that people disappear."

"You threaten me?"

Livia Drusilla dropped the *Vogue* and picked up the L.L. Bean catalog. "Of course not, my love. Merely stating fact." She looked up at Boo over the top of the mail order form and grinned. "So how about it, Boudicca? Want to disappear?"

"Ladies," Eleanor groaned. "Now, Boo, dear, please be seated. You block my view of Tomyris."

"I do not mind," Tomyris sighed. "I look the same today as yesterday."

"Please try to stay awake, Tomyris." Eleanor rubbed her eyes. "You snore so loudly."

"What is it that you want, Queen Boudicca?" Livia Drusilla asked, holding up the L.L. Bean catalog and showing her the fall jackets.

"We have less than two weeks before the Faire," Boudicca said. "Before that time, we have the Tapestry to mend, the year's embroidery to finish, and the Ritual to prepare."

"I particularly like the olive green windbreaker," Livia said. "Shall I order one for you, too?" she asked Eleanor.

"AND," Boo continued as she glanced angrily at Livia, "the Faire alone demands much time."

"We know this, Boudicca," Tomyris groaned and began texting into her cell phone. "Please tell us your point."

"My point is this: the Tapestry is failing. Almost daily I find myself battling people back into it. No thanks to any of you, who do not wish to help out."

"Why should we?" Zenobia said with a flat expression. "When you carry the hatred of forty warriors?"

"You say?"

"I say," Zenobia said so quietly Eleanor could barely hear her, "that we await you to tire of revenge." She tenderly stroked Boo's hand.

"Boo. When will you end your quest for blood?" Zen whispered as the others watched. "Your life as Elizabeth Borden did not help, nor your role as warden. You must let the past die."

The two women sat in silence, hand in hand for a minute while Eleanor scrutinized Boo's expression. The volatile woman's propensity for flashes of violence required patience when dealing with sensitive issues. To Eleanor's surprise, Boudicca remained calm, quietly looking at Zenobia. She breathed a sigh of relief. The work of the next week and a half would be difficult and draining. To be spared the additional task of caretaking a crazed blue warrior woman would be a blessing.

Just as Boo seemed to relax, Livia spoke from behind the L.L. Bean catalog. "And let us not forget about Robert de Baudricourt. He is still after Abbey." She licked her finger and turned the page with slow deliberateness. "So I agree with Zen. Remain calm. We will see to it that Abbey shan't be raped and murdered like your daughters." Instantly Boudicca was on her feet.

"Boo!" Eleanor said quietly. "Sit, dear." Boo didn't.

"He is still after us all. He would see us dead before returning to his prison in the Tapestry," Tomyris said from behind the cell phone.

"You do not know that!" Zenobia said.

"It shall not come to that," Eleanor said, motioning for everyone to sit. "You know as well as I the result of men acting as wardens."

"How can you be so sure?" Boo spat.

"I am old, Boudicca."

"I am older," Boo retorted. "He already has the Doctor on his side. Who is to say he shall not have more?"

"Unlikely," Tomyris muttered.

"Regardless…"

"Boo," Zen responded calmly, "the Doctor slayed prostitutes in England a hundred years ago. He hardly constitutes a threat."

"Besides," Tomyris said from her position on the couch, "the Doctor is only angry because he has trouble staying erect. This century has Viagra. He should be fine." She looked at the rest of the women staring at her in disbelief. "What?" She shrugged and returned to texting. "Give me a break! We did it once. Once! It was the night of the Hindenburg disaster. We were both grieving." She smirked and chuckled softly. "Besides…I was better than he was."

"I warn you," Boo said to Eleanor, "Robert de Baudricourt and his Doctor friend are coming."

"According to Tomyris, not nearly often enough," Livia quipped.

"It is *not* a joke," Boo exploded.

"No, Boo, it is not," Eleanor responded. "We are all aware of the state of the Tapestry due to Abbey's mental condition. What would you suggest?"

"Give her to me to train. Perhaps she will remember once she has a blade in her hand and a horse beneath her."

Eleanor nodded. "Very well."

Boo nodded and stormed out of the room.

"Are we done now?" Tomyris asked, leaping up from the couch.

"Yes, dear," Eleanor sighed as Tomryis trotted to the door, her dogs hot on her heels, and her feathers flapping in the current.

Eleanor turned toward Livia. "Next time, dear, if you wish to poke an injured animal, perhaps you would like to take a stick to road kill."

"For a woman proficient with politics, such as yourself, your lack of tact with Boudicca surprises me," Zen said, once again sitting down at her rolltop desk.

"And I suppose your condescension with Boudicca is motivated by altruistic love for the Family?" Livia shot back.

"Of course."

"Then we can count on your support every bit as much as your people did when you betrayed them for the man...what was his name again?"

"You dare accuse me of treason?"

"No, dear. You came to that conclusion all on your own."

"Ladies!" Eleanor shouted louder than she expected. Her arms hurt, her eyes burned, and the idea of sandwiching herself between these two Immortals upset her stomach. "Shall we deal with the problem at hand?

"We still must continue with the arrangements for the Faire and the Ritual. I'm afraid our task will be more daunting now that there is a body on our property."

"I stand behind my earlier comment. We must move the Faire's location," Zen stated.

Liv chuckled. "Impossible. Much preliminary work is already complete. The logistics of relocating now are a nightmare at best."

"Those logistics would be *your* concern, would they not?" Zen folded her arms and waited for Livia to respond.

Eleanor interjected. "I agree with Livia. The more shuffling of people and tents, vendors and the crowd, the more risk of something going wrong. Better to endure the Detective's investigation."

"When will it conclude?" Zen went over to Eleanor and began massaging the woman's shoulders.

"Oh! That feels good." Eleanor remained silent for a few moments while Zen continued. Finally, she muttered, "We should check into that detective. Mathews?"

"Mathers," Livia corrected. "Yes, I have researched him." She reached into her pocket and withdrew a small notebook. "New to the Montpelier force—less than two years. Highly regarded by his peers. Replaced retiring Detective Smythe. Quiet. Thorough. Smart. Single. Never married."

"Homosexual?" Eleanor's voice carried a trace of hope. Liv shook her head. "'tis a pity. It always becomes complicated when a human male deals with the Guild."

"I will handle that," Livia responded, closing her book. "The only problem I foresee is his intelligence." Eleanor had a questioning look. "Highly intelligent. I would hate for him to learn too much about us too quickly."

Eleanor sighed and patted Zen's hands. She couldn't risk relaxing any further. The desire to fall asleep called too strongly. She hadn't been confronted with law officials for so long she'd almost forgotten how much of a bother they were. Luckily, Livia was the Guild public relations woman.

"Handle that, will you, dear?" Livia nodded. "And Zen, darling, let us return to work. We must finish the accounts before our lives become unmanageable from the Faire. And ladies…" She paused to get their attention. "…despite the police, Robert and corpses, nothing can interfere with the Faire."

"**W**HAT ARE YOU DOING?" Whenever Heather tried to sound angry, the pouty voice reminded Lynn of her mother and, subsequently, triggered her authority issues.

"I am spreading my joy," Mrs. Bailey sang.

Mrs. Bailey, stripped naked and *sans* Feng Shi, held a towel to her shoulders like a cape and ran up and down the corridors, her multiple folds of fat jiggling in all their naked glory. From the smell of it, the shower hadn't seen a lot of glory lately either. She reeked like a cross between garbage and sewer.

"Mrs. Bailey, perhaps you would like to spread the joy in your room," Lynn suggested.

"The *world* needs my joy!" Mrs. Bailey's face contorted into anger.

"But you've been depressed lately, haven't you? I think your room needs some joy."

Mrs. Bailey nodded. "Abbey's been gone a long time."

"Almost two weeks, yes," Lynn said, thinking of the last time Abbey was in her office. She should have tied and gagged those two old psychos right there. "Are you still missing her?"

Mrs. Bailey nodded. "Two weeks is…almost…a month." Suddenly, Mrs. Bailey's face lit up. "I'll go to my room so my joy can fill it!" With glee, the woman bounded back down the residence hall.

"Thanks?" Heather questioned Lynn.

Before she could reply, a voice started screaming in the day room. "It's her! It's her!" Lynn looked up and caught Mr. Rix, looking like a dead ringer for Judy Garland in a tight, thigh-length black sequin dress with matching pearls, jumping up and down and pointing at the television.

"Mr. Rix?" Heather called, rushing into the day room.

"IT'S JUDY GARLAND, YOU STUPID WHORE!" Edna screamed. Then to Judy Garland, she said, "Quiet, please, Judy, I can't hear the television."

Lynn knew at whom Mr. Rix was pointing even before she looked at the TV: Livia Emerson. The television appearances on the local station began shortly after Lynn's visit to the Bastille. As if reading her mind, the ladies mounted a public relations blitz, kissing the ass of every local paper, town rag, neighborhood newsletter, and Elks club meeting. Lynn expected to see the woman setting up birthday parties at McDonald's next. Wouldn't that be great for the brownie-eating lesbian sadists of the Bastille?

Livia wore a tailored dress with a simple string of pearls. The woman must have contracted with Mother Nature and ordered a perfect breeze to shimmer through her hair, as it danced in rhythm with the interviewer's questions. She could practically smell Livia's cologne: something floral and expensive.

Livia flashed a dazzling set of teeth as she explained about the excitement of the Faire, how much the Emerson family waited for this time of year and the usual references to how much cash the thing would haul in for the town. She finished the interview by reminding everyone that only those dressed in authentic medieval garb could enter through the gates and local vendors were limited to ten guests per booth. Beyond that, it was restricted to the area's residents or by special invitation only. After all, she added, throwing a manicured hand through her mane, this was a personal thank you from the Ladies of the Bastille for the town's undying support.

Poor choice of words, Lynn mused, *considering the two deaths on your property*. Since word got around town about the second bag of bones— which took about fifteen minutes longer than Lynn expected—visiting the Faire consumed the minds of the populace. Only in New England does the discovery of two dead bodies add to the mystique of a place. No wonder Stephen King is a millionaire.

The phone at the nurse's station buzzed and she snatched it up. "Lynn Swanson."

"There's a phone call for you," Martha's crisp voice crawled across the line. "Do you want it there?"

"Do you know who it is?"

"Of course I do."

Lynn waited. When Martha didn't answer, she decided to play the passive-aggressive game. Her mind could use the gymnastics, as God knows her abs weren't getting any exercise. "I'd love it if you could tell me."

"It's about Abbey."

"Oh." Lynn thought twice about having the call routed to her office. She decided it didn't matter one way or the other. "Okay, thanks, Martha."

After a slight click, a smooth male voice came on the line. "Doctor Swanson?"

"I'm not a doctor," Lynn informed him, "you can call me Lynn."

"Certainly. My name is Robert, Abbey's uncle."

Lynn jumped in surprise, and spat out a mouthful of her Starbuck's double tall mocha. She snatched a few tissues and dabbed at the liquid sliding down her chin. "Oh, yes, I remember." How could she forget? For the past week, Lynn had driven around the parking lot twice and parked in the farthest stall away, hoping to accidentally bump into Mr. Perfect on his way into The Meadows. She had had no success on that front, but her calf muscles looked a hell of a lot better from wearing those heels.

"I know Abbey has left The Meadows." His voice flowed like syrup over warm pancakes. Warm pancakes? Syrup? She needed to get out more. "But I hoped you, perhaps, have checked in on her?"

"I'm sorry, I really can't discuss my patients." Lynn tried to keep her voice calm and even. She was sure his hair fell thick and heavy across his head, down his chest and… "I certainly hope you understand."

"Oh, yes," he sounded as if he didn't. Lynn thought she heard him shuffle his feet and cough. "Is there something else I can help you with Mr….?"

"Please, Miss Swanson, call me Robert. It *is* Miss?" he crooned.

"Yes. It is…it's Miss."

His laughter rippled over the phone lines and vibrated down Lynn's legs. She sat down hard on the chair. "I shall be frank with you, Lynn—may I call you Lynn?"

"Please do."

"I shall be frank with you, Lynn," his voice tickled her ears. She could see his face on the other side of the line, a slight smile radiating from behind the mouthpiece as his tongue formed words over his lips. What else did those lips do? "I am concerned about my niece Abbey, but I hoped to secure some time with you."

"I'm sorry?" *Shit.* Her voice went up at the end just like Heather's. He probably thought she was an airhead, too.

"Dinner? Tonight? We shan't discuss Abbey, as I understand your professional obligations and commitments."

"Thank you."

"So we shall keep this totally…personal."

Lynn had to pee. She was definitely going to wet her pants. "That… that…I like food."

"So do I. I shall meet you at The Siren's Call at seven? Or do you prefer I pick you up?"

"No. Siren's Call at seven is good."

"Until then." The line went dead.

Lynn leaned over and put her head between her legs. She was going to throw up. Her face felt hot. Her heart pounded in her chest.

"You don't look well, dear."

Lynn looked up. "I'm okay, Edna. Just a bit lightheaded."

"Abbey looked like that sometimes."

"Really?"

Edna nodded and sighed with great drama. "When she dreamed of death. I don't think you'll die, though. You have gas."

"I do?" Lynn asked. Edna nodded at her and patted her arm.

"I can tell. I'm pretty good at…WHAT THE HELL DO YOU WANT, YOU NOSY BITCH?"

"Edna? Is that good language?"

Edna turned to Lynn and rolled her eyes. "You take care, sweetie. Get some antacids." She brushed past Heather with a defiant, "IT WAS A PERSONAL CONVERSATION, ASSHOLE!"

"Miss Swanson?" The meek voice was barely audible above the din. Lynn turned to it and found Mr. Graves standing at the station with something in his hands. He held it out to her. "The next time you see Abbey, will you give this to her?"

Lynn took it from the man. A paper airplane made of the heavy construction paper used in art therapy. Meticulously folded, the paper creation looked far more sophisticated than folded paper. "It's beautiful, Mr. Graves. I'll be happy to get it to her."

"If I don't see her before our outing to the Faire," he said softly, "I want her to know I'm thinking of her when he meets her."

"Who? Who's going to meet Abbey?"

"The Angel of Death." With that, he turned and walked slowly back to his room.

36

ROBERT HUNG UP THE PHONE and wrapped his hand around the knife he had chosen to kill Lynn Swanson. The knife was a souvenir from one of his lives in France and an artifact he clung onto through the centuries. With this knife, he slew many an enemy of the state, a young mercenary Eleanor sent after him just prior to Napoleon's rule, and one of the witches of the Tapestry the year they moved the fabric to North America. He looked at this knife as a good luck charm in times when he needed more luck than talent. From point to butt, it measured twelve inches. The hand-carved, cherry wood handle depicted intricate religious markings of various depths. The molding contoured to fit his hand. To be stabbed to death by this knife would be an honor.

He didn't want to kill Lynn; in fact, he fancied the young lady. She wasn't too annoying, she kept her opinions to herself and had perky, firm breasts. But he needed to be sure that all loose ends remained tied.

"Who do you plan to kill now?"

Robert turned toward the voice. The Doctor stood at the door to the bedroom with a cigar in his teeth and a snifter of brandy in each hand. Robert took one of the drinks.

"The social worker, Miss Swanson, if she knows more than she should."

"What would that be?"

Robert shrugged. "I can hardly answer that now, can I? I have no idea how much she has spoken to the witches, how much Abbey has told her—nothing." He slid the knife into its sheath and laid it on the bed. He began to unbutton his shirt.

"I have the update on the corpses."

Robert nodded and slipped off his jacket, laying it on the bed and re-creasing the folds. "Here, put these on." Robert tossed the Doctor a bundle of maroon-colored clothing and motioned for him to get dressed.

"Robert," the man sighed, "your previous two attempts have proven to be failures."

"It was those damned dogs of Tomyris! Couldn't get onto the property."

"Nonetheless, Robert, you walked almost two miles in female garb looking like you stepped out of 1492. Have you no pride left at all?"

"Please change clothes while you tell me what you know of the two bodies."

"The bones from 1940 are exactly who we thought it was," the Doctor said, slipping out of his shirt and jacket.

"Elfi Reisner," Robert said, climbing out of the remainder of his clothes. He stood naked staring at the doctor. The Doctor nodded. "Which is very unfortunate. I had hoped the bones were not hers."

"Was there any doubt?"

"I guess not. Still…with Boudicca running around stabbing everything in sight, how is one to know?"

"Next time you want a hidden body, perhaps you could be so kind as to *hide* it?" The Doctor stood naked at the foot of the bed hanging his suit in the closet. He picked up the clothes Robert had given him and looked at them suspiciously.

"So many years ago. We knew so little about…"

"Boss?" Joshua's voice boomed into the room. As he knocked on the door, it swung open. "Oh, sorry, the door's not totally shut and…" Joshua stopped when he saw the naked men.

"Oh, wow. Dudes. Like totally sorry to interrupt."

"What is it, Joshua?" Robert asked.

The young man turned away and fondled the light switch. "Do you, like, need me later?"

"Yes, Joshua, we will need a ride to the Bastille within the hour," answered Robert, shoving his legs into a pair of dirty jeans.

"Oh…sure…then…I guess I'll…wait."

"Thank you, Joshua." The boy's eyes darted between the two before closing the door tightly.

"As you were saying?" the Doctor said, donning the clothes.

"First, the Bastille. Then I am to meet Miss Swanson tonight at seven."

"To what end?"

"To eat a delicious meal, extract any information I can from her regarding Abbey's mental state and, if possible, about the women of the Bastille." He finished putting on the clothes and stood admiring himself in the mirror. He made a terrific-looking cowboy. The jeans hugged his body like a second skin and faded in the crotch so the material enhanced the outline of his penis. The denim shirt's snaps shone brilliantly and the battered and frayed boots announced his riding habits. The pungent smell of cow manure still clung to them, tickling his nostrils.

"You will kill her then?" the Doctor asked, standing next to Robert and looking at himself in the mirror. He wore baggy pants, a plain brown shirt, and a baseball cap.

"I will if I must. I prefer to keep her alive." He patted the Doctor on the shoulder. "To the car, then?"

"What, pray tell, will we do at the Bastille?"

"Spy, my friend. What else?" He smiled, picked up the knife, and walked to the door. "If we are caught, you are the lost traveler brought to the Bastille by rumors of the Faire."

"And you?"

"I have...something...to retrieve from the grounds of the Bastille," Robert winked at the Doctor. "However, I have been alerted by...a... friend within the walls of the manor that the witches believe Abbey's interactions with the Frisians will aid her memory. I want to be prepared in case I 'accidentally' bump into her on the trails. If I am so lucky, I plan on commiserating with her—one horse lover to another."

"Oh?"

"Yes. And, if possible, extract her from the Bastille."

"And if you cannot? If this attempt fails like your last?"

"Then there is always Miss Swanson."

37

"I DON'T UNDERSTAND WHAT IT IS YOU WISH ME TO DO," Abbey
asked Eleanor.

"Remember," Eleanor replied, coming up behind the young
woman. The image that reflected from the full-length mirror pleased
her. Abbey stood tall and straight, dressed in a worn pilot jacket, loose-
fitting slacks, and thick-soled boots. She looked somehow…right…as if
this were the role she was born to play.

"I do not understand."

"These are the clothes you wore when we fished you from the sea.
This," Eleanor turned her attention away from the mirror mounted
on the side of the hanger and pointed to the prop plane several yards
behind her, "is the plane that crashed into the ocean. Sometimes the
body remembers what the brain cannot."

Abbey turned back to the mirror. She hated all the clothing: jacket,
pants, scarf, helmet. She looked like the Sunday comics where Snoopy
dressed up like a World War I fighter pilot. It smelled musty and the
leather didn't crackle like leather should.

Eleanor guided the girl onto the stairs leading up into the cockpit.
"Climb inside. Close your eyes. You spent many hours in this plane. Let
your body remember."

Abbey shrugged and smiled weakly at Eleanor. Seven days had
passed since the day when the horse and swordsman emerged from the
Tapestry. Seven long days she'd listened to the aunts telling her stories
from their past. Seven days of tutoring with Aunt Boo on the sword,
knife and how to kill a man with your bare hands.

Despite all this education, Abbey still didn't *feel* as if she was a part of the Tapestry's legacy. Every fragment of information was a piece of a larger puzzle, but it held no emotional weight for her. She merely memorized academic facts that she parroted back to the aunts when they asked her questions. This was particularly disheartening the day Aunt Boo put a short sword in her hand and began to spar.

"You move sluggishly," the big woman snapped.

"What do you expect of me?" she had said, throwing the sword on the stones of the hallway.

"I expect you to fight!" Boo hissed. "You spent lifetimes as a warrior; prove it."

"I cannot!" Abbey screamed. "I know I should remember how to use this," she said, pointing to the sword, "but I do not. I'm sorry."

Boo looked at her with an expression full of pity, as if Abbey had somehow disappointed her. As Boo turned, she said in a voice so quiet that Abbey almost missed it, "You are going to get us all killed."

For the next entire day, none of the aunts approached her. None of them met her eyes when they passed in the halls. None of them tried to teach her anything further about what they called her 'divine destiny.' Until this morning, when Aunt Eleanor knocked on her bedroom door, threw these ridiculous clothes at her, and told her to walk with her to the airplane hanger.

Abbey sulked all the way to the plane, then began climbing aboard. "At The Meadows, the day you brought me home, you handed me a small toy airplane with an inscription on it."

"Yes."

"This is that plane, isn't it?" Eleanor nodded. "And the initials?"

"Can you not guess?"

"Guild of Immortal Women."

"Do you remember joining the Guild?"

"I don't," Abbey confided, "Aunt Boo told me."

Eleanor sighed. "I see."

Abbey felt the hollow pit of her stomach churn in frustration. "I am sorry to disappoint you, Aunt Eleanor."

"Abbey!" Eleanor's voice stung her ears. "You do not disappoint any of us." She stared at Abbey until the young woman looked away.

"Why is it taking me so long to remember?" Abbey felt her body flush and knew her face must be red. "What is wrong with me?"

"Nothing, girl, nothing at all." Eleanor's voice struck her as calmly soothing. "Death affects all of us differently. Yours was such a... horrendous death, that it is taking longer than we expected."

"Or hoped."

"Yes."

Abbey continued climbing into the cockpit and settled herself into the pilot's seat. She lightly fingered the controls, playing her fingertips along the dials and levers. She yelled down to Eleanor standing below, "What now?"

"Nothing."

Eleanor stepped away from the plane and peered up at the cockpit. "Many of us allow ourselves to forget the circumstances following a tragic death. We have learned it is better to let the memories come back at their own speed."

"And me?"

"With you, we must...hurry the process."

"And sitting in this plane will do that?"

"I hope so."

A lingering silence stretched between the two. Abbey looked around the cockpit. The setting looked familiar, although she couldn't place it. Her stomach began to churn and she suddenly felt anxious. Where had she seen this place before? A movie in the day room, perhaps? A television special on the history channel?

"Aunt Eleanor?"

"Yes, dear?"

"Why do Emerson women live forever?"

Eleanor chuckled. "Nobody knows, child. We only know that sometimes a child is born that does not die. Unless the head separates from the body, of course."

"Always girls?"

"The occasional male. But male Immortals are few and far between."

"How is it we breed children then?" Abbey felt suddenly lightheaded and the sound of her own voice seemed far away.

Eleanor thought about this a moment. "Take care, Abbey. Unlike us, the Immortal males cannot breed with Human females. They need the Immortal females to carry their child. Some become desperate for offspring and will stop at nothing to impregnate an Immortal female."

"Against our will?" Abbey's voice floated out of her in a note she could not control. She felt dizzy and nauseous.

"It has happened. Will again, I am sure."

"Robert."

"Yes."

Abbey looked above her and saw the blue sky spread out like a painting. She looked to the sides and saw that the barn, hanger and landing strip were gone. Replacing them was a blue that was deeper in hue and went on for miles in any direction. She looked beneath her and saw herself flying over the ocean. She was finally free.

Worries over the long distance instruments, unfavorable flying weather, and the bout of dysentery made the past several days seem less like heaven and more like hell.

All that worry was behind her. Her stout immunity had beaten back the illness, the plane was in a state of perfection, and the weather had decided to cooperate. This is what flying was all about. Below her, the Pacific spanned for miles, the brilliant midday sun shooting its rays across the water's surface. It wasn't water beneath her now, but a vast blue expanse of heaven, decorated with sparkling jewels of white—diamonds on a bed of blue velvet.

Her last transmission to the *USS Itasca* had been placed, the plane's fuel reserves had been exhausted, and her whereabouts labeled in a vague manner, which was sure to cause confusion upon her disappearance. Of all the lifetimes she had lived thus far, it is this existence she would miss the most.

She had been thrilled beyond measure when she first learned of flight. The news of the successful airborne experiment in Kitty Hawk set her heart racing. Imagine! The opportunity to break away from the ruthless confines of the Earth; the ability to disconnect oneself from soil and connect to the sky, air and clouds. One step closer to God.

She looked up into the azure expanse and uttered a silent prayer to those disembodied voices who had been with her since adolescence. She long ago had made peace with her gift of seeing angels, but they never amazed her more than they had back when she was a girl—a lonely peasant wench in France. She had learned that blue was the color of the sky; therefore, the color of the heavens. God was blue.

"Hey! Hey! Torch!" the booming voice erupted, destroying her moment of tranquility. "You ready?"

She sighed deeply and returned her focus to the plane's dials. "No!" she screamed over the droning engines. Damn, how she hated to do this. Her entire life had been spent looking upward to the sky, the heavens that concealed the secret answers to her long-nagging questions: Who am I? Why am I so different from the rest? Why, God, do you choose to speak to me? Her life of flight was not so much devoted to the conquest of nature via the flying machine, but just one more step towards the Divine. One more step on a journey she began the moment of her magical birth.

Living forever had its downfalls.

"Yes, Fred," she screamed at the impatient man running navigation, "now I'm ready."

She felt him kick her seat in acknowledgement. This is a signal the two of them had agreed upon somewhere over Australia on their way to Port Darwin. After hours of screaming at each other, they had finally created a crude sign language for themselves with closed fists meaning 'good idea' and thumbs up meaning 'all's okay on my end.' The kicking of her seat was Fred's ingenious plan not only to affirm his understanding of a plan, but to keep her awake. Personally, she felt it was payback for her strict supervision of the escape from the United States during the burning of Atlanta.

She felt the plane descend slightly as she turned it towards the tiny island the Order had chosen for her. The rest of the world awaited her arrival at the Howland Islands, so the Order had decided it was best not to interrupt the flight until the last minute. Thanks to Aunt Eleanor's ability to locate just the perfect minion for any job (God knows how she was able to do that), she and Fred had been directed to a tiny outcropping of land so tiny it hardly qualified as an 'island.'

The plan was easy: to die.

It's not like they hadn't died before.

The tricky part about this death would be to avoid serious injury in the process. According to Aunt Eleanor, the piece of volcanic rock was just large enough to accommodate a small plane's landing. If the weather did not hold out, or if conditions became unfavorable in any way, she always had the option of setting down in the Pacific. Since either of these choices suited her and Fred's objectives, either one would work.

The problem was, they couldn't agree on a plan. Fred wanted to play it safe, as always, and land on the island. She, on the other hand, wanted a water landing. If she attempted to set the Electra down on the island and missed by more than a few feet, the plane's wheels would be cut to ribbons on the sharp volcanic rock. Or, worse yet, run too long for the island's short landing strip and send them plummeting over the island's cliffs down into the sea. The lifeboat aboard the plane could be utilized, but that would bring a whole host of problems should the remains of the Electra be found. Once the rescue teams discovered the missing life raft, they would surely send a search team into the area to find them. This would be unacceptable. The point was to die. But the biggest problem to her was one of fire. Although there was little fuel in the tanks, what was there could still ignite.

Fire is the one risk she refused to accept; far better to be ripped apart by ravenous sharks, or beheaded by the sharp edges of volcanic rock. Better yet, drown. At least she would survive a drowning death.

"Heads up!" Fred's voice bellowed. She felt his foot kick wildly under her seat—a frantic panic-stricken attack on her ass.

The island was beneath them now, its polished surface sparkling in the sun. One look and she knew why nobody had charted this place. The land beneath her was hardly noticeable from the air. Almost perfectly rectangular, it consisted of coal black volcanic rock speckled with a bit of vegetation. At one of its long ends, it boasted two jagged peaks, while at its other end, the flat rock which she would use as a landing strip ended at a pile of jagged rocks. Why didn't Aunt Eleanor's people tell her about the narrowness of the opening between these two peaks?

She had no time to debate the issue. The Electra's gas supply was already down to almost nothing and she must do something quickly. She glanced at her watch—21:30 GMT. The *Itasca* still had plenty of daylight to search for them. They had to land, properly cover their tracks, and take refuge before the president called upon the rescue teams.

"Come on!" Fred screamed again, kicking her seat.

She decided to set the plane down in the water. Screw it. She didn't want to fight with Fred, but he would have to accept the fact that she was in control. Suddenly, the nose kicked upwards.

"What the—" she heard Fred gasp.

The wind had unexpectedly changed. What was going on? Hadn't the weather report stated mild skies? Without warning, she felt the plane hit a wall of crosswind and the tiny plane's left side flew wildly out of control. The world before her began to shift, the horizon thrown perpendicular. She compensated but the sudden change of lift left uncertainty in her grasp.

"LOOK OUT!" Fred's frantic voice cut through the wind.

She looked up just in time to see a wall of blue rushing at her, the waves breaking on the nose of the plane as it dove into the surf. Blue enveloped her; blue, the color of God.

She banged her fists against the cold metal of the instrument panel as water consumed the cockpit. It crawled up the sides of the plane, swallowing her feet and floor panel. She pounded on the instruments, struggling against the undertow created by the vacuum of the sea. She pounded harder, her fists numb from the impact. The dull, hollow thud of her hands echoed through her, reverberating up her arms and into her shoulders.

Frantic, she thrashed about, her arms flailing wildly, smashing into the submerging nose of the plane.

Thud. Thud. Thud.

"Abbey!"

The water moved up her waist—.

"Abbey! Wake up!"

She lifted her head, desperate to keep her nose and mouth above the water line—"ABBEY!"

The slap across her face sent waves of fire through her body. She threw herself out of the water and into the open air. When she opened her eyes, she lay on the runway next to the prop plane, Eleanor kneeling by her side, her arms wrapped protectively around her.

"Aunt Eleanor," Abbey muttered. "I remember dying."

With that, darkness consumed her and she fainted.

"**W**OW, I JUST PAGED YOU AN HOUR AGO. You make better time than pizza delivery."

Matt smiled and stifled a yawn. The past few days of five-hour naps in the car were catching up with him. He straightened his belt and smoothed down his shirt, hoping the wrinkles weren't too distracting.

"You look like shit, Detective," Helen said, pushing her glasses back on her nose.

"Thanks."

"That smell…is that you?"

"I haven't showered today."

"Today?" Her nose wrinkled. "It smells like several days. What the hell is going on?"

"Stakeout." Mathers didn't lie. He had been on a stakeout. The stakeout was just interrupted by several periods of time when he went to work, then home to eat, catnap, and check his mail. And, since his stakeout involved the Emerson women, it wasn't supported by the department. He thought of it as a hobby-esque kind of stakeout.

Luckily, Janet and Sal took pity on him. Right after dinner, when he fell asleep on the couch, they cleaned out the guest room. When he awoke, Sal stood holding out a key.

"Take it. Stay here as long as you want. No sense driving back to Montpelier every couple of days."

He felt as if he was imposing on them, but accepted the key anyway. So for this week, he didn't have to worry about the drive back home and he would get more than a five-hour catnap.

Helen busied herself at the computer while he pulled up a chair and flopped down. He looked at his shoes and realized with dismay that the hole in his heel was now the size of a quarter.

"In English, or the full report?" Helen waved a thick folder in front of him.

"English. My mind is a bit sluggish."

Helen opened the file and began referencing notes. "Remember those DNA tests that you wanted re-done?" Mathers nodded. "Yes, the ones that were perfectly accurate but you wanted re-analyzed because your mind wasn't ready to accept the findings?" Mathers sighed and nodded at her. "They came back. Same results."

"I figured they would."

"Then why waste our time, Detective?"

"I wanted to be sure."

"It's good to want things," was the retort. "Keeps the brain spinning."

"And?"

"And?"

"And they prove...?"

"Detective, perhaps the dirt from this stakeout...why do you call it a stakeout? You're not staking anything."

Mathers waved his fingers. "Move along."

"Right. This proves, Detective, that the skeletal remains date back to 1941 and 2008, respectively, but the clothing, jewelry and other artifacts can be traced back to—roughly—the 1200's."

"The thirteenth century."

"Roughly."

He whistled and rubbed his eyes. "How is this possible?"

Helen shrugged. She wheeled her office chair over to the sink, opened the cabinet beneath it and hauled out a huge box of Oreo cookies. She offered them to Mathers and he took two. "My theory," she said as she twisted them apart, "is that someone knocked over a museum, stole some old clothes from a diorama, put the clothing onto a body they dug up from a grave, and left them for the ladies of the Bastille."

He rolled his eyes. "Seriously."

"I'm fresh out of theories." She chewed the white sugary center from the cookie and grabbed for another. "Oh, I think we may have a lead on who the old woman is."

"Which one?"

"The bones wrapped in the burlap bag. Circa 1941." She shoved the chocolate cookie into her mouth and picked up another paper. "Elfi Reisner."

"Who the hell is Elfi Reisner?"

Helen shrugged. "Some woman who used to work for the government during World War II." She reached into the box and hauled out two more. "Apparently, she worked in a government office that kept intricate records. When we researched the DNA data, her name popped up."

"How?"

"You're the detective. Don't you know this cop stuff?"

He sighed again. He didn't feel like sparring with her today. He was too tired and could smell himself. He smelled bad.

"How goes the stalking of the ladies?"

"Fine. Eight days of nothing." He shoved an Oreo into his mouth and chewed for a minute. "I felt sure I would find something out of the ordinary, see something odd, notice something…"

"That's a lot of somethings."

He ignored her. "But got a big fat nothing. No possible break-ins at the Bastille, no crazies saying they buried the two bags of bones. No horrendous fights between the Ladies. Nada."

"That's good."

"That's bad."

"No, it's good," Helen insisted. "You're alive. God knows what it would have been if you saw something." They chewed in silence for a moment before she continued. "I'm wondering how someone would get old clothing and a skeleton from 1941."

"I'm not," Mathers sighed again. "I'm wondering *why*."

"COME TO THE DEN! QUICKLY!" Ruth's terrified voice echoed through the empty hallways. Eleanor turned to Abbey and saw her chest rising and falling in perfect rhythm. The poor girl woke briefly about twenty minutes ago when Boo carried her into the bed chamber and the two of them were able to get her to swallow a sleeping pill. Thank goodness it worked.

Eleanor set her knitting down and raced to the door. She hadn't heard Ruth sound so panicked since the cancellation of *M*A*S*H*. Well, there were worse things a woman her age could do than watch television. When Eleanor stepped into the hallway, two of the Salukis pummeled into her, sending her careening into the wall.

"Watch it, Eleanor!" Tom said. "They're not indestructible."

"That's a pity."

"What's up with Ruth? The cable go out again?" she said, petting a Saluki.

"Would you stay here with Abbey?" Eleanor gestured toward the closed door. "She had a bad experience on board the plane earlier."

`"I heard," Tomyris said. She whistled and pointed to Abbey's room. Two of the dogs rushed obediently to the door and lay across the threshold, panting loudly.

"I would really feel better if a *Human* guarded our cherished member of the Team," Eleanor snapped.

Tomyris laughed. "They'll kill without a shred of guilt. Rather like Boo, only they smell better."

Eleanor shook her head in disgust. She didn't know why Tomyris loved these ugly dogs so much, but she had to admit, they were terribly keen watchdogs, in addition to giving Tomyris something to do. She waved to Tomyris, "Come on."

The other women stood in the large carpeted den staring at the big-screen plasma television. Ruth sat on the edge of the sofa, pink frilly apron splattered with chocolate, holding a large wooden spoon. The minute she saw them she hit the 'mute' button on the remote. "They said it would be the next story!" Ruth said in a hurried voice. "But so far, I have only seen the automobile commercials. Do we need a GMC truck? They seem so much more powerful than our limo."

"What is it?" Eleanor pleaded, ignoring the flashy GMC roaring down the beach, splashing water on bikini-clad women.

"It is the local news," Ruth's voice was thick with fear. "They have identified one of the bodies found on the grounds." Ruth threw the remote onto the couch and put her face in her hands. "I can't bear to watch!"

Zen patted the old woman's back and looked at Eleanor. "It's Elfi."

"Elfi Riesner?" Eleanor felt her mouth go dry.

Tomyris whistled a long note and the two Salukis cocked their heads at her. "Holy shit. We are so fucked."

"Impending doom is no reason to use gutter language," Eleanor snapped. "The TV!"

The lips of the local television announcer started moving and the words BODY FOUND appeared at the bottom of the screen. "The sound! Give us sound, Ruth!"

Ruth remained still, shaking her head and rubbing her eyes, banging the wooden spoon on her head. Zen used her free hand to search the couch, but her hand came away empty. With a groan, Boo stepped to the couch and shoved her hands into the cushions looking for the remote. Ultimately, Eleanor didn't need the sound to follow the story. Sandwiched between the supertitles of BODY FOUND, DISAPPEARED and MISSING SINCE 1942, were black-and-white pictures of a dark-haired beauty of twenty-eight. By the time the sound came back on, all the ladies heard was the conclusion of the report.

"...investigation is being conducted into the connection between the two bodies. Elfi Reisner's body was found underneath that of her granddaughter, Sara Reisner. Both bodies were uncovered last week."

"Well," Eleanor said after a short pause, "we now know what happened to them."

"This is Robert's doing," Boo sneered. "I can feel it."

"Reisner!" Ruth said through clenched fingers. "He said their last names were Reisner!"

"I know, dear, we are old, not deaf."

"That means..." Ruth didn't finish the sentence. She returned her face to her hands and rocked. Behind them, the dogs whined and barked once.

They turned and saw Abbey standing in the doorway to the den, flanked by the two Salukis, who wagged their tales furiously and stared up at her with anticipation. Eleanor shot a look to Tomyris. "So much for the guard dogs. Tomyris, put them outside, please!"

Tomyris whistled and pointed. The dogs scurried towards the kitchen.

"What is it, Abbey?" Zen asked, standing and walking to the girl.

Abbey swayed slightly and looked into Eleanor's face. "That woman. The one in the photos..."

"Which one dear? The old black-and-white photos?"

Abbey nodded. "I remember who she is."

40

MATHERS JERKED AWAKE WITH THE EERIE FEELING that someone was spying on him. He looked around, bringing his hand to his holster. What was it about this place? For years the women of the Bastille lived in this town under a cloak of secrecy, but never had there been a single instance of illegal activity. His research showed the last time the police became involved in the family was in 1969 when a group of post-Woodstock hippies were found having an orgy in a Volkswagen van. This was hardly the stuff of murderers.

He stretched and looked out the windshield into the wooded section of the grounds, still sectioned off by yellow CRIME SCENE tape. He was stalling and he knew it. Protocol dictated that the tape should be removed and the area cleared of all police materials by this time of the investigation. All samples had been collected, all pictures safely downloaded into the police computers, and he had no reason to refrain from turning the grounds over to the women and let them get on with planning the Faire. But he had that strange feeling that something didn't add up. How in the hell did anyone get the body of Sara Reisner into the clearing without touching the spongy ground? How did the body manage to land in the exact spot that Elfi's body lay? Why? Nothing about this case made any sense. His gut told him Abbey was keeping secrets and he didn't like secrets; secrets meant something bad.

He sighed. There was no use going over this again. He barely could stay awake, his brain hurt from hypothesizing about motives and facts of the case. Better to head back to Sal and Janet's for a beer and a good night's sleep. Tomorrow, he'd think of something.

He pulled out onto the private drive and headed back towards town. If Abbey knew either of the Reisners, she would have met them through the aunts. How did the aunts know them? The locals assured him that the ladies rarely socialized outside the elaborate fundraisers and altruistic work that made the Bastille so beloved. None of them could remember a single time that the locals went into the mansion except for the yearly Faires. Even then, the locals kept to the money-making jobs running food booths, selling goods, or acting as entertainers. There had to be a connection. There had to be something he was overlooking. As he stopped for the red light, Mathers groaned and rubbed his eyes. Maybe this was one time where his innate curiosity was not going to do him any good.

Out of the corner of his eye, he spied the Dairy Queen. Just what he needed—a peanut buster parfait. He swung into the parking lot, steered the car into the first vacant stall, and headed into the building.

"Detective Mathers?"

He spun towards the voice.

"Miss…Swanson, right?"

"Just call me Lynn."

He hadn't seen Lynn since he interviewed her last week. At that time, she darted around a crowded office, stepping over piles of manila folders while clutching a huge Starbuck's cup. She looked haggard and tired, her hair pulled back into an oily ponytail that she tried to hide under a faded Red Sox baseball cap. She seemed hesitant to talk, as if one slip of the tongue would damage a career or get her fired. He chalked it up to her job. It couldn't be easy being someone's shrink and walking a tightrope between the desire to help and confidentiality issues. He found himself taken in by her childlike franticness and pure honesty. He doubted there was a mean bone in her body.

Today, however, she looked spectacular. Her freshly washed hair lay primped against her head and she wore a tailored dress accented by black high heels. Her eyes darted no more. Instead, they pierced through him like lasers and he found himself becoming the frantic one with eyes darting everywhere. Damn! He really needed a good night's sleep. He was a mess. He looked into her eyes and nodded. Had she always been this much of a knockout?

"Lynn," he said, trying to sound calm and avoid staring at her chest. "Nice to see you again."

"Yes," she giggled nervously. Too many Starbucks? "How is the mystery going?"

He shrugged. "Still a mystery."

She laughed and pulled at her necklace. "I was wondering…"

"Yes?"

"I was wondering…did you ever interview Abbey? At the Bastille?"

"Why do you ask?" Man! This woman had some high cheekbones.

She shrugged and looked around her with jerky, almost paranoid, movements. "Just curious. You know…if things looked…normal there."

"Normal?"

Her eyes darted around the parking lot. "Well…I see unusual things in my line of work."

"I bet."

"The last time I was there…the air seemed…tense." She coughed a cough meant to consume time, not clear the throat. "As if…"

"What are you trying to say, Miss…," he caught himself, "Lynn?"

"What's your opinion of the relationship between Abbey and the aunts?"

"Why do you ask?"

"Please don't." She dropped the formality and stared at him, her hand on her hip. "Please don't answer my questions with questions. I'm a therapist. I can do it better than you."

He laughed and shrugged. "Occupational hazard."

"I would like it if someone else noticed an odd relationship between the family members."

"Would you care to elaborate?"

She shook her head. "Occupational hazard."

"Understood." He stared at her. Were her eyes always so blue? "Yes. The answer is yes, it seems like an…unusual relationship." She nodded. He continued with, "and there's no need for you to worry about speaking with me. I realize you are in a unique predicament with your job."

She grinned. "All right then." She took a spoonful of her sundae and a drop of it dribbled on her chest.

"Careful. Awfully nice dress. Your dessert is spoiling it."

She swallowed. "Not dessert. I'm on my way to dinner." She toasted him with the sundae. "I'm starving, but I don't like to eat too much when I'm on a date."

"Ah, that's the secret."

"Little-known fact about women." She ate another bite of the ice cream and threw the rest away. "Nice seeing you again. I have to hurry. Robert will wonder where I am."

He nodded. "That's my uncle's name, Robert."

"Really?" she asked, dabbing her mouth with a napkin. "Do I have parfait on my face?" He shook his head and she looked relieved. "Well," she cleared her throat, "'bye now."

He followed her with his eyes as she got into her car and laughed as it backfired twice before turning over. When she shuddered out of the parking lot and onto the street, he decided that she needed a new clutch. And a boyfriend with a different name. He never liked the name Robert. His Uncle Robert was a jackass.

WHEN ROBERT SAW THE UPSTART DETECTIVE drive away down the private road, he crawled down from his hiding place in the trees. He looked at his watch. Damn. He hadn't expected to be here this long. It was a simple job: go in, retrieve the piece of hidden Tapestry, and leave. The only acceptable deterrent would be meeting Abbey. Otherwise, he had dinner reservations with Lynn and he would have to rush.

He dashed to the far side of the clearing to an ancient oak tree which stood on the easternmost side, its two immense trunks splitting just above eye level. The darkening sky didn't slow him down, as he knew this tree well and could easily make out the black ridges of the hollow crevice in the fork of the split.

His fingers closed around the fabric hidden within and he tenderly withdrew the rolled up piece of Tapestry. The last time he ventured into the Bastille, he used his dagger to hack away a corner piece of one of the panels in a spontaneous act of desperation. Despite the fact that he now had a spy within the walls of the Bastille, each time he trespassed onto the grounds, the percentages of being caught grew. With this stolen panel, he could get inside without being detected.

He unrolled the fabric and scrutinized it in the fading light. Perfect! Exactly as he had left it. The two feet by two feet section held four embroidered memories, two of them his and two of them the Doctor's. After years of study, he had mastered the magic necessary to access and separate these particular memories from any other memory of the Tapestry—a forbidden and difficult feat. But due to the winter's flooding, the Faire was being moved to this location and the oak had now lost its allure.

From behind him a dog growled. Then another. Then a third and fourth. Robert slowly turned to face Tomyris' Salukis staring at him. He froze.

He lifted one foot. The dogs stood up. He lowered it. They sat down. He pulled the knife from its sheath. So be it—man against beast.

Suddenly, they scattered into the darkness. Robert took off like a shot, running towards the road. He was almost through the clearing when the first dog attacked. His left leg disappeared from under him and he toppled onto the moist ground. Instantly, a second dog sank its teeth into his right leg. Before he could react, a third clamped down on his left sleeve. He wielded the dagger in his right hand, stabbing blindly, but the mongrels stayed out of range. He felt himself being dragged backwards by the two creatures on his legs, while the third tugged him to the left.

He flailed wildly, and he felt a mouth loosen around his left ankle. He kicked upwards and felt his foot connecting with the jaw of one of the dogs. He felt the thing release his leg and he tucked it under himself protectively.

"NO!" he screamed, thrusting out with the knife toward the flurry of fur and fangs. He felt the blade piercing flesh and one of the mongrels howled in pain. With renewed vigor, he slashed at the air. With his free leg, he kicked towards the Saluki holding his other ankle, and heard the CRACK of bone and a frantic yelping. As if on cue, they released him. He flipped over, lifted himself onto his knees, and found himself staring at one of the dog's hindquarters. Before he could react, it lifted its leg and let loose with a stream of urine that soaked his hair, rolled down his neck, and saturated his shirt. The smell struck him like a brick and he choked back a gag as he felt droplets of the dog piss coat his lips. He jabbed out with his knife and felt it sink into the soft tissue of the animal's underbelly. Another loud whimper shot through the dark as he jumped to his feet. Wiping the liquid from his face, Robert limped towards the road, digging into his pocket for his cell phone.

This was quite enough. Being attacked, then pissed on by dogs was the last straw. They had to die. While he was at it, he'd kill that bitch Tomyris as well. She was a terrible lay anyway.

"WHERE ARE THOSE DOGS?" Tomyris asked, fingering the feather in her hair. "They always come the first time I call."

Fred shrugged. "How's Abbey?"

"You mean besides fainting every time she begins to remember something? Just dandy." Tomyris whistled again.

"She'll come around."

"We're running out of time." Tomyris spun toward him. "She didn't remember you. The plane is here—she didn't remember it, either. Hell!"

"Boo reports that the yellow police tape is down. The area is ready for the Faire."

"You better inform Livia. Goddess forbid, one of us plebeians talks to the public."

"I will when I go inside."

Tomyris reached into her pocket and withdrew a wadded-up napkin and revealed its contents. "Want a cookie?" He shook his head. "Pumpkin square?" He waved it off. "An oatmeal bar?" He thought a minute and took the oatmeal bar.

"I've been asked to leave," he said. She looked away quickly before replying weakly, "I know."

"Eleanor thinks it would inhibit Abbey's memory to keep me around. She's afraid if Abbey does remember me, the shock of recalling the crash will…"

"I know. Eleanor told me."

He nodded. "I'm leaving in the morning." She whistled for the dogs again. "I won't be here for the Ritual. You know what that means."

She nodded. "You can cross over next year. What's a year to an Immortal?"

Fred nodded and chewed on his oatmeal bar. "I need a rest. It's been almost a hundred years since I returned to the Tapestry."

She touched his hand tenderly, then jerked her head towards the woods. "Here they come."

"They're carrying something."

"Something's wrong."

They stepped towards the animals as the dogs raced out of the trees and headed for Tomryis. Two of the beasts bounded ahead, growling playfully, but her eyes were glued on the other two. They hobbled slowly, each dragging a leg behind them, their heads hanging. "They've been injured. Stab wounds."

"I'll call for the others," Fred said, heading for the mansion.

43

LYNN KNEW SHE SHOULDN'T HAVE ORDERED the third Lemon Drop; she always became instantly stupid when she drank too much vodka.

"I think you have a marvelous sense of humor," he said, turning his perfectly formed, perfectly colored eyes to her.

"Well..." she said before she burped loudly. She jumped and covered her mouth. "I am so terribly sorry."

"For what?" Robert asked. "It is I who should be sorry. Was it not I who arrived late?"

"Only half an hour," she said, waving him off. "I've waited longer than that." She didn't add 'for less of a man' like she wanted. Even though her luck was taking a turn for the better, she still knew that discretion was the better part of valor.

"I want to prove how truly sorry I am for my ill manners," he said, placing his hand upon hers.

Lynn flushed. His moves were kind of cliché, but his timing was perfect.

"I see you need another drink," he said, waving down the waiter.

"Oh, no, I shouldn't," she said. He flashed his mouthful of even, white teeth and she felt herself blush. "Well, are you having one more?" He nodded. She sighed and said, "All right then."

"Very well!" He motioned to the waiter. "After all, you've had a horribly taxing week." He leaned back, letting her hand fall to the table with a thud. "It must be difficult seeing Abbey again."

"How did you know I saw Abbey?"

"Just a guess." He winked. "I understand, believe me." He shot a glance around and leaned forward. "Those aunts of hers..." He rolled his eyes.

"I know!" Lynn leaned in. She really shouldn't be talking about this, but he was family. Perhaps he had some insight to the situation that might help Detective Mathers with his investigation. If Abbey was being abused or tortured, shouldn't the uncle be able to provide some evidence? Maybe he could provide a safe place for Abbey to stay.

"Were they always...this way toward Abbey?"

He bowed his head. Abbey reached across and took his hand and he looked up at her. A single tear rolled down his cheek.

"It has only gotten worse since she began remembering..." he stopped himself and hiccupped back a sob. Lynn gripped his hand tighter. His face froze. The poor man looked terrified. She squelched the urge to wrap her arms around him. "You know...all of it...."

"No, I don't know. I'm sorry," she whispered. "Abbey told me nothing."

He lowered his head and sniffed. "Then Abbey didn't tell you about...her life...before The Meadows."

She leaned in and lowered her voice to a barely audible whisper. "The last I heard, she hasn't remembered a damned thing. That's why I think the aunts are...you know...doing what they're doing."

He looked into her face, his lips turning upward into an enthusiastic grin. "I know she would tell you if she did. You're such a great comfort to her, Miss Swanson."

"Lynn."

"Certainly." He wiped a tear from his eye. "Lynn."

He caressed her hand, applying gentle pressure to her joints. She closed her eyes and allowed herself to relax into his touch.

"Your Lemon Drop?"

Lynn pulled her hand away from Robert and took the drink. Without looking at him, she downed half of it in one gulp. "Now, where were we?"

"I'm sorry, but I really must take this." He jumped up from his chair and stepped away from her, opening his cell phone which Lynn never heard ring. After a brief moment, he walked back to the table and touched her shoulder. "I'm terribly sorry, Lynn, but I must go."

"What?"

"Yes. It seems there is an urgent matter…a death…with a client. I am sorry, but I must leave and attend to this issue."

"Oh," Lynn tried to hide the disappointment in her voice.

"I assure you, the dinner companionship was exquisite." He leaned over and kissed her cheek. He lowered himself onto one knee and looked into her eyes. "Perhaps next time, you shall be the one to kiss me?"

Acting on impulse, Lynn gulped the second half of the Lemon Drop, grabbed Robert's face in her hands, and brought his face to hers. She kissed him hard, feeling his tongue inside of her mouth, playing with her lips. When he pulled away, she wished she had another Lemon Drop.

"Well…" he stuttered standing up, "I see you and I shall have a much more… interesting…second date."

"Second?" Lynn tried to hide the excitement in her voice.

"Oh, yes."

He threw a wad of bills onto the table and left the restaurant.

"Will there be anything else?" the waiter asked.

"Hell yes! Another Lemon Drop!" she said, handing him the empty glass.

THE MINUTE ROBERT SETTLED INTO THE BACK OF THE LIMO he flipped open his cell phone.

"Hey, boss!" Joshua said as the window slid down. Fragments of rock music blared from the front of the limo and Joshua quickly turned down the volume. "Sorry. It's from their Sticky Fingers album. Great tracks. So…early date, eh? Not…what you wanted?"

"Oh, she's exactly what I want."

Josh's eyes narrowed as he thought about this. "Oh," he said hesitantly, "a woman who doesn't put out?"

"On the contrary," Robert smiled. "Put out exactly what I needed."

"All right man!" Josh whistled. "See ya later, dude!" As the window slid shut, the Doctor's voice came onto the line.

"Yes?"

"We are clear. Abbey remembers nothing."

"Are you sure?"

"Yes," Robert said, lighting his cigarette. "Lynn would have known. Which means the witches are as clueless; we can commence with the plan for this weekend."

"Are you sure this Lynn girl does not lie?" The Doctor sounded strained.

"My dear doctor," Robert said, exhaling smoke, "women are the most predictable creatures. Easy to manipulate once you know the trick."

"Trick?"

"Tears," Robert said flatly. "A single tear gets them every time." He paused while the Doctor laughed. "One more thing—those mutts of Tomyris' must be killed."

"I don't know if it will be convenient."

"Oh, trust me," Robert said, extinguishing the cigarette. "It will be convenient. No matter how much work it takes."

45

"**I**'M NOT DEAF YOU FUCKING BITCH!" Edna squeezed the last pair of socks into a tight ball and set it into the left portion of her sock drawer, making sure it didn't touch the white socks lined up on the right side of the drawer. There was nothing worse than a sock drawer that wasn't divided into 'colored' socks and 'white' socks.

"Edna?" Heather's voice filtered through the door, "I thought we weren't going to use any more bad language? That's what we agreed?"

Edna gently slid the drawer closed and straightened the lace doily on the top of her dresser. With one last glance around the room to make sure everything was in its place, she reached for the doorknob. "I'M COMING OUT, YOU SWINE, SO MOVE BACK!" She shot a parting glance at the bare mattress where Abbey used to sleep and opened the door.

Without waiting for any more of Heather's prattle, she moved towards the day room, where Mr. Chow stood with his penis peeking out through his zipper.

"Put him away before I chop his head off," Edna whispered as she passed him. Mr. Chow gave her a nervous glance and stuffed himself back into his pants.

Lynn stood at the white board and looked up as Edna entered the day room. "Hello there, Edna."

"Why do you call her Edna and the rest of us 'Mr.' and 'Mrs.'?" a shrill voice shot out from the back of the room.

"Well, Cher, it's because…"

"Liza. Can't you tell the difference between Cher and Liza?"

"No," Lynn shook her head and winked at Mr. Rix, "not when they're both so beautiful."

"Oh, okay," Mr. Rix said, patting his hair into place.

"Like I was saying," Lynn began again, "we have received an invitation to be part of the festivities at the Faire held on the grounds of the Bastille. I thought it would be a good outing for us."

"What are we going as?" Mrs. Bailey asked, petting Fung Shi.

Lynn stifled a laugh. "The Freak Show" didn't seem an appropriate title. "I have some ideas, but what are yours?"

"Well, I ain't doing anything stupid like wearing those dumb costumes," Mrs. Bailey said defiantly. "I don't want to look like no retard. Neither does Fung Shi. He's very sensitive."

This from a woman who ran around naked and had an imaginary... what was Feng Shi, anyway? "It's all in the spirit of fun, Mrs. Bailey."

"I know!" Mr. Rix screamed, straightening the Liza wig. "I can do Katharine Hepburn from *Lion in Winter*!"

"If he does that, then Peter gets to go in costume too!" Mr. Chow unzipped and whipped out his peter and began wagging it. "Look at me! I'm King Arthur!"

"Everyone?" Heather's voice erupted from the corner, "Let's not get crazy?"

Too late, Lynn thought, as Mrs. Bailey stood and began stripping. "Let's spread some joy!"

Lynn sighed. It was going to be a long day. When she felt the tap on her shoulder, she jumped.

"Oh, Mr. Graves."

"He touched you." Mr. Graves voice sounded raspy and worn.

"Who did?"

"The Angel of Death," Mr. Graves croaked.

Lynn looked at him, wondering what to say. Finally she decided on, "If he had, Mr. Graves, wouldn't I be dead?"

He shook his head and pondered her, his eyes boring into her. After what felt like an eternity of silence, she opened her mouth to speak, but he held up his hand. "I will go."

"Go where?"

"To the Faire," he said and walked away.

"Are you sure?" Lynn asked, ignoring the bedlam in the day room. "You hate going out in public."

He spun around to look at her. "I can see Death through his disguise. I need to protect Abbey." He paused for a moment then continued, "And you."

Lynn felt suddenly guilty. She had made a promise to Mr. Graves last week to check up on Abbey. How could she counsel the patients to follow through on promises if she wasn't going to do it herself? What kind of role model would that be for them? Did it matter? Yes, she decided firmly, it did.

46

HIS TEETH COMPLETELY MUTILATED THE END OF THE STRAW
before Mathers realized he was chewing on it. He pulled
the fragments of plastic from his tongue and flicked them
into the bag with the rest of the fast food wrappers. He gathered up
the stray French fries, unused catsup packets, and dirty napkins and
shoved them in the bag as well. Janet and Sal would kill him if they
ever found out he ate drive-thru burgers rather than go back to their
house for 'real food,' so he double-checked the interior of the car
for stray sesame seeds before opening the door and walking to the
trash can.

He was positive Abbey and the aunts were involved with the
dead bodies of both Sarah and Elfi Reisner. What was Abbey's role?
He brushed the remnants of salt from his trousers and headed back
to the car. Elfi Reisner, the second body found, turned out to be the
grandmother of Sarah Reisner, the first body found in the glade.
What were the odds? Both women were known as the 'black sheep'
of the family, famous for their late-night carousing and flagrant
disregard of the rules; both cut from the same cloth. That much
explained why they weren't reported missing until weeks after their
disappearance. But what was their connection to the Bastille or the
Emerson family?

He sighed and got back into the car. If he couldn't find the missing
link soon, then he would have to close the case as unsolvable. There
was nothing he hated more than closed cases that didn't feel closed.
He sat behind the wheel and rolled over the theories. One: The two

Reisners were murdered and Abbey was directly involved. This was impossible. Elfi Reisner died before Abbey was born and Sarah's death occurred while Abbey was placed in The Meadows. This led to theory number two: The two Reisners were murdered and Abbey knew the killers. This was much more plausible. Perhaps the aunts were the guilty parties and young Abbey stumbled across something that would indict the old women. In an effort to discredit her, the crazy aunts placed her in The Meadows. Not only would anything Abbey said come under scrutiny, but it would also provide the aunts with privacy and time to cover their tracks. Something in The Meadows (Lynn's counseling, perhaps?) jogged Abbey's memory and now the horror of the act was coming back to her. This caused the aunts to pull the girl from the loony bin and bring her home.

He glanced around the intersection, letting his eyes wander over the landscape. This didn't feel right. He spotted a dented, rusty Ford making an illegal left-hand turn into the driveway of the Dairy Queen. There was a time when he would have rushed to apprehend the driver, intent on fulfilling his duty as…

Dairy Queen. He ran into Lynn, Abbey's therapist, coming out of the Dairy Queen, didn't he? When was that? The days blurred together lately. He remembered how stunning Lynn looked in her heels and dress, and how her hesitant, darting eyes belied the calm voice she used when she spoke with him about the women of the Bastille. What were the words she used? '…the air seemed…tense.' And '… we all have our secrets.'

Did the therapist know something she wasn't telling him? He rolled his eyes in disgust. How could he have been so stupid? Of course Lynn knew something! That's why she acted so oddly the first time he interviewed her last week! She must have been trying to raise his suspicion without betraying her ethical responsibilities. Damn, what an idiot he was. She was on to information about Abbey and her relationship with the aunts back then. Why didn't he pay more attention? Because he was tired. Because he wasn't listening. Because he was distracted by the way her dress was cut off her shoulders and dipped into her chest. Damn! That dress left little to the imagination. Maybe he'd be in luck and she'd have it on the next time he saw her.

Right. Like his luck was that good. When was the last time he had a date, anyway? A year? Two? Pierced tongues were nice, but the Vermont winters got awfully cold. He started the car. He needed to get a move on. He needed to talk to Abbey without the aunts.

"**O**VER HERE!" TOMYRIS SCREAMED, swinging her sword at the tall tattooed man in a loincloth. He stumbled into the stone wall of the hallway as Boo grabbed him from behind. The man yelled in surprise as Boo's strong arms swung him around and threw him back into the Tapestry, where he merged into the thick fabric with a whoosh.

On the opposite end of the hall, a black Frisian reared and flailed his hooves at a gray stallion standing half in and half out of the wall. As the Frisian's front legs came down on the stone floor, two of Tomyris' Sulakis rounded the corner and leapt at the stallion, fangs bared. The stallion's eyes opened wide in a look of horror as it backed up into the wall and disappeared into the embroidered portrait of the Crusades.

"Is that all of them?" Boo's voice belied her exhaustion.

"Yes," Tomyris answered, replacing her sword on the wall and adjusting the feathers in her hair. "Fuck! I lost my earring."

"Damn the jewelry!" Boo hissed, descending upon her.

Tomyris strode within inches of Boo's face. "I like my jewelry."

"Ladies!" Eleanor spat as she rounded the corner. "Enough!" She reached out and laid her hand upon the Frisian. "Let us do what we can with that fissure before anything else slips through time." She pointed to a gash in the Tapestry that cut through the embroidered soldiers of the Crusades and continued for several inches into a picturesque scene of a young redheaded woman sitting next to a grey stallion.

No sooner had the words left her mouth then the redheaded woman in the picture stood, stretched, and stepped towards them. As the tiny body became larger, a foot emerged from the fabric, followed by the body. Within moments, she stood in the hallway looking around in amazement.

"Hello, Eleanor!" She waved at the rest of the group and grimaced when she spotted Boo. "Boudicca."

"Luna," Boo hissed.

"Luna, dear," Eleanor said, resting her hand on the young woman. "It pains me to be the one to tell you this, but you must return. It is not yet time."

Luna looked at her in surprise. "But…?"

"Dear, it is a long, tired story." She pointed to the Tapestry and Luna followed Eleanor's gesture.

"Good Lord! The Tapestry is torn! Eleanor, did you see the rips in the Tapestry?"

"Nothing escapes your keen sight, does it, dear?" Eleanor droned.

"Those should be fixed, should they not?"

Eleanor smiled weakly and nodded. "We still have four days."

"Four days?" Luna shook her head. "Oh, dear. But there is little that Eleanor of Aquitaine cannot do."

Boo coughed and Eleanor shot her a harsh look. Luna patted Eleanor on the shoulder. "Should I go now?" Eleanor nodded and gestured to the Tapestry. Luna waved to Tomyris, grimaced at Boo, and stepped into the wall.

"Ruth, please see to it that the larger of the repairs are sewn up first. We can seal them later." Eleanor turned and headed down the corridor. "Tomyris," she called over her shoulder, "please find Abbey. It is time for drastic measures."

ABBEY FELT THEM WATCHING HER. One moment she stood gazing at the private landing strip and the next her skin crawled with gooseflesh and a chill shimmered down her spine. When she turned around, the only things watching her were Fire and Water, standing at opposite ends of the corral. Those two horses hated each other. It took no brains at all to see that. Just yesterday, she walked in to find Fire biting Water's neck. Why did the aunts keep them here?

As she stood watching them, Fire reared up and crossed to the opposite side of the corral. Water, on the other hand, trotted over to the fence and moved his head up and down while stomping his foot in the turf. Abbey went to him and he laid his head on her shoulder.

She suddenly felt like riding. She hadn't been on horseback since she and Boo rode the trails a few days ago and that trip was not at all relaxing. During the whole ride, Boo harassed her about posture, form and speed, all the time bombarding her with questions about The Meadows. For God's sake, the woman visited The Meadows herself several times! Why all the questions?

Abbey looked around and found herself alone. Could it be possible that she had escaped the watchful eyes of her aunts? Where was Fred? She hadn't seen him since the night Tomyris' dogs were injured in the woods. She missed the man. They hadn't spoken often, but the brief conversations they shared relaxed her and left her wanting more. She enjoyed his quirky sense of humor, low-pitched belly laugh, and crooked smile. She wished she could remember what their relationship was like before her accident, as he felt so…familiar and safe. She grabbed a pair of reins from the hook near the door and decided against lugging the saddle from the tack room.

She hoisted herself on Water's back and set out into the woods.

WITHIN THIS TEN-ACRE AREA OF THE BASTILLE, the answer to his case sat waiting to be discovered. He could feel it. Mathers backed up to the newly strung rope bearing the sign: FAIRE WORKERS ONLY BEYOND THIS POINT and retraced his steps.

An arch constructed from tree limbs and tied together with vines stretched across an eight-foot-wide path that signified the entrance to the Faire. In four days, the town's invited guests would line up outside the 'Market Square' to greet the 'Royal Gatekeeper' and receive an entrance medallion. This year's theme was "Peasant Craftwork" and the Gatekeeper would be Mrs. Collins, the owner of the town's only specialty bakery. Mrs. Collins' contribution to the Faire would be her own idea of a "Peasant Craftwork": her freshly baked sourdough dinner roll strung on a length of hemp rope. He wondered how the theme of "Craftwork" related to dough on string, but he didn't have the heart to question poor Mrs. Collins, who relayed the idea to the reporter while grinning at the photographer through a face full of flour.

The townsfolk who weren't on the VIP list were vendors and had already invaded the glen with their tents and signage. From where he stood, Mathers could see a dozen canvas tarps with little wooden signs with the names: Glenburn's Glop (baked goods from old lady Glenburn who made the best blueberry pies in the county); Dorne's Delusions (how in the hell Betsy Dorn would pass off her new age crystals and incense as 'delusions' he had no idea); Sucking Sappy (sounded more like porn than candy); and Michael's Miracle Mudd (an overpriced facial cream he himself had purchased for the Secret Santa gift last year and later found in the booking department's bathroom. Apparently they preferred their Miracle Mudd with a bit of toilet paper). Several other unnamed tents stood empty, waiting for the big day when their owners could haul wares from the stores on Main Street to the tables under the trees. Dominating the scene, smack in the middle of the acreage, was a large, round canopy of brown burlap with a single sign: ALE. He guessed that in the fifteenth century there wasn't much to do besides drink and make babies.

The rest of the grounds looked like a movie set. Colored fabric ran from tree to tree to establish the boundaries of the Faire and a makeshift walkway of tree bark meandered through the maze of vendor tents. To his left, back behind a small clump of firs, was a line of Honey Buckets pathetically camouflaged by branches of pine trees. In front of him at the other end of the glade was the spot where Janet found the bodies. A small stage for musicians stood over the spot where the corpses were found, directly underneath a magnificent ancient oak tree whose trunk split just at eye level.

This year, the sewing circle was set up under the trees far from the center of the Faire. He could see twelve three-legged wooden stools set up in a circle around a short, round wooden table. One of the highlights of the Bastille's Faire was when the women of the Bastille came out of the huge stone mansion dressed in full Renaissance regalia and sat for the entire day chanting, humming and sewing some kind of Tapestry made of black fabric with small pictures embroidered into it. Apparently it was rather old, as every year the ladies would repair the Tapestry while the townspeople watched. For some reason, it was a huge hit. The area around the sewing circle was packed shoulder to shoulder with spectators. Apparently, the invited VIP group included a herd of closet quilters.

Not that being invited to the Faire was that difficult. In fact, Mathers didn't know of anyone who *wasn't* invited. He always assumed the term 'invite' made the event that much more appealing to the townspeople, getting them to open up their wallets and buy some of this junk that they wouldn't think of buying should they see it downtown. Regardless, the Faire was always a hit with the locals, as every year people made plans to attend. People seemed to crawl out of the woodwork for this shindig; there were always more Faire-goers than Faire-workers.

He stood at the musician's stage, looking up into the massive old tree. Could anyone have shimmied out on the tree's limb and dropped the bodies onto the ground? The tree, while old, still seemed sturdy enough to hold a slightly built woman like Tomyris or Abbey. He examined the tree closer. The rotten portion of the trunk, where the main trunk split into two large branches, emitted a foul stench that smelled like spoiled shit. As he poked into the crevice with a pen, a swarm of flies lifted into the air and he waved them away to prod at a nest of some kind, built into the rotten piece of wood. Nothing seemed odd at all.

The snap of a twig behind him rang out like a shot. He spun around, reaching inside his coat to grab his gun.

"Detective?"

"Abbey?"

The young woman smiled broadly and walked towards him, leading a horse that seemed too huge for her to manage. He noticed she rode with no saddle.

"What are you doing here, Detective?"

"I might ask the same of you."

"You might," she said, stopping only when she was a few feet from him. "But you will not, as I live here."

Another snap of a twig sent them both reeling around this time.

"Must have been an animal." Abbey's voice was even and metered; emotionless.

"Must have," Mathers said.

"You still feel the connection between the two dead women lay with my family." Her eyes bore down on him.

Her bluntness startled him. He wasn't prepared for an honest question. He decided to reply in kind. "Yes."

She thought about this for a moment. "I would suspect someone in the Emerson family, too." She turned her back on him, patted the horse's head, and walked away. "Come. Walk with me."

ROBERT HELD HIS BREATH as Abbey and Mathers passed beneath him. He was certain they heard the snap of the twig when he shifted his weight, but as they walked under his hiding place, he breathed a sigh of relief. He was still undetected. Sweat poured out of his underarms and ran down his sides and he cursed himself for not being more prepared. But he had purposely waited until he saw the last of the townspeople leave the glen and that wretched creature, Livia, do a final walkabout with the crazed Boo before setting foot on the grounds. He knew that once those two had left the scene, he would easily have an hour or two before that insane maniac, Boo, returned with her damned blue paint and bloodlust. Didn't that insipid woman ever tire of hacking things to pieces?

When the two witches left the Faire grounds, he quickly raced from his hiding place on the far side of the access road where Joshua had left him (he must remember to remove that CD player from the limo) and into the Faire grounds. He dawdled slightly when the sound of a car drew his attention. Without looking at the car's driver, he climbed the nearest tree and settled into the crook of the two huge limbs directly over the portable toilets. Here he had sat patiently for the past twenty minutes. First, he watched Mathers as the detective walked the area, then strained to hear the conversation between him and Abbey.

Damn, those toilets stank! Everyone knew the vendors used them during the day while they arranged their tents and tables. He imagined Livia, the money-pinching wench, demanding that they be left reeking until Friday's festivities. The woman had no class.

He put a handkerchief over his nose and breathed through it while he waited for the two to walk farther away. What was Abbey doing out alone? Why did the witches let her go riding without supervision? His spy inside the Bastille told him the witches knew he was after the girl. He replaced the handkerchief into his breast pocket and his fingers brushed the knife's sleek handle, filling him with a reassuring courage. He looked around the glen. From his vantage point, he could see no other people. Wonderful! It would be a disaster to be caught this close to the end of his quest.

Suddenly, a realization flooded through him—he could kill the detective and take Abbey on his way out. Abbey weighed little and it would be no great chore to carry the girl back to the limo.

He smiled. Maybe this wouldn't be a wasted trip after all.

"YOU SUSPECT THAT I LIE," SHE SAID.

"I never said that."

Abbey responded quickly in a sharp, efficient tone. "You think it."

"How do you know what I think?"

"Because that is what I would think."

"Then you are a suspicious woman."

"Am I?" Her voice sounded miles away. "I wish I could remember."

"If you can't remember, then how do you know what you'd think?" He intended it to be a joke, but the look in Abbey's eyes was anything but amused.

"While it is true I cannot remember much of the things that happened to me, I know who I am."

"Oh?"

She thought for a moment before answering. "I know that I do not like liars. I do not find evil acts against others acceptable. The mere idea of injuring an innocent person causes my heart to ache. Does that not say something about who I am?"

Mathers turned this over in his mind. Years of patrolling the streets showed him how cruel people could be to each other. As a detective, he witnessed brutal acts that made him surmise pure evil did exist. Did he see too much? "I think you can't change the spots on a leopard."

She grinned and her whole face lit up. "When I was in The Meadows, there was a man named Mr. Graves."

"Yes, I've heard of him. His family owns a chain of Burger Kings. Very wealthy."

She nodded. "He was a fierce man. Frightening to look at. Prone to violent outbursts. Many of the others were afraid of him. But one day, after my first recollection of…" she paused and her eyes lowered. When she spoke again, her voice was soft. "…I fled down the corridor to my room and I stumbled into him. Usually, Mr. Graves dislikes people touching him. It sends him into fits of fury. But he stood aside and let me pass. Later I asked him why he did not lash out at me. Do you want to know what he said?"

Mathers shook his head and she continued, "He said, 'It ain't honorable to kick a person when they're down.' Amidst all the chaos, pain and confusion that he endures, he still could not violate a truth of his soul."

"Is that true with everyone?"

"I have to believe so. Otherwise, why would any of us continue?" She looked at him and he realized she wanted an answer.

"I don't know *why* we continue living."

She stopped. "We are all part of God's plan. Our souls remember who we are, Detective. Even when the mind has forgotten." She looked away for a moment, then quickly back to him and smiled. "God has planted a seed inside each of us that, given the chance, blooms into the flower."

He smiled. "I've been a weed before…"

"A weed is a flower to God." She reached out and touched his shoulder and Mathers felt like a small child.

ROBERT DUCKED BEHIND A LARGE BUSH and pulled the dagger close. The sun hinged on the horizon and in a few moments it would be dark. He gripped the dagger in the palm of his hand as he weighed his options. She didn't have a sword, but he had a gun. He would have to kill him first and hope she was so startled that she couldn't react in time to protect herself.

He had killed people under worse circumstances. Just as he headed out from around the bush, he heard hoofbeats in the distance. Someone was coming.

At the sound of the hoofbeats, Mathers jerked himself out of the semitrance state he had fallen into and stepped away from Abbey.

"That must be one of my aunts," she said with a sigh. "It was so good to see you again, Detective Mathers." She held out her hand.

He took her hand just as a rustle of branches erupted from behind him. He spun around and thought he saw a shadow out of the corner of his eye.

"Must be jumpy," he said.

He pulled away from her just as the woman on horseback arrived, flanked by two large Saluki dogs.

"Good evening, Detective Mathers," Tomyris said, brushing a feather away from her face.

"Good evening, Ms. Emerson."

"Tomyris, please. I don't do fucking formality."

He nodded. "Tomyris." He noticed she had changed her belly button jewel. A huge diamond flickered in the fading light.

"You are missed," she said sternly to Abbey. "Your aunt sent me to find you."

"I needed some air."

Tomyris' eyes darted between Abbey and the detective. "Uh-huh. Sure."

Before Mathers could respond in Abbey's defense, the dogs stopped their sniffing of the ground and set off at a run towards the Faire grounds. Tomryis jerked her head up and said briskly, "Go to the Bastille. The horse will be dealt with later." She turned and sped off into the darkening woods.

As Tomyris galloped away, Mathers saw Abbey looking at him. "Abbey," he asked, "are you...all right?" Abbey cocked her head, questioning. "I mean with your aunts. Are you...do you feel safe with them?"

She nodded. "With them, yes." She opened her mouth to say something else, but instead of speaking, she jumped on the horse's back, grabbed the reins and, in a flash, was riding back towards the mansion.

Mathers turned his attention back to the Faire grounds. He pulled his gun from its holster and ran after Tomyris.

When Robert saw the Salukis, he turned and fled, inadvertently rustling the bush. He did not intend to tangle with those insane beasts one more time despite the fact he could have killed the detective. He made it as far as the Honey Buckets when he heard the dogs barking. Damn those things! The next time he could, he would kill these last two. He would kill them very slowly. He took stock of his situation; if he tried to make it to the road, the beasts would overtake him. If he stayed, he would not be able to triumph over two huge dogs and whichever witch was on horseback. The barking was coming closer.

He spied a folding table with several coolers, packages of paper cups, and various culinary items. Next to one of the coolers was a huge can of pepper. He snatched it up, opened it and poured the contents on the ground, making sure to cover his footprints with the spice. Then he opened the door to one of the portable toilets and went in. He closed the lid of the toilet and stood with one foot on either side of the toilet seat. He put the knife in his mouth and pushed his hands along the sides for additional support. He heard the dogs outside. They began to bray loudly, bark and sneeze. A moment later, he heard a horse approach.

"What is it?" the voice asked—Tomyris.

She began sneezing along with the dogs and the horse neighed loudly. Robert chuckled to himself. He wished he could see the spectacle—the view must be priceless!

"Whoa, Fire. Down! Down, boy!" Her voice sounded frantic and he heard the horse kick and stomp. The dogs were going wild, braying, barking and sneezing in a cacophony of confusion.

Then he heard a dog clawing at the door of the toilet. Suddenly, loud banging came from all around, as if the beasts were hurling themselves at the toilet's sides. He felt the small shed shift slightly as the horse reared and pounded on the structure.

"Fire! What are you doing?" Tomyris' voice screamed over the racket.

The horse neighed violently, Tomyris screamed, the dogs bayed and Robert felt the square porta-potty tipping over onto its side. As it crashed down onto its back, the toilet seat opened and the brown, fetid contents splashed everywhere, covering him in days-old piss and soggy turds. Outside the capsule of feces, he heard the dogs' howling and the hoofbeats of the witch's steed fade as they retreated into the distance.

He pried himself off the wall of the structure and felt his clothing sticking to the plastic. After slipping in the slimy liquid a couple of times, he managed to push the door open and climb out, where he fell with a plop onto the grass of the glade.

"YOU SHOULD HAVE TOLD US, DEAR," Aunt Ruth chided as she slid a waffle onto Abbey's plate. "We were terribly worried! Do you want blueberries or strawberries, dear?"

"I am sorry, Aunt Ruth," Abbey replied, avoiding Aunt Boo's eyes by staring at Ruth's Star of David.

Boo screamed, slamming her fist onto the table and sending the glasses rattling. "Have you gone daft as well as blank?"

"Boo," Ruth patted Boo's hand, "go easy on her."

Boo jerked her hand away. "Have I taught you nothing this past week?" With a grunt, she turned and stormed out of the kitchen. Ruth shook her head and sighed. "You must excuse Boo. She's been… tense lately."

"I know," Abbey whispered as she picked at the blueberries.

"So," Ruth said, pulling out the measuring cups from under the counter, "you have not spoken to me about what happened inside the airplane." She stared at Abbey while measuring out the flour.

Abbey picked up her fork and began pulling her waffle apart. Ruth waited patiently for the girl to choose her words. "I saw something. A plane crash."

"Yes…."

"I felt as if I were watching a terrible experience."

"That would be a memory, dear."

"It wasn't. Memories trigger emotions…feelings…. I did not feel anything. I… saw a terrible crash, but felt no emotion…this is so difficult to describe."

"So you isolate yourself from us." Abbey nodded. "Dear, dear Abbey. How hard this must be for you." She emptied the flour into the bowl and opened the sugar container. "Take care, sweetheart, as when the visions do evoke an emotional response, the results will be devastating. Do you think I should use honey instead of sugar?" Without waiting for an answer, she reached for the glass bear filled with the amber liquid. "I shall."

A crash reverberated through the house. Ruth wiped her hands and motioned for Abbey to follow. "Not again! I shall never complete all my baking!"

54

"R OBERT?"

He turned around and glared over his shoulder, squinting against the car's bright headlights. "Miss Swanson?" He heard a car door open and footsteps on the hard pavement moving towards him.

"You look terrible!" she lied. He had stripped down to a pair of shorts. Tiny shorts. Shorts that left little to the imagination, or, in Robert's case, a lot to the not-so-imaginative imagination. His toned body was covered in fine chest hair, muscles rippled around a tight six-pack. He looked fucking fabulous. She took a step closer when the smell hit her like a brick. "Oh, God! You smell worse. What happened to you?"

Robert tried to keep his phony smile plastered to his face. "One of my clients… let us say, she is angry with me."

"I would imagine so!" Lynn turned away, gagging. "You can't walk around like this in the middle of the night. Here," she pointed to her car, "I have a tarp I use for firewood. We'll put it on the back seat and I'll drive you home."

He watched her walk back to her car. She wore baggy jeans and a loose sweatshirt with frayed sandals that showed her fiery red nail polish. A baseball cap hid her hair, which, he guessed, lay hidden in a frenzied mass.

"You stay there until I spread it out and roll down the windows." She motioned for him to stay.

"How can I ever thank you?"

"By not leaking that…whatever it is…onto my back seat. What are you doing out so late?"

He shrugged. He normally abhorred signs of weakness such as a shrug, but his experiences in the twenty-first century taught him that a shrug had become an acceptable form of communication. Ambiguity had replaced critical analysis. "Client emergency. You?"

"Oh, Fung Shi bit someone," she chuckled. "Never mind. Long story. Just take it from me—what you don't see *can* hurt you." She closed the trunk and hauled a thick green canvas tarp to her rear door and handed him a gallon of water along with a towel. "This is my winter emergency water. It's not winter and, let's face it, you're an emergency." She began spreading the tarp onto the back seat.

"You keep unusual hours, I see."

"Well, I'm on call a lot, if that's what you mean. But it's okay…The Meadows is flexible. I'll be working this weekend at the Faire, then take Monday off. It all evens out." She finished spreading the tarp and leaned against the car's roof.

"The Faire?" He felt his heart beat faster. "You are attending the Bastille's festivities?"

"Yes, some of the folks from The Meadows are participating in a field trip. Community service kind of work." She patted the top of the car and motioned for him to get in. "It's ready for you."

He remained frozen to his spot. "I thought the Faire was by invitation only."

"Well, over the past couple of years, the ladies have been rather lax about 'invite only.'" She smoothed her sweatshirt.

"Is that so? I assumed it was strictly enforced." She motioned for him to rinse his hair and he began pouring the water over his head.

"It *was* for a long time." She frowned. "But for some reason they began to loosen up the rules a bit. Now, almost any of the townspeople who want in can manage it. Don't say anything, though. It's a small town secret."

An idea came to him and he smiled broadly. "Had I known that, I might have gone last year."

"Well, there's always this weekend."

"Yes." He flashed his smile and locked eyes with her. He held his gaze until she broke it.

"You…" her voice sounded quiet and hesitant. "You could always join us." She cleared her throat. "The clients have jobs…juggling, passing out free pastries…things like that…but I'm there to supervise."

"You will have plenty of free time?" he asked. She nodded. "I would like that."

"Good. Then we can meet you at the main entrance…the archway. Do you know where that is?" He nodded. "We'll see you there. Come on. Get in."

He sloshed his way towards the car and she moved around to the driver's side.

"Oh," she said as an afterthought, "I forgot to tell you. You need to come in costume."

"Oh, that will not be a problem," he said, sliding into the back seat and wrapping the towel around his shoulders. "I have many costumes."

His nipples poked out from under the covering and Lynn wondered what they would taste like. Maybe just a little nibble. She wiggled into the front seat and slid the key into the ignition. As the car started up, she thought she heard Mr. Graves' voice and jerked her head to the passenger seat. Feeling stupid, she put the car into gear and pulled out onto the road. She could have sworn she heard him whisper, "Angel of Death."

55

"HER HAIR WILL DO," Helen said, shoving her glasses up onto her nose. "Unless you want to get a skin sample?"

Mathers laughed. "No. Here." He handed over some of the hair samples he had snatched from Abbey's shoulder and Helen took them gently, as if she was handling fine china. While she placed them into a small plastic bag, he looked at the charts hanging near the metal tables and craned his neck to read them.

"Don't snoop." He pulled away.

"Simple DNA analysis. We need time, though."

"Time, we don't have."

She shrugged and yawned. "Depends on what you want, I guess." She looked at the phone and suddenly screamed, "RING ALREADY!" She shrugged. "Sorry. Just had to say that."

"Late night?"

"Another project. Not as much fun as investigating four hundred-year-old skeletons." She cleaned her glasses on her lab coat. "Talk fast. As soon as I hear that phone ring and the lab tells me what I need to know, I'm out of here."

"I suspect the Reisner family is connected to the Emerson family. Blood relation maybe. The DNA should tell me."

"How will that prove if Abbey or her aunts killed those two women?"

"It won't," he answered. "But I need to know."

"Curiosity killed the cat."

"Satisfaction brought him back." He slid his business card across the table. "I don't give up on a case. I'm like a bulldog that way."

"Or a piranha." She picked up the card and looked at it. "Private cell phone number?" He nodded. "How do I rank?"

"You have information I need." The phone's shrill ring filled the room.

"Okay, gotta go."

"Mathers," she said as he headed for the door. "I still don't understand how this is going to help the case."

"We all do what we have to do," he said. "It's what makes us who we are. It's in our nature." He pointed to the phone as she grabbed the receiver. "It's like our souls remember what we have forgotten."

"WHY IS IT YOU BROUGHT ME HERE?"

"Watch, my dear. Just watch."

Abbey turned away from Eleanor and backed up until she felt the cold stone wall of the turret press against her. The chill settled around her and she rubbed her arms, wishing Aunt Eleanor had warned her about the cold. Less than a quarter hour ago, Eleanor found her in the hallway watching Boo battle another fugitive from the Tapestry. Her aunt looked at her in disgust.

"I needed to clear my head," Abbey said, looking to Ruth for support.

"Any more clear and you would not have a head to worry yourself about," Eleanor snapped tersely. "We had to look all over the estate for you."

"Tomyris found me…" but Abbey got no further in her explanation before Eleanor strode over to her.

"I am distressed to admit this, but perhaps Boudicca was right. We have been too easy on you."

"Easy, Auntie?" Abbey shot back, sounding more angry than she felt. "For days I have sparred with Aunt Boo, shot hundreds of arrows with Aunt Zenobia, thrown knives with Aunt Tomyris, and relived a terrible experience with you. Perhaps you forgot about our trip to the plane? How is that easy?"

"Because, you silly girl, that is child's play compared to what could happen." Eleanor grabbed Abbey and Abbey shook the woman off.

"When you met me in Lynn's office at The Meadows, you told me you could tell me who I am. Yet this you have not told me."

"No?" Eleanor asked, pulling herself taller.

"Please!" Ruth said. "Let's all have a matzo ball and a glass of warm milk!"

"No," Abbey said.

"I shall get you both a warm bagel."

"I do not know anything!" Abbey countered Eleanor, her face flush and her heart racing. "I have no pictures of my past. You offer no history other than a mysterious fabric on your walls and some fairy tale of how I am a witch with the power of magical quilt-making," Abbey shouted, her anger rising to full force. "I do not even know if you are truly my aunt!"

"Abbey," Ruth whispered, her hands clutching the serving spoon. "We love you. We protect you. We care for you."

"Do you?" Abbey's anger crested and she felt herself speaking without thinking about the words. "You care for me by keeping me imprisoned in this house? You love me by telling me I have forgotten memories that only you can help me recall?"

"Have you learned nothing from the Tapestry?" Eleanor sounded defeated and tired.

"I have learned that this house has terrifying, amazing things happening within its walls. But for all I know, you are the devil beguiling me with lies and coercing me with false visions."

This struck Eleanor like a boulder. She stared at Abbey for a moment then calmly said, "Come with me, child."

Eleanor led her to the far end of the Tapestry into a corner of the intersecting hallways that Abbey had never investigated. She pointed to an embroidered picture and Abbey saw a scene depicting two women who looked like Eleanor and Ruth standing in a small stone turret, looking out into a marketplace through a stone window. Eleanor grabbed Abbey's arm and the two of them walked into the Tapestry.

Now, Abbey found herself standing inside the stone turret depicted in the Tapestry. The air nipped at Abbey's flesh, the wind whipped around her ankles and the sounds of a mob filled the air. The stench of horse droppings and rancid food permeated the air. She turned to whisper to Eleanor, "Where are we?"

"France. May 30th. The year is 1431. We are watching the death of a heretic." Just then the crowd outside in the courtyard sent up an outraged cry. Eleanor sighed. "Watch quietly. You will soon feel what the heretic feels," she said as she pointed to the second version of herself, standing at the window. "You can hear her thoughts. You can smell her smells and know what she knows." Another roar from the crowd. "It begins."

Abbey turned and looked out the window. As she watched, Abbey felt herself drawn into the events, as if her soul merged into the scene playing out below them in the marketplace. She felt the dizzying sensation of falling and in a sudden burst of intuitive knowledge she knew why the throng beneath them gathered. She felt herself remembering...

In just moments, the King's guard would escort the heretic into the courtyard, tie the young blonde woman to the burning post, and set her ablaze. The Guild knew they were too late to stop the burning, but with a bit of luck and quick action, they might save Eleanor's granddaughter from permanent death.

Eleanor's physiology kept her warm atop the castle wall, despite the bitter cold wind gusting over the parapet. She felt only the pulsating rhythm of her heart as it pounded in her chest. She frantically scanned the courtyard below, praying to catch a glimpse of a member of the Guild.

"There!" Ruth's weak voice gasped. The old woman appeared next to Eleanor and pointed her shaking finger to the crowd below.

Neither Ruth nor Eleanor had eaten for two days. When word of the young heretic's fate reached their ears, they were in the foothills of the Auvergne, deeply enmeshed in the work of the Guild. If only she had stayed closer to the girl! Why had she let the foolish child gain so much popularity and attention? Eleanor had seen much in her centuries of life—she should have protected her.

Eleanor followed Ruth's finger and spotted Zenobia standing ready at her post near the church door, and next to her, Boudicca shuffled restlessly, doing a fine job of hiding her sword beneath her cloak. Eleanor reached her hand out to Ruth. Ruth fell into Eleanor's arms and they hugged each other.

Of all the members of the Guild, Boudicca would glean the most from this rescue. It had been decades since the warrior had seen a battle. While replacing the charred body of her granddaughter with some unknown girl's carcass wasn't a battle, it would require stealth and courage.

With one movement, the guard's torch touched upon the wood beneath the burning stake, sending showers of sparks into the air. The twilight came alive with dancing shadows of flame as the fire burned through the twigs and ate its way toward the girl, who continued to pontificate to the throng, even as the mob screamed, "Sorciere!" "Diable!" "Pecheresse!"

For a brief moment, Eleanor saw the flicker of recognition flash across the girl's eyes as she spotted her grandmother and Ruth. Then the moment was lost. Fire ate up the body, blocking Eleanor's sight with its smoke. Eleanor could bear it no longer. Tears burned her eyes and she turned away.

Ruth hugged Eleanor tightly, stroking the woman's hair delicately. Then, in a voice thick with emotion, she whispered to Eleanor, "Come, dear. We must intercept the remains before it is too late to save her."

Abbey felt a hand upon her arm and someone pulling at her. She looked around and uttered a gasp as she realized that she and Eleanor stood in the hallway of the Bastille. Her knees felt weak and she fell to the floor. Eleanor did not move to help her, but instead stood over Abbey.

"They burned you at the stake, Abbey." Eleanor's voice sounded gruff and frustrated. "We rode for days to make it there before the burning, but we arrived too late. Someone knew Ruth and I were on the way and sped the execution. Someone betrayed you."

Abbey said nothing. Her guts churned and nausea washed over her.

"That wasn't the first time you died, Abbey. And it wasn't the last."

"The plane crash," Abbey groaned.

"Among others. Several times you lived lives too flamboyant for an Immortal, girl. We warned you. You ignored us. The lives that do not survive in the history books can be dealt with, but two personas—TWO—that live in the history of mortals is inexcusable!" Eleanor knelt down to stare into Abbey's eyes as she berated the girl.

"Most of us live *several* during those centuries that fade away into the bowels of time without fanfare. But you? Two conspicuous, attention-seeking, famous personalities. Is it any wonder their violent, untimely deaths drove you to madness and the Guild over the edge of patience?"

"What have I become?" Abbey cried.

"You are stubborn, child. You are reckless. You are impossible to control. You have driven yourself into a state of convenient amnesia and we are all paying the price for your selfishness."

"You call me a coward?"

Eleanor laughed. "You flee into forgetfulness when the rest of us live with our mistakes. That, my dear, is the definition of coward." Eleanor turned her back and strode away.

"I am no coward!" Abbey declared, rising to her feet.

Eleanor stopped and said, "You want the life of a hero? Then accept your role in this cosmic joke God has played on us and fulfill your duties."

Just then the Tapestry billowed out a huge gust of wind and the pungent scent of seawater filled the corridor. A petite woman, dressed in only a bra, panties and a sailor's hat jumped out of the Tapestry, clutching a bottle of champagne. She stood for a moment looking around with an expression of bemusement and confusion. Abbey detected the distinct odor of alcohol.

"Aurora?" Eleanor asked.

"Eleanor!" She threw her arms around her and hugged her tightly. "Is it the new year already?" Giggling uncontrollably, she turned and saw Abbey standing in the hallway. "Abbey girl?"

"Stop," Eleanor commanded. "Abbey, go to your room. Aurora, get back into the Tapestry. The new year is not until Saturday."

"But..."

"We shall see you Saturday." Eleanor shoved the half-naked woman back into the wall. She then turned to Abbey. "You see what we have to contend with? All because of you and your silly desire for attention. I can take it no longer. We shall assume you worthless to us now."

"I am *not worthless*!"

Eleanor flew into a rage, her hands clawing the air as she descended upon Abbey. "Can you do your part to repair the damage to the Tapestry? Can you remember the chants? Can you remember the threads? How about those of us who are allowed out of the Tapestry, or those who are to be kept inside during the Great Ritual? Can you even remember why the chosen are imprisoned in the Tapestry to begin with?"

She stared at Abbey who stood with her mouth agape.

"I thought not. And the two weeks since you have been here, what have you learned? To go riding alone. Near dusk. With Robert out there in the world." She shrugged. "You are as stubborn as you always were. I can bear it no longer."

With that, Abbey stood alone in the hallway.

She stumbled to her room in a half-comatose state and undressed. Ever since her return to the Aunts and to the Bastille, she had watched events unfold around her as a spectator. The strange properties of the Tapestry, Aunt Boo's fondness for nudity and the color blue, Tomyris' penchant for feathers and ugly dogs, all of the unusual qualities of the women washed over her as she watched, confused by their surrealism. As she washed and slipped on her silk pajamas, she realized that not once in the past two weeks had she felt connected to herself. She felt no responsibility, no sense of relation, no part of the drama at all. Instead of trying to figure out her role in the mystery of the Tapestry, she pushed herself away from the strangeness like one refusing to participate in a game.

She pulled back the covers and slipped into bed. This place, these people, this Tapestry was her destiny. So why did she feel nothing?

The sound of hooves clacking on the hallway drew her back to the present. She sighed. Not again. She lay listening to the echoes of the sounds and realized that they were growing louder. They sounded like they were right outside her door. Then the horse stopped. A brief moment of silence passed and Abbey heard her doorknob rattle. Someone was trying to enter her room.

She flung back the covers, ran across the room to the wall where the weapons hung displayed. She grabbed a broadsword and dashed to the door. She could see the knob jiggling, but not turning. It stopped. After another brief pause, there was a loud knock on the door.

Keeping the door between herself and the hallway, Abbey turned the knob and opened the door a crack. Standing in front of her was the huge black Frisian. Abbey stared at the beast.

"I hate to intrude after such an exhausting argument, but would you mind terribly if I came in?"

Without thinking, Abbey opened the door and the horse strode through into the center of her room where it turned and looked at her. "Thank you. I am determined to work those damned doorknobs at least once in this form. I must admit, though, they are a bit tricky without opposable thumbs."

Abbey stepped closer to the Frisian. "You? These past nights…you have followed me."

"Would you mind lowering your weapon, please? Swords make me rather nervous."

Abbey lowered her weapon.

"Followed, no. Watched, yes." The horse paused looking to her for recognition. "I should not clatter down the hallway, I suspect, but the Tapestry demands so much attention these days!" He cocked his horse head at her and leaned closer.

"You do not remember your old friend Merlin?" The horse stuck out a foreleg and bowed low, shaking its mane. It stood back up and looked at her. "Would you like to go for a walk?"

B Y THE TIME ELEANOR RETURNED TO HER STUDY, the rest of the women had taken the biggest slices of Lemonseed cake, leaving her the small corner pieces. As Eleanor put them onto her plate, she noticed that they had less frosting than the other slices, as well as fewer colored sprinkles. She shook her head in disgust. The least they could do was save her one with lots of sprinkles. Eleanor loved the sprinkles.

"Well at least we know what became of Elfi," Tomyris said, cutting up her large piece of cake with the most sprinkles Eleanor had ever seen on a single slice of cake. "I had much worse things in mind than death." With a flick of her wrist, Tomyris flung a piece of cake to each of the Salukis. They caught the treat in mid-air and gobbled them down. Two of the dogs sat with Tomyris on the leather couch, looking even uglier than usual now that Tomyris had provided first aid to them after their confrontation with Robert. Silky white bandages covered most of their midsection.

"I have the newspapers covered," Livia reported, showing a typed press release. "I concocted a story of Elfi's employment with the Bastille and how it was eliminated due to her excessive health problems. Seeing as how during the time of her supposed 'employment' a war was going on, I doubt anyone will question the exact nature of her illness." Eleanor noticed that Livia had not touched her piece of cake. It, too, had more sprinkles than hers.

"Excellent," Zenobia smiled, forking more into her mouth. "The question is, who killed her?"

"As if that is a question that needs an answer!" Boo laughed, alternating between the two pieces in front of her. "Robert. The Doctor would have hacked them to pieces."

"I agree," Liv nodded. Then to Zen she said, "This means security will have to work extra hard this weekend. It is guaranteed that he will show."

"I hope he does," Boo said, finishing the second piece of cake. "I can't wait to cross swords with him again."

"I have it under control, Boo," Zen snapped. "I have handled security for six years. Has there ever been the slightest problem?"

"Has Robert ever shown up before?"

Zen snorted. "Is Robert ever a problem for me?"

"Oh, please stop, both of you," Eleanor shouted as she sat at her desk. "I cannot take any more bickering right now."

"Eleanor and Abbey just had quite a row," Ruth said, passing out napkins.

"Can we just focus on Elfi Reisner?"

58

"SHE WAS YOUR...LET'S SEE NOW...would that be your cousin or your niece?" Merlin said, rubbing his head against Abbey's shoulder. "She was a descendant of Ruth, but wasn't born until just before World War One."

"She was of Ruth's blood?"

He nodded his mane. "Yes. A direct descendant." He continued to walk down the hallway and turned the corner at the end. Abbey had never examined this hallway before, as it housed only the linen closet and the archway into the east wing. "She was quite the character! I adored her! It was her idea."

"What was?" Abbey asked.

"During the war, the Tapestry was displayed in the Bastille, exactly as it is today!" Livia said as she laid out two stacks of papers on Eleanor's desk and began collating them.

"No, dear," Ruth said with a giggle. "Remember? During the war, we closed off the east wing. Portions of the Tapestry lay wrapped up in sealed bags under the waterproof tarp on the grounds." She lifted the teapot and poured the steaming brew into Livia's cup.

"Exactly where the remains were found," Boo finished the thought. Ruth nodded.

"Which explains why we lost Elfi's trail in Germany," Tomyris said, adjusting the bandages on one of the Salukis.

"I must admit," Eleanor said quietly, "I assumed she had been sent to the chambers along with the other unfortunates."

Tomyris laid one of the Salukis across her feet. "I assumed she was caught by the Gestapo."

❖ ❖ ❖

"The Gestapo?" Abbey asked the Frisian.

"Yes, they were a special police force who worked for Hitler."

"I know."

"You remember the Gestapo, but you don't remember yourself?" The horse turned its long head to her and glared with its huge eyeball at her face.

"We have many books at The Meadows," Abbey explained. "And television. And old men who survived the war."

The horse nodded and continued. "I see. Television. What a wonderful invention. I watch the daytime soap operas with Ruth and long to join her on the couch. Have you ever seen *Days of Our Lives?*"

"The Gestapo," Abbey redirected Merlin and the horse shook its huge head.

"Yes, I do digress, don't I?" The horse sounded as if he chuckled. "I do that often."

❖ ❖ ❖

"I feared that she wasn't up to the task," Boo said and helped herself to another huge glass of lemonade. "She never handled the sword well enough."

"Boo, dear, she was trying to murder Hitler in Germany in the year 1941. A sword would have been a bit…obvious…don't you think?" Livia said with a smirk. "Here, Eleanor darling, help me fold these VIP passes." Eleanor sighed and began to fold.

❖ ❖ ❖

"Her husband was killed in the gas chambers," Merlin said, poking his nose at a finely embroidered picture of a handsome man in his mid-twenties. Next to the smiling face stood a curvy young brunette in an evening gown. "She wanted Hitler dead more than anything else in the world."

"Surely she knew she would die," Abbey whispered, fingering the golden threads of the embroidered picture. "Infiltrating the Gestapo would be suicide."

"Yes, but, you see, she was a direct descendant of Ruth's line," Merlin said. "Although she was not Immortal herself, she did possess some of the recuperative powers of an Immortal. In addition, she also had the ability to tolerate extreme temperatures, was faster than a normal human, and had an acute sense of balance. She counted on these heightened physical traits to assist her in her task."

"So she set out on a mission to murder a murderer."

"Revenge is the oldest of motivators." Merlin thought for a minute and added, "along with sex, but I sincerely doubt sex with Hitler was on her mind."

"As do I," Abbey said.

❦ ❦ ❦

"She had the best training we could provide," Ruth said, picking up her knitting. "We can rest assured of that." The women nodded in agreement.

"She maintained excellent control of her powers," Boo agreed. "They rivaled those of an Immortal."

"There is nothing we could have done," Eleanor said, stapling a program and laying it on top of the growing stack. "The girl was determined to try the assassination and nothing could stop her. We trained her to our best ability, we funded her mission and we provided her with transportation, contacts and as much protection as we could. What's done is done."

"Amen, sister," Livia responded.

"Why are we discussing Elfi anyway?" Tomyris asked, stroking one Saluki with her hand and another with her foot. "I thought we were worried about Robert."

"Oh, that's right!" Ruth laughed and placed the knitting in her lap. "We started talking about poor Elfi and her quest to kill Hitler and, by gosh, we got sidetracked." She paused and cleared her throat. "I must admit. I'm confused about how she went to Germany and wound up on our yard. Do we need more Lemoncake? Tea? Anyone?"

"That's the point, dear," Eleanor struggled against frustration, "how did she?"

"Robert! He must have something to do with it!" Ruth shouted excitedly, as if discovering this fact for the first time.

Boo glared at her. "Yes, Ruth. Yes. Now you are back with us."

❦ ❦ ❦

"I have a theory," Merlin said as he pushed Abbey farther down the hallway. "You see, one comes out of the Tapestry at the exact moment that they went in. Surely you have noticed that yourself?" Abbey nodded. "Regardless of the time spent in the past, no time at all has passed on *this* side of the Tapestry."

"I understand. But the question remains…"

"I'm getting there," Merlin sounded irritated. "As far as we at the Bastille know, Elfi had no interest in going into the Tapestry at all. She had no reason to believe she could survive the trip back, you see."

"Trip back?" Abbey asked.

"Immortals flit in and out of the Tapestry at will. Mortals can make the trip into the past with no problem, but when they return to our time, they age. Ten years for every century."

"So the bodies that were found… the detective said one looked to be eighty. If the woman was twenty or so in the present time…?"

"It would be sixty years of present time, or six centuries."

"That would mean…"

"Approximately 1408." Merlin sounded proud of himself. "I already did the math."

"So somehow, Elfi went to Germany to kill Hitler and wound up going to the year 1408?"

"Approximately."

"Approximately. Why would she do that?" Abbey asked.

Merlin stared at her. "That, my dear Abbey, is the question of the moment."

⟡ ⟡ ⟡

"Robert was the only one who could do this!" Boo insisted.

"No, dear, he is not. However, the odds are in his favor."

"It could be the Doctor," Livia said as she finished with the programs.

"Impossible," Tomyris yawned. "He couldn't go back to the fifteenth century. He was born in the nineteenth."

"Fifteenth century?" Eleanor's head jerked up.

"I did the math," Tomyris said, unbraiding her hair and taking the feathers out. "iPhone app."

"Ridiculous! Why would Robert want to go back to the fifteenth century?" Zen said quickly.

"Don't defend him'" Eleanor said sharply.

Zen sat back and shook her head. "I'm not defending him."

"We all know why he would want to go back to that time," Eleanor said.

✤ ✤ ✤

"So you think he has something to do with me?" Abbey stopped abruptly.

Merlin nodded. "The Tapestry was not in Europe. It had been moved to the United States many years prior. Elfi had no way of getting into the Tapestry from Germany. Nor could she have done so on her own." Merlin stopped in front of another section of Tapestry and continued.

"I hypothesize that Robert tricked her into the past from the United States. She never made it to Germany. He wanted her here in America for some reason."

"I have heard so much about him. Who is he?"

"Oh, you have met him. You will meet him again soon enough," Merlin sounded serious. He nudged another embroidered pattern and Abbey looked closely at it. This picture depicted a dark London street, covered in fog and illuminated by a dim light. A man, face and body covered in a long cape stood hidden in a doorway. Under the streetlight, a scantily clad, buxom woman stood.

"Robert is here because of him. The Doctor."

Abbey examined it closer, but saw no face. "Who is he?"

"An evil man who used...dear, how do I say this? Women of the night...is that the expression? To experiment upon."

"Why?"

"His theory is that the blood, or DNA, of the Immortal can be controlled in the laboratory, converting any human into an Immortal. He and Robert became fast friends. Both sought the same thing." He glared at Abbey before continuing. "An heir."

✤ ✤ ✤

"I wouldn't mate with that man in exchange for the return of Rome's glory days," Livia spat.

"We speak hypothetically, Livia, not realistically," Eleanor groaned.

"I didn't know there was any man you'd refuse to mate with, dear," Tomyris sneered.

"All we're saying," Eleanor continued, holding up her hands, "is that Robert and the Doctor have both tried to sire a male heir with mortal women before."

"Because they know not a single Immortal female will bear their child," Boudicca said.

"Regardless of the reason," Eleanor continued, "the only sure way of siring an Immortal child is when both Immortals are the biological parents. Males as well as females know that. This is most likely the reason Robert is after Abbey."

"That's ridiculous!" Zen laughed. "Abbey would never mate with him."

"Not willingly," Eleanor's voice carried no emotion.

"Since he cannot convince an Immortal female to carry his child, he was hoping to create his own," Merlin said.

"In the laboratory," said Abbey. Merlin nodded.

"With this man." Merlin nodded again.

"The only other option is to convince an Immortal woman to… dear….how to say…agree to become impregnated."

"What did I tell you?" Boo exploded, descending on Eleanor and pounding the desk. "If you had let me kill him last week…"

"You'd have been a murderer," Eleanor said calmly. "How many police detectives were hovering about last week? How many mysterious deaths can the Bastille survive, Boudicca? Two? Then we have hit our quota."

"You suggest Robert hopes to kidnap Abbey for the purposes of impregnating her?" Zen laughed. "That's absurd!"

"I see nothing absurd about it," Boo turned on Zen. "Men have been forcing pregnancies on women for a thousand years."

"Yes, in extreme circumstances."

"Oh? The mere fact that a woman is married means she wants to be pregnant?" Boo asked. Zen shook her head in disgust.

"Let us assume Robert is here, he has followed Abbey, and is stalking the Bastille," Eleanor said, turning to Zen. "This means he must strike during the Ritual. We need appropriate security."

"I have stated a hundred times I can handle it."

"Let us hope so," Eleanor said, "for all our sake."

"Once a year, there is a…dear, how to say it? A changing of the guard." Merlin nosed another of the finely embroidered scenes, this one showing a circle of women sewing. "The guardians of the Tapestry—that's you, Abbey—gather into a circle and sing the ancient chants. It is during the Ritual that Immortals wishing a respite go into the Tapestry and those wishing to start a new life with a new persona return from their respite, all the while ensuring that those serving penance stay inside the Tapestry." Abbey nodded and pointed to the scene. "That's the reason behind these scenes!" she said excitedly. "These memories are where the respites occur."

"Has nobody explained this part?" said Merlin. Abbey shook her head. "Each lifetime, the Immortal chooses one memory they wish to take respite in. They embroider it during the Ritual and here it remains as a safe haven in which one can relax for a lifetime. Sometimes two lifetimes."

Abbey gasped and turned to Merlin. "So *these* are where one takes their vacations?"

"But be careful," Merlin warned, "you become another physical being in that time. You must never—repeat *never*—allow your past self to see your current self. You also must not change anything."

"But my point is this," she said, waving him aside, "why did Aunt Eleanor embroider a scene of my burning? Why would she want to use that as a respite?"

Merlin shook his head. "Ask her."

⬧ ⬧ ⬧

"Here," Zen said, placing a list of names on Eleanor's desk. "These are the names of those being released from detention."

Eleanor gazed at the names and nodded. "Fine."

"Ladies, I bid you goodnight," Zen said.

"Are we done here?" Tomyris asked, sitting up. The dogs jumped to their feet, tails wagging.

Eleanor nodded. "I'm exhausted. Let's all remember that we have less than forty-eight hours before the Ritual. Be on guard."

"I am," Boo said, grabbing her sword and heading out.

"She always is," Tomyris said, following the woman.

"I'll meet with reporters and have a cover story ready regarding the bodies," Livia said, picking up her papers.

"I think I'll make crêpes for breakfast," Ruth chimed in, still knitting. "Fresh strawberries, blueberries, and some whipped cream."

"That sounds delicious," Eleanor agreed.

59

"I TOLD YOU I'M THE BAKER'S WIFE, YOU STUPID WHORE, ARE YOU DEAF?" Edna snatched the dress, apron and hand towel from Heather and disappeared down the hallway. Just as she grabbed the doorknob, Lynn turned the corner.

"Edna, can I speak with you?"

"Oh! Good morning, dear. You look nice today," Edna said, brushing lint off Lynn's blouse. "Is that new? Red looks so good on you, why don't you wear it more often? Or is this a ... special occasion?"

Lynn felt her face go flush. It had nothing to do with the fact that Robert casually mentioned his fondness for red. Nothing. It was a coincidence. "No, I don't know…just felt good."

"When I said that about swallowing a handful of Valium, you told me I was full of shit," Edna smirked.

"Ah, well…" Lynn stuttered. "Well, about the party…"

"Faire, dear. The women of the Bastille are very stern about the terminology."

"Faire," Lynn corrected herself. "We have all the positions covered except one." Edna stared at Lynn coldly. "You can still be the baker's wife…"

Edna broke out into a smile. "Good. I like carrying bread. I ask cute guys to squeeze my buns."

"That's great. Clever," Lynn lied. "But we need a person to help herd the visitors to the quilting demonstration." Edna's eyes squinted. "You know, when the women sit in a circle and chant?"

"That's so boring! I've seen it before!" Edna whined.

"Mr. Graves and Mr. Rix—sorry, Joan of Arc—are on trash duty with me; Mrs. Bailey is monitoring the inside fence with Mr. Stewart."

"Monitoring the...?"

"If they are struck by the need to strip and dance with Feng Shi, the chances are minimal that they'll be seen by anyone other than Heather," Lynn explained.

All I do is get people to watch the sewing circle and then stand there?" Lynn nodded. "Can I bring my buns? I love to say, 'Want to knead my loaves, sir?' Last year, some guy did. He was a cutie pie, too."

"Sure. Ask them to touch your buns all you want."

"Fine! I'll do it!" She looked at Lynn and lowered her voice. "Want me to find a cute guy for you, too? I'll share my loaves with you." Her eyes flitted over Lynn's shoulder to Heather. "WHAT DO YOU WANT NOW, YOU TRAMP?"

"**D**RESSES?" THE DOCTOR CHUCKLED from behind his paper and sipped more café au lait. "You have quite the fondness for dresses, don't you?"

Robert modeled his dress for the Doctor. A wig of long, thick blonde hair looked so realistic it could have easily passed for real. A fresh shave erased his normal stubble and a thick scarf hid his predominant Adam's apple. The loose-fitting peasant's dress hid the hairy arms and rounding out the façade was a bodice and falsies that formed an enormous cleavage. Robert looked sexy.

"This will enable me to go anywhere and do anything I like during the Faire," Robert said proudly, petting his own breasts. "Tell me...shall I dress this way?"

The Doctor nodded, "I'd ravage you."

"You would ravage anything," Robert chuckled.

"Like, don't mean to interrupt the ravaging," Josh's voice interrupted, "but there's a Lynn Swanson on the line?" The boy stared from Doctor to Robert with wide eyes and cocked head. "Um…what do you want me to say, boss?"

"I'll take her in here." Robert strode to the phone.

"So, she's…like…your girlfriend...or something?" Josh asked hopefully.

"Or something," the Doctor answered as he closed the door on the boy.

"Hello, there, my dear." Robert's voice sounded smooth and soft. Silk on air. He shot the Doctor a thumbs up. "That time works perfectly for me. I must warn you, however, of my choice of costume. I must attend as a woman. I assure you, the minute we leave the grounds, I will don pants."

"No," she said quickly, "you don't have to do that for me."

"Not for you, my dear. For me," he crooned. It shouldn't be too difficult to reel her in again. She was old and desperate. "I should like to dine with you looking as masculine as I can."

As soon as Lynn put the phone back into the cradle, Martha stormed into her office, laid a manila folder on her desk, and cleared her throat.

"The Faire's VIP passes," Martha's sandpaper voice ground across the room, "are not to be trifled with."

Lynn smiled at her. Trifled with? They were badges to a freaking Renaissance Faire, not the Willy Wonka Golden Tickets. "I'm sorry?"

"The Faire passes that Livia Emerson sent over. She wants an information sheet filled out for each of these VIP passes. Name. Contact information. Emergency contact."

"Yes, I remember." Lynn barely heard the Nazi. She had to get to Payless Shoes and get a pair of boots for tomorrow. There was no way she was walking around the Faire in her new sneakers. Besides, her new brown cords would look outstanding with those new hiking boots she saw in the window of Payless.

"I don't have enough forms for the number of VIP passes," Martha said, crossing her arms and leaning against the door frame.

"Okay, I'll get right on it."

"In *duplicate!*"

"Well," Lynn laid down her pen and looked at Martha. "How about if I fill out the top information sheets once and copy each one so you'll have two copies?"

"I need two copies of each form. I don't care how you get them." Martha smiled fiendishly and said, "So now you can tell that to Livia Emerson. She's on line two." She coughed into her hand and headed out the door. Lynn snatched up line two. "Ms. Emerson?"

"Lynn," the crisp, efficient voice said, "good to speak with you again. Abbey is doing fine. We are all a bit hectic with this Faire business…"

"Thank you so much for letting me bring my patients." It was out of her mouth before Lynn thought. She had interrupted Livia Emerson. Livia Emerson didn't like interruptions.

The pause before Livia responded was just long enough to let Lynn know that the interruption was noted with disapproval. When Livia spoke again, the voice clinked like ice in a glass. "Due to the recent series of events, we would very much like to know everyone who has access beyond the guests' area of the Faire grounds. As your people will be assigned duties requiring them to have full access to the grounds, it is imperative we have their contact information. A protection, you understand."

Lynn waited a few seconds to make sure Livia was done talking. "Yes, I am finishing them up now."

"Lovely." Livia paused and lowered her voice. "Lynn, may I ask you about something else?"

"Shoot."

"The detective…that one who is investigating the…." Livia let the word 'bodies' lie unsaid in the conversation.

"Detective Mathers. What about him?"

"Has he seen you recently?"

"Yes. I can't remember when…yesterday? Two days ago? He needed some hair. Something about DNA…"

"Abbey's?" Livia's voice rose in surprise.

"Hers too, yes. He went into her old room. I thought you knew?"

Livia hesitated. "I see."

"I'm sure it's all perfectly normal. He took some hair samples from Abbey's old dresser."

"I see. All right then. We shall see you tomorrow."

Lynn searched through the folder. Martha had taken a yellow highlighter and highlighted the ADDRESS line of each of the patient's emergency contact form. Was she kidding? A child could look at a stray dog, mutter 'The Meadows,' and the mongrel would lead your ass here. She sighed and began writing in the address when a thought came to her: She forgot to tell Livia about Robert taking Mr. Chin's VIP pass. She had gotten permission from Livia Emerson at the Bastille for her patients, but she had neglected to get Livia's approval for him. Should she list him as 'Visitor'?

Her pen hesitated over the application. Surely Livia wouldn't have a problem with Robert being there, would she? The guy was Abbey's uncle, for heaven's sake. To hell with it. Family is family. They would be more than happy to have him.

She picked up the pile of papers and headed out of the office. If she hurried, she'd still be able to stop and buy those hiking boots before the shoe store closed.

ABBEY JERKED AWAKE as strong hands pulled her from the warmth of her bed.

"Aunt Boo!" Abbey gasped as Boo tossed her into the hallway. From behind her, she heard Merlin's voice.

"Boudicca! Stop it!"

Boo snapped. "My patience has flown."

"What do you think you're doing?" the horse said, putting himself between Abbey and Boo.

"Get out of my way, old man. I have no time for you today."

"You will have time for me or…"

"Or what?" Boo stood before the Frisian, meeting his eyes with her own venomous glare. "Your power wanes as quickly as the Tapestry's does."

"This behavior is utterly unacceptable."

"Look at me and tell me you have not thought of this yourself."

The two stood glaring at each other in the dull gloom of dawn. Neither said a word. Neither blinked.

"See?" Boo whispered, "even the great Merlin is on the verge of desperation. You cannot even summon the power to return to human form."

"I keep this form out of respect for—"

"Do not lie to me," Boo's voice carried an edge of anger. It reminded Abbey of the staff at The Meadows just before they put a patient into restraints. "You are as weak as the rest of us."

A tremendous ripping sound erupted from the Tapestry to Abbey's left. From the lowest panel of embroidered scenes, a young woman stepped out of the fabric, stumbled across the hallway, and fell into a heap on the floor. She wore a bright red, tight-fitting flapper dress, a single string of pearls, and a tiny hat.

"Boudicca?" the woman slurred, tipping a huge bottle of champagne. "Boo! How good to see you!" She sloshed through the puddle of champagne to throw her arms around Boo. "I *love* this era!"

"It is not time, Alucia," Boo said. "Go back to your party."

Alucia looked at Boo with glassy eyes and pained expression. "But I don't want to go back, dear. The police are coming. The party's over."

"Yes," Boo hissed, "it certainly is." With that, she leaned over, grabbed Abbey, and threw her into the Tapestry.

The roar of the crowd scared Abbey. Never before had she heard such vile and vulgar words as those yelled by the crowd in the center of the courtyard. Hundreds of filthy people milled around a pyre of sticks at the foot of a thick post. Abbey recognized this scene—it was the same location as Aunt Eleanor's memory. Only this time, instead of standing high above and away from the burning post, Abbey stood barely a hundred yards in front of it.

"Aunt Boo, I don't want to be here."

"Nor I."

"Get me out of here."

"No," Boo said, spinning towards the girl. "Just stay out of sight. If the crowd spots you, you'll be dead before they burn you."

"I do not wish to see this again."

"Oh, my dear," Boo said, "trust me when I say you are correct." She pulled Abbey into the shadows of the stone wall and held the girl tightly against the sharp, cold stones. She forced Abbey's face toward the pyre of sticks.

"This is where it all began, girl."

"I died here, I know."

"Not died. You set into motion an entire series of events that must be stopped before it leads to the downfall of the Tapestry's Guardians."

"I saw this scene with Aunt Eleanor!" Abbey felt the pain in her chest growing. She could hardly breathe. "I don't remember anything about this lifetime."

"You are a warden of the Tapestry, Abbey," Boo said in her ear. "We lack the luxury of forgetfulness."

The crowd roared as the King's men emerged from the sanctuary. Abbey remembered from her visit with Eleanor that next she'd see herself emerge from within the church walls, bound and trussed, and the crowd would pummel her with rocks, taunts and jeers.

"Please, no," Abbey said, feeling Boo's fingers dig into her jaw. She saw the guards marching towards the pyre. "What do you want me to do?"

"I need you to feel what you felt on this day. I need you to remember what you saw before you burned to death. Whatever you saw holds the key to repairing the Tapestry."

"This is torture."

"Yes. Which is why Immortals do not draw attention to themselves. Haven't you learned that lesson yet?" The crowd roared. Abbey smelled the scent of burning wood combined with burning flesh as a wave of hot air brushed past her.

"You had barely regained consciousness when Eleanor allowed you to play with that aircraft," Boo hissed.

"But those years in between—"

"It is not spells that bind magic, girl, but intent. For almost three hundred years you lacked the gusto of a warden. You could not focus on the magics and Eleanor allowed you to weave your half-hearted attention into the Tapestry. It weakened us."

Boo pulled Abbey towards the doorway where minutes ago the army had emerged. Abbey could hear the cries of the crowd above the din. She heard herself screaming in pain. After an eternity of being dragged through the throng, Abbey felt Boo shoving her into a dimly lit chamber. "Watch, Abbey. Watch what happened while you burned."

Abbey looked up. The room contained only a small wooden bowl and a stool. A wall opposite them opened. Two figures entered the chamber and unfurled their hoods, revealing Eleanor and Ruth. After a moment, the main door from the courtyard opened and Boo rushed in, followed by Zenobia. The four women stood staring at each other in silent understanding.

At the sound of approaching guards, the four women split into two pairs, each pair flanking one side of the main door. The door opened and four of the King's guards entered, carrying a body wrapped in a thin, white garment—the charred remains of what used to be Joan of Arc. As the soldiers passed, Boo and Zen jumped them from behind, slitting their throats and kicking the lifeless bodies into the dark corners. With quick precision, the four Immortals transferred Joan's charred carcass to a thick, dark fabric and in its place exchanged a thin, decaying body in Joan's shroud.

Eleanor and Ruth picked up the dark fabric and hustled out of the camouflaged side door as Zen and Boo slipped back into the courtyard through the main one. Seconds after their disappearance, an elegantly dressed man—Abbey guessed it to be the King—walked into the chamber. He stared at the lump of white fabric and sighed. He gestured to the white shroud and the guards picked up the carcass and exited back into the courtyard amongst cheers of glee. Only when Boo and Abbey were alone again did Boo dare speak.

"The King ordered your body burned repeatedly. We barely had time for the switch."

"I do not understand."

"The body that was burned a second and third time was not yours. Your charred body was removed from this room while another pyre was built. This is a fact that was lost to history. It was, however, our saving grace."

"What did you do with me?"

"We saved you."

"For what?" Abbey asked, frustrated. "For a half life defined only by my half memories? It is our memories that dictate who we are."

"You remember nothing. You mean to say you *are* nothing?" Boo stared at her. "You were betrayed, murdered, and murdered again. Who was it who betrayed you? Did this," she gestured to the small room, "not stir any memories at all?"

"You had no right to show me this."

"We risked our lives to switch corpses. It is imperative we know who betrayed you!"

"I want to go home."

"And where would home be?" Boo asked.

Abbey felt herself falling backwards. As she landed in the hallway of the Bastille, she scooted to the wall and rested against it.

Merlin looked to Abbey and stared at her for a moment. Then he said to Boo, "It didn't work."

Boo shook her head and glared angrily at Abbey. "I know."

JOSHUA SHUFFLED FROM ONE FOOT TO ANOTHER while avoiding Robert's eyes. "Look, man, I don't care what you do in your private life, you know? But," the young man paused and looked up, "I'm straight."

Robert frowned and leaned toward the boy. "You are what?"

"I...don't...you know—swing that way."

Robert looked down at the Doctor who kneeled in front of him, measuring tape in hand. "Do you wish to say anything?"

"He believes we are lovers," the Doctor said without lifting his eyes. "Just a moment and this hem will be completed."

"I can, like, totally drive you there and wait but..." Joshua stumbled as he searched for the words, "...can I drop you off where nobody will see me?"

"Joshua," Robert began, "your concern is noted. You are, however, still in the employ of myself—"

"Robert, drop the dress."

Robert followed the Doctor's request while speaking to Joshua. "The most important task we have in front of you right now is to remain nearby. Should we summon you, it is imperative that you appear within minutes to collect us."

"I don't have to wear one of those, do I?"

"One of what?"

"A dress."

"Robert," the Doctor asked from his knees, "we shall need to tighten your bodice."

"This is a costume for the Faire," Robert laughed. "You are not invited. Monitor the phone. Be prepared. And if need be…"

"Turn around and pick you up near the old Faire site on the other side of the Bastille, don't tell anyone you are there, and don't be seen. If the police ask me who I am, tell them I'm with security." Joshua sighed. "Kind of 0-0-7, super spy-like, isn't it?"

"Perfect, Robert. Take a look," the Doctor said, pulling the bodice tighter.

Robert turned to the mirror and looked at himself. He nodded. He was an extremely attractive woman. "Yes, Joshua. Super-spy it is."

"CONSIDER IT AN EARLY BIRTHDAY GIFT," Mathers said as he pulled over to the side of the road. He could practically see Helen in her lab, sitting atop her swiveling chair, poking her glasses onto her face with her index finger.

"Do I get cake?"

"If you feel like celebrating."

"Okay, here it is." Helen's voice suddenly turned cold and professional. "Want the long version or the short?"

"Short."

"They all match," Helen said. "They're all the same family."

"Abbey, Elfi and Sarah?"

"All of them; Elfi, Sarah, Abbey, Eleanor, Ruth…all the subjects whose samples you sent to me a couple of days ago."

"Holy shit," Mathers said. "I sent you samples from the women of the Bastille. Are Ruth and Eleanor blood-related? I thought they were in-laws." He paused and ran the faces of the women through his mind. "And what about Zenobia? She's black. And Livia? She's—"

"Yep. All of them a clean match. Just another mystery surrounding the women of the Bastille," Helen said.

"Okay…if Ruth and Eleanor are sisters, then it makes sense they share some of the DNA of Abbey."

"Technically, Abbey would share *their* DNA."

"Helen, work with me."

"Sorry. I'm a scientist. I'm telling you, enough pairs of chromosomes match for me to say with utter confidence that all the women are all related by blood."

"Okay. Got it. Thanks, Helen."

"That's why they pay me the big bucks. Oh, there is one thing, though."

"What?" Mathers asked.

"There was one bag of hair strands you gave me labeled 'Abbey.' It had three hairs in it. Where did you get it from?"

"From Abbey's drawer. I collected them from her room at The Meadows. Why?"

Helen hesitated for a moment. "Well, two of the three strands were from Abbey. The other wasn't. But whoever owned that hair is also related to the women."

"Whose was it?"

"Damn. My other line is ringing. I have to take it. I think it's that murder-suicide case from the pig farm. Do you know what analyzing pig shit is like?"

Mathers laughed. "No."

"Count your blessings." The phone went dead as Helen disconnected. Mathers sat in his car plotting his next step as another beat-up VW bus passed him on its way to the Bastille's Faire grounds. As he watched, the Grim Reaper stuck his head out the window and waved.

64

"I KNEW A HORSE ONCE," Ruth sighed as she placed the plate of Rice Krispy treats on Eleanor's desk, "but it died. I think it was brought to a factory and they ground him into glue."

"That is a myth, Ruth," Livia said, rolling her eyes. "Glue is not made from horses."

"Oh?" Ruth turned and walked out of the room, saying over her shoulder, "I'm going to watch *The Price Is Right*."

As soon as Ruth left the room, Livia turned to Eleanor. "I tell you, that detective concerns me."

"Yes, dear, I know," Eleanor said, signing the checks Zenobia held out for her. "He is investigating the death of two women found on our property. I should think that is cause enough for concern."

"He will be a problem, mark my words," Livia said, settling into her chair.

"That is the problem with police, isn't it?" Eleanor said. "They seem to hover around illegal activities."

"There is nothing illegal here, Eleanor," Zenobia interjected.

"My love, we are a group of Immortal witches guarding a magical artifact. I am quite certain somewhere within that scenario are one or two illegal activities."

"You do not seem upset, Eleanor."

"What would you have me do, Livia?" Eleanor snapped her head toward the Italian.

"I would have you issue a warning about Detective Mathers and, should he show up on the grounds tomorrow, have him ejected."

"I don't think that will be necessary," Zenobia sighed. "After all, wouldn't that look a bit…suspicious?"

"Zen, dear," Livia said, turning on her, "throughout this whole ordeal, you don't seem to think anything or anyone is dangerous. Why is that?"

Zen's voice cut like ice, "It must be exhausting to see assassins in every shadow. Are you not tired of that?"

"Enough, both of you," Eleanor said, handing the checks back to Zenobia. "I quite agree with Zenobia. Banning Detective Mathers from the Faire would be much too suspicious. Zen can keep an eye on him."

"I would be happy to do so."

"You have the Watch List?" Livia asked sharply. Zenobia nodded. "Pray tell, what is your plan to keep track of those on the Watch List?"

"I have my ways, Livia," Zenobia replied, as she sat down again. "Rest assured, the only people on these grounds tomorrow will be the ones I allow."

Livia snorted. "I hope so." She pulled herself to her feet, smoothed her skirt, and grabbed her briefcase. "I spoke with that social worker, Lynn Swanson. Her people will be here wearing identification badges."

"Oh, delightful!" Eleanor smiled. "Abbey will be surprised to see her friends."

Livia nodded. "I hope so." She checked herself in the mirror and ran a hand through her hair. "I am off. I have a media tour beginning in fifteen minutes. Have you read my statement about the bodies?"

Eleanor nodded. "I think it's splendid."

"Yes, it is." Livia strode out of the room.

Eleanor turned to Zenobia. "Do you really feel the Bastille is as secure as you say, despite the fact that Robert may show up?"

"I'm counting on it," Zenobia replied.

THE ENTIRE CONTENTS OF LYNN'S PURSE lay spread across the glass counter before she found the credit card stuck in a crease at the bottom of the bag. She shrugged and smiled at the pimply-faced, chubby woman. "I thought I'd lost it."

The girl nodded and continued to chew her gum with ferocity. Lynn held out the Visa card as her cell phone began to ring. She reached over the counter to grab it and knocked her lip balm onto the floor. Lynn watched it spiraling under the wooden rack and shrugged as she flipped the phone open.

"Lynn? It's like, Heather?" The girl's voice sounded stressed.

"Yes, Heather?"

"I'm having a problem with Mr. Graves, okay? He thinks he's going to die?"

"Here," the pimply sales clerk said, thrusting a pen and receipt at Lynn.

"Why? What's wrong?" She took the pen with a smile.

"Nothing," the girl responded.

Lynn covered the phone with her hand and shook her head at the sales clerk. "I'm talking to my work."

"What?" Heather asked.

"Mr. —" She glanced up at the sales clerk watching her and stumbled over the name. "The…uh…our client. What's wrong?"

"He said that Death is coming to visit him and he has to save Abbey. He said you'd understand?" Heather continued as Lynn handed her pen back to the sales clerk.

"Step aside, please," the clerk snapped as she popped her gum. Lynn nodded and scooped the purse's contents back into her bag.

"Heather, I don't understand what the problem is."

"I don't think he should go with you tomorrow?"

"Heather, he is *not* dangerous," Lynn said as the salesgirl looked at her in disgust. "And he's going with us. It would devastate him not to see Abbey."

"That's another thing?" Heather continued. "He says he can feel Abbey and she's in trouble?"

"He always says that. Don't worry." Lynn looked up at the pimply girl and added, "I'm leaving."

"What?"

"Nothing, Heather, I'm talking to the clerk in the store." Lynn knelt before the sock rack. She stuck her hand under the wood to retrieve her stray lip balm.

"He's going with us. He'll see Abbey and everything will be fine. Don't worry."

"Well, if you're sure?"

"I'm sure. Besides, he is one of the only people that Abbey will open up to. It will be helpful to have him there if she's in trouble." Lynn thought of the trunkful of torture devices and shuddered. She hadn't spoken to Detective Mathers about her suspicions and pangs of guilt washed over her. What if he didn't understand her concern and never investigated Abbey's safety? That thought had never occurred to her before.

"Heather, I've got to go. I'll see you in the morning." She slid her hand farther under the rack. As she did, she heard her pants rip. Great. Just great.

She gave up the search and sat on her heels. Well, at least she was going to keep her dignity and wait for the customers to leave. She'd be damned if she was going to show her ass to the whole town. She dialed Mathers' number and waited for the pimply clerk to finish waiting on the last of the customers. She had never been happier that she wore clean underwear.

MATHERS SAID GOODBYE TO LYNN SWANSON, closed his cell phone, and sat on the shoulder of the Bastille's private frontage road waiting for the pickup truck filled with fairies to pass. He noticed that the fairies shared the bed of the Ford with an ogre and a court jester. Can fairies and ogres coexist in peace? When he spotted a fairy handing off a bottle of Guinness to the shirtless ogre, he had his answer: world peace is achieved through Guinness.

The sheer flamboyance of the pre-opening hubbub made him chuckle. The once-innocuous green field had been transformed into a medieval village. A primitive log fence outlined the boundaries of the Faire grounds, set off by the huge arch constructed of woven tree limbs and vines. WELCOME ALL YE WHO ENTER screamed out from a burlap banner displayed over the leaves and stray twigs. Colorful tarps covered the empty booths he had passed last night. Approximately twenty or thirty people in period costume wandered the grounds, setting up tables, hanging signs from tree branches, and preparing for opening day; among them he counted two lances, endless bottles of Guinness, and several swords. Did they have permits for the weapons? One particularly busty young maiden wore a bodice under her tunic, making her look top heavy and lopsided.

Suddenly a realization struck him. Whether they were ogre, fairy, peasant or royalty, all the people walking around looked like they had stepped out of a medieval fairy tale. Just like a fantasy movie. Just like Elfi and Sarah Reisner.

Maybe he was taking the wrong tack. He had been using his research time to look into the past of the women of the Bastille. He had screened DNA, interviewed people, and scoured crime scenes exactly as he had always done on a case. Maybe the key to the case was not the *people* attending the event, but the event itself.

A convertible of Grim Reapers riding in a Ford Mustang zoomed by, the radio blaring "Angie." He bet Abbey was going to play a prominent role in this Faire, along with the menagerie of aunts. They were the constant in all the Faires stretching back through time.

The call from Lynn Swanson was just the break he was looking for. Ever since he spoke with Helen, he had sat in his car wondering what to do next. Then, like a gift, Lynn gave him his answer. She was afraid for Abbey's safety at the hands of the aunts, no matter how much she danced around the issue trying to be ethical. If she wasn't fearful, she wouldn't have called him again.

A horn honked and he looked out the window at the truck that had parked alongside his vehicle.

"Hey, stranger," Janet Gage shouted from the truck. "Don't you know you're holding up traffic?"

"Am I?" Mathers joked. "Some cop should give me a ticket."

"I'm headed up to the Faire site to sign off on extinguisher placement. Want to tag along?"

Mathers smiled. "Yes. Yes I do. I may have to be there a while, though."

"Sal's going to be there. He's grilling burgers for the vendors who will be unloading after dark." She unlocked the passenger side door and ushered him into the truck.

"Hurry up!" she joked. "Lots to do before the Faire opens in the morning."

"THEY ARE AMIABLE HORSES, but terrible conversationalists," Merlin said as he trotted to Abbey. "I've never been one for formalities, but these two are a bit…full of themselves." He jerked his head toward Fire and Water, who stood staring at Abbey from the center of the corral.

"I wish to be alone," Abbey said, walking into the barn and barely noticing the warmth of the stone tiles heating her feet.

"So do I," Merlin answered as he overtook her. "All wishes cannot be granted, however." He brought his head down to rest on her shoulders, his eye locked onto hers. "At least not immediately."

She flung the horse off her shoulder. "Do you not understand English? I said I wish to be alone."

"And I responded in equally good English that not all wishes can be granted. Perhaps your excursion into the Tapestry erased your ability to listen?"

She flew at the horse and grabbed him by the mane. "Do you realize I watched myself burning to death twice?"

The horse stomped in frustration, not wanting to crush the girl's feet. "I do."

"Do you realize I have also seen myself drown?"

"I do."

"Do you realize these are two images I would never wish to see again?"

"Do you realize," Merlin said, struggling to hold still as Abbey twisted on his mane, "that these are the two most important scenes in history? Dear," Merlin said through clenched teeth, "would you mind letting go? I do not wish to hurt you, but I feel the urge to trample you right now."

Abbey let go and touched Merlin's neck. "I'm sorry."

"You are still very strong." Abbey's lips went up slightly and Merlin nudged her shoulder. "Ah! I see you still can smile." Abbey threw her arms around him. "Not in front of *them*," he nodded to Fire and Water who stood in the corral glaring at them. "They get jealous."

"Always talk to yourself?" The voice startled Abbey and she spun around, tripping over Merlin's hooves.

"Detective Mathers?"

"Sorry to interrupt, but the Faire workers said you'd be up here."

"I do not mind the interruption."

"Abbey," Mathers said, "can we chat?"

She nodded and stood against Merlin, who stood glaring at the detective. "If you don't mind walking."

He shook his head and held out his hand to her. She ignored the hand and followed him out of the stable. "I'm not sure how to say this, but we don't have a lot of time, so I'll be blunt," he stammered before continuing. "Are you getting along with your aunts? Are they...good to you?"

"Why do you ask, Detective?" He stopped and she followed suit. Merlin, who was following too closely, ran into her and she had to flail to keep upright. "Are you concerned for me, or the case?"

She thought she saw a flicker of a smile before he answered. "I'm always concerned about people's safety."

"Safety?"

He paused, weighing his answer. "If anything is happening that causes you to feel...scared...would you tell me?"

"Do you care?"

"I do."

Abbey nodded. "I see. You are a man as well as a law enforcement officer."

He grinned. "Don't tell anyone. I have a reputation to protect."

"From what Aunt Livia tells me, your reputation is well-protected."

"Oh?" He sounded shocked.

It was her turn to grin. "Aunt Livia...let us say that nobody learns anything about this family without my Aunt Livia finding out." His smile faltered as he considered this. "I know much more about you."

"That...probably isn't a good thing for a cop to hear."

"No," she agreed.

"So...Abbey." He leaned close to her. "I don't know much about your family, but I do know this: They're involved with these bodies somehow." He studied her face for a reaction but she stared at him blankly, a model of neutrality. "Well, if you need help, or want to tell me anything, here." He handed her a business card. "Please call. My cell number is on the back."

He paused for a moment and thought he saw a flash of something across her face. He leaned in to her. "Abbey?" The girl looked at him with a vague, distant expression. "I'll figure out what's going on sooner or later."

She nodded and turned back to the horse.

Reluctantly, he headed back towards the Faire grounds feeling more helpless than he had in a long time. He hated grasping at straws.

68

ROBERT SHIFTED HIS WEIGHT FROM FOOT TO FOOT as he waited for the damned detective to move away from Abbey. How long had that vile man been speaking to her? It seemed like hours, although barely an hour had passed since Joshua dropped him off at the intersection and he nearly died beneath the wheels of the convertible full of Grim Reapers. Disgusting costumes, but an idea struck him as they drove past: If he donned a black cloak, anyone who caught a glimpse of his face would see the face of a woman! He couldn't resist the deliciousness of wearing two disguises and set about separating a costume from its owner. After several minutes of arguing with the pimply teenager, he decided to be done with the bickering and kill the lad when the young man decided to sell the cloak for a hundred dollars. The transaction left Robert feeling empty. He hadn't killed anything in days and the youth cheated him out of a kill.

He hadn't wanted to bury another body anyway.

He feared for a moment that the treacherous bitch, Livia, spotted him as she conversed with a group of vendors, but his luck held. Just as he was about to cut back towards the Bastille, he noticed Detective Mathers.

Gambling that the detective was not here for a social visit, he followed the man under the ropes defining the Faire's boundaries and into the woods. Just as he suspected, the detective led him to Abbey. He hadn't anticipated the two of them talking for long and he felt himself growing impatient as he spied on them from the trees next to the stable. At last they parted and Robert re-covered his head with the cloak's hood, placed the piece of Tapestry inside his cleavage, grabbed the knife in one hand and the syringe of the Doctor's concoction in the other. Thus prepared, he bolted towards Abbey.

What the hell was he thinking? Mathers stepped under the rope strung between the trees and entered the flurry of activity around the Market Square, which would be the center of commerce when it opened to the public in the morning. From this square, the patrons could move left to purchase handmade goods, watch the wandering artists perform, or buy food. Veering to the right would enable them to observe the sewing circle where the women of the Bastille sang period songs and demonstrated quilting techniques. Mathers leaned up against a huge old oak tree and pondered his discussion with Abbey. Wasn't it time to admit that he was less obsessed with Abbey's safety than he was with uncovering the truth? Could he stop asking himself so many questions?

No. He was a detective and asking questions was second nature. He couldn't explain why, but he suddenly needed to talk to her again. He turned and retraced his steps under the ropes. He picked up his pace as he headed back towards the stable. Within minutes, he found himself running.

Water smelled the interloper when Robert was a few yards from Abbey. The horse reared back, hooves kicking the air. They would have hit their target, but Immortal blood gave Robert the edge he needed to dodge the horse's legs and to come within striking distance of Abbey.

"Abbey! Run!" Merlin shouted as Robert came up next to Merlin's rear flank. With inhuman speed, Robert sank the knife into Merlin's hind end and Merlin screamed, stumbling backwards as his hind leg collapsed under him.

Robert looked up and saw Abbey hesitate atop Water. The pause was the opening Robert needed. Gripping the syringe tightly, he grabbed her leg. She kicked at him, but he held her shin and plunged the syringe into Abbey's leg. He uttered the Spell of Passing and the two of them disappeared into the Tapestry.

Mathers froze, unable to believe what he had just seen.

One minute, the Grim Reaper had been running towards Abbey and her horse; the next, they disappeared.

What the hell was going on here?

Eleanor screamed as a bolt of pain shot through her. "The Tapestry's been breeched!" she screamed when she found her voice again. "Abbey's gone into the Tapestry." Sounds of hounds braying echoed through the house and Tomyris entered the office followed by the dogs, Ruth, Boo and Zen. Eleanor looked up and motioned for Tomyris to sit down. "Shut them up," she said, pointing to the dogs. Turning to Ruth, Eleanor continued. "Ruth, dear, where was Abbey when she crossed over?"

"The stable," Tomyris said, putting her iPod into her pants pocket. "Merlin is with her."

"The stable?" Eleanor demanded. Tomyris gestured to the dogs. "Of course."

"Merlin speaks canine. The dogs, however, are not so fluent at horse," Tomyris began. Eleanor cut her off.

"Boo-"

Boudicca was already out the door and into the hallway. Eleanor turned to the other women. "Tomyris, send the dogs to Merlin. Find out what happened. Ruth—" she turned to the crying woman, "dear, can you please alert Livia?" Ruth nodded and trotted out of the room behind the hounds.

"This is Robert's work. He has taken her," Zenobia said, sitting down at the desk. "It's hopeless."

"Dear, if that is all you have to say," Eleanor said, heading for the doorway, "then it is best we hear only silence."

WHEN ABBEY AWOKE, she lay naked between the sheets of a wide canopy bed, thinking that she had urinated on herself. Her head pounded, her thighs quivered like jelly, and she felt as if she were going to vomit.

She sat up and immediately regretted it. Her vision blurred, her head swam, and blood pounded through her ears. After her nausea passed, she slowly looked around. She lay within a castle. Heavy wooden furniture filled every inch of the room and tapestries hung on the walls of the cavernous room. From her vantage point in bed, she could see out the great arched window and into some kind of public square.

She scanned the floor and saw no clothes, no robe or anything with which to cover her nakedness. She wrapped the bedsheet around her as she stood up, making sure to move slowly to keep the nausea under control.

She inched her way to the window and her blood ran cold. The familiar pyre of wood and burning stake stood just yards away.

"Ah! You are awake!" a voice said from behind her in a thick French accent. She swung around to see a handsome, dark-haired man carrying a silver tray. He wore a finely detailed doublet, an embroidered shirt, wide leather belt, and sturdy leather boots. Around his waist hung a large knife sheathed in a fine scabbard. "I figured you may be hungry, my love."

Abbey stared at the man. She had seen him before, but she couldn't summon his name from the recesses of her mind. The fuzzy balls of memory bounced through her mind, but they slipped through a fragmented past. "Who are you?"

He smiled and the sight of his perfectly white teeth struck another bell within her.

"Of course you wouldn't remember me." He shook his head and placed the tray on the dresser next to the door. He backed up to the entry door, never turning his back on Abbey.

Abbey's blood ran cold as she heard the sound of the lock sliding into place. "Why am I a prisoner?"

The man held out his arms. "No, my love!" He wrapped her in a warm embrace. "They took your memory and with it, they took us. My love, it is me—Robert. You are my wife. And..." he laid his hand on her stomach, "at long last, you now carry our child."

"**G**ET THESE DOGS OFF OF ME BEFORE I SHOOT THEM!" Mathers screamed, waving his badge and gun.

Tomyris sighed and hit 'pause' on her iPod. "Men. Always playing with guns." She whistled and the pair of dogs immediately backed away and sat at her feet. She turned to him and rolled her eyes. "What do you want now? More hair samples?"

"Oh! Dear, me!" Ruth's voice floated from the interior of the Bastille. "I shall call for Eleanor."

After Mathers watched Abbey and the Grim Reaper disappear into thin air, he set out for the Bastille at a full run. He hadn't gotten halfway to the mansion when two large dogs appeared out of the woods that separated the mansion from the stable and herded him like a sheep towards the Bastille, where they kept him confined to the garden that separated the woods from the kitchen door.

He looked at the woman with beaded hair wearing the sports bra. "Tomyris, right?" She nodded and reached into a leather pouch on her belt, withdrew pieces of meat, and tossed them to the dogs. "Abbey... she...disappeared."

Tomyris nodded and sighed. "Yeah. Pisser, isn't it?" She adjusted the jewel in her belly-button and straightened the bells strung across her neck. "Do you like the jingle bells, or should I get fairy bells instead? The jingle bells are fucking grating on my nerves, but—"

"Detective Mathers!" Eleanor said, rushing out of the kitchen and onto the lawn. "What on earth are you doing here?"

"Abbey..." he had no time to finish as an arm wrapped around his neck and another wrapped around his chest. "Ow! That hurts," he hissed as the elbow closed around his throat.

"Boo, dear, please don't strangle him until we know what he's seen," Eleanor said calmly. "And pray tell, why are you not searching the Faire grounds for the Doctor?"

"Because Robert is no longer here and you know it!" the gruff voice behind him said.

"Oh, dear!" Ruth whined, "please don't kill him. He needs food. Shall I set another place for the detective at dinner?"

Eleanor looked at Mathers. "Are you hungry, Detective?"

"Abbey," he gasped. "She's gone."

Eleanor nodded slowly. "Yes, we know. We've already begun searching for her. When Merlin arrives, perhaps he shall give us more information about Robert." She turned to Tomyris, who stood re-braiding her hair. "Have the dogs found Merlin?"

Tomyris nodded. "They are bringing him now. Merlin is injured. Stabbed."

"Dear!" Ruth said, clamping her hands over her mouth. "I shall get the healing potions."

"Robert?" Mathers tried to say through his clenched windpipe. Eleanor motioned to Boo and the grip on his neck loosened. "You mean Abbey's uncle Robert?" The arm wrapped itself around his neck again. "What do you know about Robert?" Boo shouted. "Where is he?"

Mathers tried to shake his head. "I...don't...know!" He gasped for air. "Lynn Swanson mentioned him. He is coming to the Faire with her tomorrow. She asked me to check on Abbey because her Uncle Robert told her Abbey was in danger."

"From who?" Boo demanded.

"From you."

"Well," Zenobia said, appearing in the doorway, "why should we take the detective's word for it?" She looked to Eleanor. "I say we keep him in the basement until tomorrow night."

Livia appeared out of the thicket of trees. Her business suit remained perfectly pressed, although bits of leaves and twigs clung to the hem. "I have researched the detective thoroughly. I say we question him regarding the disappearance."

"Agreed," Eleanor nodded at Boo. "Besides, a police officer would be missed if he disappeared."

"Damn," Tomyris sneered at him, "he would look fabulous in chains."

"Can…you…let…me…go…now?" Mathers gasped.

Just then a crash through the trees silenced them. Stumbling through the undergrowth was the horse that Mathers saw stabbed in the field by the Grim Reaper. It favored its hind quarters, where blood ran down its flank. Two of the large dogs that had herded Mathers towards the mansion accompanied it. The horse stopped, looked to the group, and spoke.

"I seem to have run into a bit of trouble."

Mathers felt the arm around his throat loosen and he collapsed onto the grass, staring up into the eyes of the talking horse.

"Well, Detective," Ruth's voice came from behind him. "Do you like roasted chicken and Couscous?"

ABBEY CHEWED THE DRIED MEAT and stared into the man's deep brown eyes. "I'm your wife?"

His head lowered onto his chest. A sob escaped him and he wiped a single tear from his eye. "You were taken from me." He pointed out the window to the burning stake and the pyre. "The shock of the…" he paused before continuing in a broken whisper, "of your death was too much for you. I became erased from your memory. I have been pursuing you through time ever since."

"Why didn't you contact the Bastille? Aunt Eleanor—"

"It was your Aunt Eleanor who aided in this fraud!" Robert spat, leaping to his feet. "She was against our union from the beginning! When the King ordered your death, I tried to save you but those wicked women stood in my way."

Abbey swallowed the meat and shook her head. Her stomach began to churn and the headache began pounding again. "I saw what happened to me from the window. She took me through the Tapestry and she showed me…"

"Showed you what?" Robert demanded. "Showed you burning as she stood watching with that whimpering Ruth? Showed you screaming in pain as she hid safely in the shadows?"

"She said she arrived too late."

"She lied." He knelt before her and rested his hands on her knees. "She wanted you to die, Abbey."

"But Aunt Boo—"

"Boo is a crazy—"

"NO!" Abbey screamed at him. "She showed me how the women replaced my charred corpse with an unknown girl's, because my body was to be burned twice."

Robert's eyes flashed in anger for a moment before more tears flowed. Within that moment, a key twisted in Abbey's mind, unlocking visions of forgotten events. Hazy pictures flooded into her. She remembered Robert's expression of hostility, his eyes narrowing into slits, his lips parting slightly as his teeth bit into his bottom lip.

"Oh," he said. "I did not realize they showed you that memory." He looked into her eyes and smiled. But his eyes belied any sense of humor or compassion. His eyes reflected a glazed, distant rage. She suddenly felt afraid.

"I suppose they also told you that you are Joan of Arc?" He sighed when she nodded. "I was afraid of that. Dear, you are not Joan of Arc. You never were. Immortal, yes. Fierce, yes. Desirable, yes. But a warrior child?" He smiled broadly and shook his head. He leaned in and hugged her tightly.

"You are nobody important to the world. Only to me."

"**M**ORE LAMB, DETECTIVE?" Ruth cooed, holding out another chop toward Mathers. He shook his head.

"So Abbey chatted with a horse, disappeared into a piece of fabric, traveled through time, and now you're going to find her with magic?" he asked the group. The women around the table nodded.

"You need more wine," Ruth said, filling his goblet. "These things make more sense with wine."

"Kinda sucks you have to find out this way," Tomyris said, tossing a bone to the dog on her right, "but it's a shitload of work to search through time. It'll be a while before we find her."

"I shall brew coffee!" Ruth smiled. "We need coffee with the cobbler. Detective, do you like cherry cobbler or peach?"

"Excuse me," he said, standing up, "but I'm going to find Abbey."

"Detective," Eleanor asked as he stormed out of the room, "how shall you do so?"

He spun around to stare at her. "Start at the scene of the disappearance. Standard protocol."

"And then what? You saw her disappear. That is what you said, is it not?"

He stared at Eleanor for a moment before responding. "I said that's what it *looked* like."

"And we are telling you that is what it is," she said, wiping her mouth on the silk napkin.

"But that's impossible."

"And we are telling you that it is not." Eleanor patted the table. "Please sit down. Have some of Ruth's cobbler."

Ruth nodded. "I have Rice Krispy treats, oatmeal bars—"

"This is going to be a P.R. nightmare," Livia said, laying her head on the table. "We must get a gag order against the detective now."

"Livia, you must relax. This is not the first time a mortal has become embroiled in the business of the Tapestry." Eleanor reached out for Mathers' hand. "For example, look at Elfi and Sarah Reisner."

Mathers stared at the woman. "I knew you knew something about them."

Eleanor laughed. "My dear man, I know everything about them."

He leaned in closer to her and stared into her eyes. "Then explain to me how they share your DNA."

"Oh, dear, no!" Ruth said, emerging from the kitchen with two cobblers. "And Elfi and Sarah are my descendants. Be careful, those are hot." She motioned to the cobblers. "They are born from my granddaughter's granddaughter. See, she bred with an Immortal as well and…"

"Eleanor!" Zenobia cried as she rushed into the dining room. "I have a location on Abbey."

S HE FORCED A SMILE as Robert tapped the end of her nose lightly with his finger. "Shall I bring more water when I return?"

"Yes, please."

"Very well, my love." He replaced the dishes on the silver tray. He leaned in to kiss her and Abbey turned her cheek to him.

"What? No passion for your husband?" He grabbed the silver tray and headed to the door. "I shall only be gone a moment. Can I get you anything else?"

"Only the tea, please," she said, shaking her head. "This headache distracts me so! As well as upsets my stomach. I fear I do not feel well."

"Many women with child feel the same way," he said with a wink. He left, locking the door behind him.

Abbey leapt to her feet. She had no guarantee how long fetching tea would keep him out of the room. Before he returned she needed to see what, if any, she had at her disposal. She reached out to an enormous dark mahogany dresser with deep drawers and elaborate gold knobs. She flung the middle drawer open and explored its contents. Articles of clothing, scarves and other miscellaneous garments spilled out, but nothing to help her. Robert was lying. But lying about what? What was he hiding? She needed something to trigger her memory and fill in the missing pieces of the puzzle. More than that, she needed a weapon.

She found nothing unusual in the second drawer, so she moved onto the next drawer with the same results. She repeated this maneuver with the remaining drawers but found nothing but clothing and trinkets.

As she turned away from the dresser, her eyes fell upon a small bejeweled box sitting atop the dresser. Constructed of hammered metal with crudely constructed bolts, it looked out of place in these lavish surroundings. She snatched it up and flipped the top open. Several articles of women's jewelry lay inside.

Then she saw something lying on the bottom of the pile of jewelry. She dug into the necklaces and drew out a broach of wildly colorful jewels. Mickey Mouse. She had seen much of that icon lately, most recently in the Bastille while Aunt Ruth watched the evening news on television. The body discovered buried on the grounds of the Bastille bore a tattoo of Mickey Mouse. It struck the police odd that an old lady would have such a thing.

Abbey dug around at the box and withdrew another chain. A thin piece of gold, perhaps eighteen inches in length, made of thin links. Strung in the middle of the chain was a single word—SARAH. Sarah. She knew that name, too. It was on the same news broadcast. The television anchor spoke of the unusual coincidence of the two bodies belonging to the same family.

Abbey stiffened as the sound of the lock turned. Robert had returned.

"**N**O!" Zenobia insisted, crossing her arms. "It is much too dangerous."

"I agree," Tomyris said, kicking the pile of fabric.

Eleanor sighed and crossed her arms. "Zen, dear, why did you prepare this section of the Tapestry to be repaired first? Surely you knew that this was the logical place to begin our search for Abbey. Once the preparations for repair have begun, we cannot use it to locate her."

Mathers thought he saw a flicker of anger flash across Zenobia's face. "It had the most damage, Eleanor," the woman responded. "It is the most in need of repair."

"If the Spell Zenobia cast showed Abbey can be reached through this section, we must unfold it and—" Boo began.

"No! There is no time! If we unfold it now, then we must recast the spells before it is moved to the Faire site!" Ruth exclaimed. "We cannot break that spell!"

Boo sighed. "Yes," she said, turning to Ruth, "but we must have Abbey's energy during the Ritual, which we will not have if we do not unfold the Tapestry tonight." She turned to Merlin, who stood against the wall, scratching his hind end. His flank showed no signs of the earlier attack, yet the horse favored that side of his body.

Merlin shook his mane and looked at Boo. "I must agree with Ruth. We wait until the Ritual has begun before we unfold this section of Tapestry."

Boo bolted over to him and aligned herself with his eyes. "That is almost twelve hours!" she screamed. "Abbey is in danger *now*."

"The annual Ritual is the coven's first priority."

"She could be dead!"

"If she is dead," Merlin said firmly, "we would have felt her spirit within us. Abbey is very much alive."

"Dear, Robert did not snatch her back through time in order to kill her. He could have done that when he was in this century," Eleanor said.

Boo turned her aggression on Eleanor. "They why did he let her live?"

Eleanor shook her head. "There is something he wants from her. That is how he operates."

"I find it appalling that we allow the girl to fend for herself for the next twelve hours while we do nothing."

"Dear, we will be doing much," Eleanor corrected. "So much that I expect nobody will sleep tonight."

Boo turned and stalked down the corridor stopping only long enough to glare at Zenobia before disappearing around the corner.

"Will someone please tell me what the hell is going on here?" Mathers asked.

"Of course, my boy," Ruth said cheerily. "You can help me with the dishes while I tell you. Oh," she put her arm around him, "you didn't get your dessert, did you?"

"WHAT ARE YOU DOING?" Robert's eyes flashed between Abbey and the dresser. "Were you looking for something?"

Abbey smiled and wrapped the blanket around herself. "A dress. I'm chilly."

Robert smiled and walked towards her holding out a cup of steaming water. "Drink this. It will help your headache and warm you up." Abbey took the mug from him and his eyes flitted from her to around the room.

"It does seem like you were looking for something...specific."

"As I said...something for the chill." She turned away, desperately seeking someplace where she could pour out the tea. She would drink nothing that he brought her. She stood facing the window when she felt his hands caress her shoulders.

"No need to be," he whispered in her ear. "I shall warm you." He grabbed the blanket and pulled. Abbey tugged the blanket out of his hands and wrapped it tightly around herself.

"I told you, I am cold."

"And I told you that I shall warm you." Again, he pulled and she resisted. "Why are you doing this to me?"

"I do nothing to you, Robert," Abbey said. "I am cold."

"Are you saying I cannot be with you? I cannot have you?" He spun her around to face him. Abbey took the opportunity to let the cup slide from her grip. It fell to the floor with a loud clang and the liquid spilled out over the stone.

"Look what you did," his harsh voice rang out. Abbey backed away from him, but he grabbed her by the arms.

"Robert, you're hurting me."

"You are my wife. I told you we will go to bed again and you'll be warm."

"I don't want to." Abbey jerked away. "I hurt. I'm tired."

The slap came without warning. His hand landed squarely across her face and stung her flesh. "Look what you made me do. If only you would listen. You never listen to me."

"Don't do that again, Robert."

"I am your husband. I will do as I see fit, woman." This time when the hand connected, it was a fist. Abbey felt her head jerk and her legs give out from under her. Then the world went black.

MATHERS TOOK THE DISH FROM RUTH and placed it in the dishwasher. "You're talking about time travel."

Ruth giggled. "That sounds so...television-ish!" She squealed in glee.

"So, really, it doesn't matter when you go to find Abbey, as the Tapestry will take you back to whatever time you want."

A horrified look spread across her face. "We love Abbey! The sooner we see her safely back to the Bastille, the better!" She handed the silverware to him. "These load on the side, dear." She watched him slip the forks into the bin before continuing, "We don't know where or when she is. We step through the Tapestry and we may find ourselves arriving at a place before she does. We go back to the exact time that you see in those little scenes sewn into the Tapestry." She took a tall glass from him and set it in the sink. "These I wash by hand. They were gifts."

"So...but wait..." Mathers said, twisting the drying towel around a freshly washed set of forks.

"It is really very simple, actually," Ruth said, sitting Mathers down at the kitchen table. "Let us say you have this fork." She took one of the forks from him and set it on the table. "In the old days, we made them ourselves. Nowadays, it is all machine-done. What a pity!" She sighed and stared off into space for a moment.

"What was I saying? Oh! Yes!" She took the second fork from him. "Now, you cannot use *this* fork because it is the one I made. But you can make one just like it for yourself." She laid the two forks side by side. "This is how the embroideries in the Tapestry work. One can only enter through a scene they themselves have created. So, another Immortal sews their scene which takes place at approximately the same time."

Mathers nodded. "That way, there are always two entry points to any event. And they would only be moments apart."

Ruth smiled and patted him on the head. "Now you've got it! This is the reason the witches of the Tapestry share a similar history." She brushed his cheek. "Whatever time Abbey finds herself in, one of the women in this house will be able to travel back to the same time. Give or take a couple of hours."

"Why are you telling me this?" Mathers stared at her with his hands on the counter. "Why tell me anything about the Tapestry, or...what you ladies do here? Isn't that...dangerous?"

Ruth smiled and pinched his cheek. "Normally, yes."

"But I'm not normal?"

"Oh, my boy, you are anything but normal." Ruth lifted his chin and looked into his eyes. "There is a reason for everything, Matthew."

Her gaze weighed heavily on him and he pulled away after a few seconds. "So we wait?" She nodded. "Until tomorrow?" Ruth nodded again. "What do we do until then?"

"We prepare for the Ritual. You?" She looked him over. "Will shower and go to bed. You'll need your strength."

"Why?" Mathers asked, "what will I do?"

"Why, help save Abbey, of course."

"But you said I couldn't." Mathers shook his head and backed away from Ruth. "I don't get it."

"Dear, you forget. We are witches. We can do so many things. Except camels. Working with camels is...oh! I digress. Just trust me, you never want to work with a camel. But as for traveling back through the Tapestry..." She shook her head and sighed. "Any human can travel back in time." Ruth sounded like she was speaking to a child. Mathers supposed that he must be a child in her eyes. "It is the return trip that kills you."

"Literally," he said quietly. "Just like Elfi and Sarah were killed when they returned from the past."

Ruth nodded. "You'll be trapped in the past if you step through the Tapestry. Try to return and you age proportionately. Here, hand me those, will you?" She reached for the wine glasses and placed them in the dishwater.

"So do I help or not?"

"Oh, yes," Ruth whispered. "Everyone has their part to play. That's God's will." She drained the sink and began to rinse out the suds. "Go, now. Wash. Sleep. There's nothing more for you to do tonight." With that, she watched the suds flow down the drain and began to hum to herself.

LYNN AWOKE THE SATURDAY OF THE BASTILLE'S FAIRE feeling like a truck had run her down. Her muscles ached, her head throbbed, and she felt so agitated that she wanted to hit someone. Where was Martha when she needed her? Backhanding that anal-retentive controlling wench would make her day just a bit brighter.

She rushed through her shower, threw on her new hiking boots (she overpaid but they looked fabulous and felt even better), and topped her outfit with a loose-fitting blouse reminiscent of the medieval period. By the time she arrived at The Meadows, she was nursing her second double mocha and was feeling much better about the day's prospects. She had even lost her urge to pummel Martha.

"Lynn? So I have everything together, right? And the patients all have their passes and stuff?" Heather looked awake, vibrant and ready for action. It seemed to Lynn that no matter what time of the day the girl was working, she always managed to look great. *Bitch.* "Did you sign out the van or should I?" Lynn asked, going into the nurse's station.

"It's done. And it has gas in it and parked out back, you see?"

"What time did you get here?" Lynn asked, glancing at her watch. It was only seven o'clock.

"Oh, just about…half an hour ago?"

"All that in a half hour?" Heather nodded and readjusted the diamond bracelet on her perfectly manicured hand. *Double bitch.* "Let's load 'em up, then."

To Lynn's surprise, the group was so excited about the excursion that they offered no resistance to Lynn's directions. Even Mrs. Bailey and Feng Shi posed no objection to the seating arrangement. "Feng Shi is excited," Mrs. Bailey said. "He doesn't get out much. He wants to run free in the weeds this afternoon."

"That's great, Mrs. Bailey," Lynn smiled. She made a mental note to alert Heather to the heightened probability that they would be chasing down a naked Mrs. Bailey as she spread her joy through the field.

"I love this outfit!" Mr. Rix said, twirling so Lynn could see his clothing. She had to agree with him; he looked like he stepped through a time machine. Decked out in cotton pants, a doublet, and sporting a short haircut, he looked exactly like the picture of Joan of Arc from the encyclopedia. Not that she would have any idea what Joan of Arc actually looked like.

Edna was the last to board. She wore a simple peasant's costume made of burlap and held two huge, round loaves of bread in her arms. "My daughter brought these from Hannaford's," she explained. "My granddaughter made these in her home economics class." She modeled the dress for Lynn. "Want to touch my buns?"

"Maybe later."

Edna looked around. "Where's Heather?"

"She's on her way. Paperwork." Lynn glanced at her watch. She was due to pick up Robert by 7:30 and it was almost 7:20 now.

"HURRY UP YOU IGNORANT BITCH!" Edna screamed. As if on cue, Heather toddled out of the door, pulling it shut behind her. "WE'RE ALL WAITING FOR YOU, STUPID!"

"Edna? Your language?"

Edna patted Lynn on the shoulder. "We can go now." Then, back to Heather, "BE CAREFUL, YOU MORON! I'M NOT STOPPING AT THE HOSPITAL BECAUSE YOU'RE CLUMSY!"

"Edna? I like your bread...it's cute, isn't it?"

Edna stared at Heather with her mouth agape. After a moment, she closed her mouth, got into the van and settled down with the others, being extra careful not to awaken Feng Shi who was deeply asleep in Mrs. Bailey's bosom.

78

MATHERS AWOKE TO THE FEEL OF WETNESS ON HIS NECK. He opened his eyes and stared into the huge marble eyes of Merlin.

"If you want to break your fast, I dare say you are on your own." Merlin nudged him lightly. "The women have begun the Ritual."

Mathers sat up and looked at the clock. Seven-ten. "So early?"

The horse nodded and chuckled. "They were gone before dawn. Boudicca has been awake all night." Merlin backed up and clapped his hoof on the ground. "Let us be off. There is much to do."

Mathers stumbled out of bed and looked for his clothes. "Where are my clothes?"

Merlin trotted to the door. "Ruth decided they needed to be washed. But nakedness violates the Faire rules. Come. I have more appropriate clothing for you."

"Can I have a robe or something? I'm naked."

"I am over eight hundred years old," Merlin chuckled. "I have seen much. I doubt you will show me anything new." Merlin walked out the door adding, "I cannot bring clothes for you—I temporarily lack opposable thumbs."

Mathers sighed and followed, walking naked down the corridors of a castle following a talking horse. Definitely a first.

As they walked through the kitchen, Merlin paused outside a door leading into a small laundry room. Behind it, Mathers spied a folding table with a pair of medieval-looking pants, shirt and vest hanging from a rack above it. As he crossed the kitchen linoleum, the door burst open and Tomyris' dogs bounded into the room. They spied him and ran to his side, sniffing at his crotch. "I do not understand why you organized them in this order," Ruth's voice filtered in.

"I…was so upset by the events, I wasn't thinking clearly," Zenobia said as she entered. She glanced at Mathers, nodded, and continued walking, disappearing into the depths of the Bastille.

"Ruth, have we anything for food?" Boo asked as she thundered into the room. She was also naked except for a huge broadsword around her waist, Mathers noticed, making him less self-conscious about his own nudity. She was also painted blue, making him feel somehow inadequate.

"Of course," Ruth said as she spied Mathers. "Good morning! Cinnamon roll?"

Mathers couldn't decide which was more embarrassing, standing naked in front of several women or the fact that none of them noticed his nakedness. He looked down. Well, there was that shrinkage factor to consider.

"Yes, please. Coffee?" he asked. One of the dogs stuck a cold nose into his butt crack and he jumped. "I'm going to get dressed."

"Don't let me stop you," Tomyris said from behind him. Jeweled fringe hung from her sides, her top barely covered her breasts, and thigh-high boots made her legs look like they extended into her shoulders. She stood leaning against the kitchen door and eyeing him up and down.

Mathers nodded and pushed past Merlin into the laundry room to fetch his clothes.

"You shall have to drink it on the go," Ruth called into the laundry room. "There is much work on the Faire grounds to do. You can eat while you walk."

"Merlin!" Boudicca's voice cried. "We need your strength!"

The horse snorted and backed out of the kitchen. "I am an Immortal, woman! Not a pack horse."

"Well, dear, you do look like one," Ruth crooned, handing Mathers his coffee and cinnamon roll. "I have that nasty pistol of yours if you want it."

Mathers nodded and followed Ruth into the kitchen. He felt comfortable in the Faire clothes. They hung loosely around him and the cotton felt soft against his skin. He wished he had some underwear, though; he liked more support. It bothered him to have his equipment flopping around. He shoved his feet into the boots as Ruth reached for an ornate ceramic sugar container. She lifted the lid, reached in and pulled out his gun. She blew the granules of powder from the barrel and handed it to him.

Just then Merlin came back, a huge section of the Tapestry upon his back. Tomyris, Boo and Zenobia followed, each with a hand on the fabric to steady it.

"Come," Boo said, motioning for Mathers to follow.

79

AT 7:45, THE VAN FULL OF PEOPLE BEGAN TO GET IRRITABLE. Joan of Arc began changing the lyrics of Barbra Streisand songs to match the fourteenth century ('don't rain on my armada!), Edna had relinquished one of her buns to Mr. Graves, and Feng Shi had awakened horny.

Lynn sighed and looked around for Robert. She had been stalling, suspecting he had awakened late, or perhaps had car trouble. But at 7:47, she had to admit that he wasn't joining them. Just her luck. Not only had she been dumped in the twenty-first century, now she could be ignored on her way to the fourteenth. Well, at least she had the receipt for the boots. If they didn't get destroyed she could always return them.

80

"THE RITUAL HAS BEGUN," Eleanor whispered to Mathers. "Just in time. The Faire workers will arrive in an hour."

"And you don't do this inside?" Mathers whispered. The Tapestry lay a few yards from the central hub of the Faire grounds on an enormous, round wooden table, surrounded by small three-legged stools. Several women whom Mathers did not recognize sat around the table with Tomyris, Boudicca, Ruth and Livia. They all had their eyes closed and were chanting softly. As they worked, nimble fingers sewed the tears and rips in the Tapestry using a heavy thread that resembled yarn.

As he stood whispering to Eleanor, a loud hum sounded and a large, bearded man wearing silk clothing and a cloak emerged from the Tapestry and stood looking around the knoll. Livia whispered in his ear and the man nodded. He immediately stepped behind the seated women and began to chant in time to their stitching. Two of the seated women stood up and moved to either side of him. They joined hands, creating a human shield between the Faire grounds and the Tapestry's table.

"Partly due to tradition," Eleanor answered, "partly pragmatics. Since we don't know who and what emerges, we need space. What if a knight and steed leapt out of the Tapestry?" She gestured to the woods. "Why do you think we needed so many acres?"

"I thought it was for privacy."

Eleanor smiled and grabbed his hand. "That, too."

Suddenly the Tapestry billowed and hummed. The women stopped sewing and clutched the edges of the fabric, holding it onto the wooden table. The chanting grew louder and a loud *POP* crackled through the air.

"Someone tried to exit who should not have done so," said Eleanor. Mathers had a quizzical look. "The Tapestry functions as a prison as well."

"For?"

"For those who are imprisoned, of course." Eleanor broke away from him and joined the group, blocking the view of the Tapestry. She closed her eyes and began chanting along with them. Mathers stood dumbly for a moment until he felt a presence at his side.

"There is no more for you to do," Merlin said in his ear. "When it is time, we need your help to cover Boo and Eleanor. When they enter the Tapestry to save Abbey."

Mathers turned back to the small table and watched as another figure sprung from the Tapestry. How in the hell did the women hide the fact that people emerged from a huge piece of fabric on a low wooden table?

81

"**M**Y CONTACT WAS LIVIA EMERSON," Lynn told the petite woman dressed in a lion costume. The young woman's skin was deeply tan, rough and scarred, like she had spent years foraging in the woods for survival.

"Livia's busy," the woman's accent sounded familiar to Lynn, although she couldn't place it. Without another word, the woman gestured to two other women dressed in animal skins and the three approached Lynn's patients.

"I'm sorry, but if I could just speak to Livia for a moment?" Lynn asked. The three cave women stared at her in disbelief and murmured to each other in a foreign language.

"Please leave her alone," the petite one said. She then motioned for Mr. Graves, Joan of Arc and Edna. "Follow me. I will show you your duties." While the lion woman motioned to the three, the remaining two fur-clad cave women ushered Mr. Chow and Mrs. Bailey towards the opposite side of the Faire grounds. Lynn suddenly found herself alone with Heather.

"Well, that was weird."

"Oh?" Heather cooed. Lynn turned to see a tall, thin, geeky-looking man with thick glasses dressed as the Grim Reaper stride up to Heather. They kissed passionately before Heather turned to Lynn. "This is, like, Harry?"

Lynn didn't think she was able to hide her shock. She had Heather pegged as someone who would date only rich New England doctors.

82

JOSHUA SWORE AND TURNED DOWN THE VOLUME ON STICKY FINGERS.
"Boss?"

The Doctor turned from the window and looked at Joshua through the rearview mirror. "What is it?"

"It's totally freakin' crowded already," Joshua said, waving to the officer directing traffic. "I thought the Faire didn't open until nine." He screamed at nobody in particular.

"Let me out here."

"Are you sure? It's like...totally far to the entry gate," Joshua said. "It's got to be...wow...probably half a mile."

"I can walk," the Doctor said, opening the back door. He walked to the driver's side window of the limo and leaned into Joshua. "Just remember what I told you."

"I know," Joshua nodded. "The rendezvous, the time, I know, I know."

The Doctor stared at Joshua a moment before saying, "you are becoming rather cocky, my young friend." Joshua felt the man's eyes boring into him before the Doctor turned to go.

When he saw the Doctor shuffling towards the entrance gate, Joshua cranked the Stones and idled through traffic. Maybe he'd go grab breakfast downtown. If he was a few minutes late to pick up the Doc and Robert, it was no big deal. What? They would kill him?

83

SHE STOOD AT THE STAKE, bound so tightly she couldn't feel her fingers. Around her the people taunted her. She felt no anger, only pity. For those who prey upon the weak deserved nothing else. They have lost their way from God. But God had not lost his way to them.

She felt its heat beneath the soles of her boots. As her clothing caught fire, she smelled the scent of burning flesh. She called to God and pleaded with him for a quick death. It was then, as she lifted her head to the heavens, her eyes stinging with smoke, that she saw two things simultaneously.

First, she saw two figures staring at her. One man and one woman. The man, tall, dark, stunningly handsome with perfectly white teeth stood grinning at her. He pulled a woman towards him and pointed. The woman, red-haired, young, plump with chubby cheeks, waved as Abbey felt the flames crawl along her arms. On the girl's plump arm, Abbey saw a colorful imprint, as if the woman had a picture stenciled on her skin.

Something caught her eye to her other side. A woman stood watching her; a woman with flowing white dress and angelic face. She wept uncontrollably, sobs wracking her body. Her guardian angel! God had heard her cries and answered by sending this—

Then a second figure appeared next to the angel. This figure was a short woman, thinner and older. She held something in her hands… could it be bread? Did this second angel offer baked goods at the time of her death? Would she meet God only to be greeted with sweets?

The flames licked at her clothes and she cried out in pain as the burning consumed her legs. She looked directly at the angel and screamed the Lord's name. Miraculously, the angel looked at her and their eyes met.

It was no angel. It was Eleanor. Beside Eleanor was Ruth. She turned her head towards the strange red-haired woman and handsome man. She remembered his name: Robert. Robert and his captive, Sarah, kidnapped from the future, during an era when Robert lived in a country across the ocean. The flames ate at her shirt now and her breasts began to bake. The events of the past months rushed through her mind. She had learned of a plot by Robert and the Doctor to snatch women with Immortal blood from the future and impregnate them in the past. They planned to wrench control from the women of the Bastille and use the Tapestry's power for themselves. They had already killed one woman— Elfi—and now kidnapped Elfi's descendant. Abbey tried to reason with Robert, but their talk turned violent as he hit her. He tried to rape her, driven crazy by the idea of fathering a child. They fought.

This was not a new issue of contention for them; Abbey had rebuked him many times over the years; each time she was the voice of calm reason and his was the voice of a man driven to the edge of sanity by lust. He claimed Abbey as his property years ago, back before she was the mouthpiece for God. Back then, she was young and ignorant to the ways of men and stood her grounds as a girl would—with coy words and avoidance. Now the time of the girl was through.

She should have killed him that day long ago. But her heart defied her rational mind and rather than kill him, she solicited a promise that he would stop his misuse of the Tapestry. He betrayed her. Now he stood watching her burn, relishing the death of the only person who knew his secret. The only person who had the knowledge and strength to stop him. She knew Robert would make sure she didn't resurrect from this death. This was the end of her Immortal life.

As the flames ignited her hair and boiled her arms, she tried to cry to Eleanor and Ruth. "ROBERT! STOP ROBERT!"

The roar of the crowd drowned her out. Her words became lost in the din of the crowd. The last thing she saw as the smoke and flame consumed her was Eleanor and Ruth crying in despair.

MATHERS STOOD TRANSFIXED BY THE SIGHT. For the past hour, he watched as the Immortals worked with smooth precision. Before the main gate opened and the townspeople filtered into the living museum, some twenty or thirty people emerged from the fabric. Instantly, they crowded behind the sewing women and took their position among the throng, joining hands and chanting. After that lot stepped out, several people wove their way from the crowd onto the table, disappearing into an embroidered scenario. When through, the women around the Tapestry stood, folded the section of fabric in an elaborate pattern, accompanied by a song of loud rejoicing, and carried it away to the base of the ancient oak tree.

The first wave of Immortals, having just emerged from history, picked up the next section to be repaired and brought it to the low table. In less than an hour, the Immortals had repaired three of the twenty-five by twenty-five sections and were working on their fourth. There were many more exiting than entering, thus leaving a huge crowd of onlookers to block the view from the general public.

Mathers looked behind him and noticed many familiar faces from town: Janet and Sal, the mayor, the busty high school girl from the Dairy Queen, and the waitress from the diner. Lynn Swanson stood at the edge of the throng, looking dynamite in her peasant shirt and tight jeans. He smiled at her, but she didn't see him.

"It's time," Eleanor said.

He looked at her and she nodded. He nodded back. As she led him to the huge wooden table, the group of seamstresses stood, folded the fabric and carried it away. They were replaced by women who unrolled another huge section of Tapestry that was particularly tattered and torn.

"Remember," Eleanor said, "stay here. I do not know what will happen when we emerge, but it is sure to be exciting."

"I want to go with you."

She shook her head. "Impossible."

"Eleanor," he said in a quick, hushed tone.

She squeezed his arm. She looked up as the women spread the fabric out and flattened it onto the table. "The spell I cast should give the embroidered entry point a soft golden glow to it."

Mathers glanced over. Exactly as Eleanor had said, there was a faint glow hovering over a section of the fabric. "What will happen if you… you know." She shrugged. "I shall be lost to history. But that is of little consequence. We are already lost to history, are we not?" She broke away from him and patted his shoulder. "If we do not see each other again, it was a pleasure, Detective Mathers." He watched her weave through the crowd and stand next to the table. The women began their chant. Then Mathers saw a flicker of light from behind Eleanor and looked up to see Zenobia standing within a cluster of Immortals, chanting. Her eyes were wide and she stood peering at Eleanor with an odd grimace on her face. In her hand, she grasped a huge knife which reflected the sunlight streaming through the trees.

He acted on instinct. He leapt forward and shoved through the crowd. He threw the prone bodies aside and reached the table in three strides. "No!" he shouted, reaching for Eleanor. Then several things happened at once.

The chanting stopped and he heard someone scream. Zenobia shoved the knife into Eleanor, who stumbled from the impact, flailing at the air. Eleanor grabbed Mather's wrist to stabilize herself, but the momentum from the thrust sent her tumbling into the Tapestry and through the glowing embroidered patchwork.

And Mathers fell into the Tapestry with her.

S HE OPENED HER EYES and found herself staring at the stone floor. Her head pounded and her face ached. Images spun through her mind: Robert, Elfi, Sarah, smoke, fire, flashes of swords, fists hitting her face, blood running down her shoulders—memories spinning into a kaleidoscope of visions.

Then it stopped. Like a curtain rising, she saw all of her Immortal lives in a clear dawning of understanding.

She remembered who she was.

She felt a tickle on her chin and scratched herself. Blood stuck to her fingertips. Robert had broken her skin.

"Do you see what you made me do?" he asked. "If you would listen to me, I would not have to hit you!" He stood over her, fists clenched in rage, his eyes flashing in anger.

"You need to learn your place! Who do you think you are?"

"I am Jehanne d'Arc, daughter of Jacques and Isabelle d'Arc. I am Amelia Earhart. I am Abbey Emerson. I am an Immortal witch and a woman of the Bastille."

With a quick jerk, she brought her foot up between his legs, connecting with the soft tissue. He doubled over in pain and she bent both her legs, then let fly with a double kick to his stomach. Robert flew backwards, landing with a loud thud on the stone floor. He rolled in agony as she stood over him.

She stepped to him and placed her foot on his throat. "And you, Robert de Baudricourt, are a traitor."

Detective Mathers felt the hard stone slam into him and he rolled across something cold and wet. He lay on his back, staring up at a high beamed ceiling in what appeared to be some kind of small storage room.

"I see you came along for the ride," Eleanor's voice came from beside him.

He tilted his head and saw her grinning at him. "I didn't have anything else to do today."

She reached down and offered him a hand. "This does cause problems, Detective." He went to take her hand and saw blood covering her palm.

"Zenobia. She stabbed you."

Eleanor nodded. "I know. Merlin and I have long suspected Zenobia of such treachery, and this confirms our suspicions. Will you take my hand or not?"

"You need help. How bad is the wound?" He stood up and tenderly lifted her arm, inspecting her side for the entry point.

"Detective," she snapped, "I cannot be killed by this, I assure you. And as for the blood," she wiped her hand on her dress, "my son led one of the bloodiest massacres in history. Perhaps you've heard of him? His name was Richard?"

Mathers saw a smirk spread across her face and smiled back. "Sorry. I...it's an occupational hazard."

"No," she said, taking him by the hand. "You are a male. And it is delightful to see chivalry these days. I thought it had gone the way of the boot strap." She tugged him towards the door.

"Eleanor," a thought suddenly striking him, "if Zenobia knows that wound wouldn't have killed you, why did she stab you there?"

Eleanor's smile faltered for a split second before she tugged at his arm and said, "Come. Let us find our girl."

Abbey never saw the punch coming. One moment she stood on Robert's throat, staring down at him, the next she flew across the room and landed on the floor, her head cracking on the stone. By the time the black spots before her eyes disappeared, Robert had made it to the door and out.

She jumped to her feet and ran after him. She tackled him as he half-ran, half- limped down the corridor. They tumbled across the floor, the rough masonry tearing at her shoulder and skinning her knees. He recovered quickly, kicking her aside and sending streaks of pain down her arm where his boot made contact. She screamed. Robert chuckled.

"France's best warrior, eh?" he spat on her and ran.

She clawed at the wall, pulling herself to her feet. Robert hobbled around the corner towards the streak of sunlight ricocheting off the walls in the intersecting hallway. Her hand brushed against something and she looked down. The wall she had used for leverage contained several weapons hanging from crude metal hooks. She snatched a foil and a long dagger and took off after Robert.

Eleanor and Mathers inched down the corridor. They had just turned the second corner when they heard a woman's scream coming from behind them.

"Abbey!" Eleanor gasped.

Just then they heard Robert's voice resounding in a fierce, angry tone. "France's best warrior, eh?"

Eleanor nodded to the detective and they turned to run towards the voice.

Abbey caught up to Robert as he approached the doorway inside the small recess of the wall. She threw herself at him, knocking him off-balance and the two of them crashed through the door and into the tiny storage room.

Abbey clawed at him as Robert scrambled along the floor towards the arched window. Just as his hands reached up to grab the windowsill, Abbey swung around on her butt, connecting her foot with his gut. The force sent him rolling onto his back, his head resting against the wall underneath the small porthole.

"Want an Immortal child, do you?" Abbey sneered. "Be my guest." She plunged the small dagger into his crotch, where it pierced his genitals and stuck into the crevice between two stone blocks.

"Immortal women decide with whom to conceive."

"Abbey?"

Abbey spun around to see Eleanor and Mathers standing at the doorway.

As Mathers reached the doorway to the small room, the first thing he noticed was that Eleanor wasn't going inside. The second was that from his vantage point behind Eleanor, he could see Robert sitting beneath a window with a dagger sticking out of his crotch and blood oozing across the stones.

"What have you done?" Eleanor gasped.

"I am Jehanne d'Arc, and I do what must be done."

Eleanor rushed into the room and lifted her from the floor. "Welcome back." She wrapped the young woman in her arms and held her tightly.

Mathers stood transfixed, not knowing if he should address the fact that Abbey was naked, or that Robert had a knife sticking out of his crotch. He slipped off his doublet and stepped into the room, holding the garment out in front of him. Eleanor took it graciously and wrapped it around Abbey. Thankfully, it was too large for him, so on Abbey's small frame it hung like a very large T-shirt.

As he turned back towards Robert, Mathers spied him pulling a piece of fabric out of a crack in the wall beneath the window.

"Eleanor!" he shouted as he leapt at Robert.

"You think I had no escape plan?" Robert laughed as he unfurled the Tapestry.

Then all went black.

M<small>R. GRAVES SIGHED AND WISHED</small> Mrs. Bailey would either shut up or go back to making love to Feng Shi. He didn't care which one the crazy coot did, but if she started talking about spreading her joy one more time, he would have to—

He saw movement in the trees several yards on the other side of the rope that separated the Faire grounds and the Bastille's woods, which he knew were the ones that were off limits to the public. The small clump of foliage was too far away for him to get a good look, so he ducked under the yellow nylon rope and strode towards the scene of the disturbance. As he walked towards the area, the bushes parted and he saw a young man emerge, smiling broadly and counting bills as he walked towards the Faire grounds. What the—?

After taking another few steps, Mr. Graves saw a second figure emerge from the shrubbery and he froze, his blood running cold. The Grim Reaper was here. The Grim Reaper had found his way to the Bastille and stood less than a hundred yards away.

Abbey. He must save Abbey from Death. As Mr. Graves stood wondering about the best way to approach Death, the Grim Reaper lit a cigarette. Why would Death be smoking a cigarette?

He had no time to lose. If he didn't stop Death, the Reaper would pay a visit to Abbey and that was not acceptable. As the cloaked figure headed back towards the Faire grounds, Mr. Graves broke into a run, closing the gap between himself and the smoking Death. He may die today, but at least he would die saving Abbey.

FOR THE SECOND TIME TODAY Mathers fell through time. One moment he felt himself reaching out to Robert, the next he felt himself being pulled through a black emptiness. When he opened his eyes, he found himself sitting in the middle of the small wooden table on top of the Tapestry while the near-naked Abbey tumbled out of Eleanor's embrace and onto the grass amid the gasps of surprised onlookers.

"Robert the traitor!" Boo screamed, leaping out of the crowd, sword in hand. She wore only blue paint and an angry expression. Boo flung herself against Zenobia, who clutched a knife in one hand and drew a sword from within her dress with the other. Instantly, the two women began flailing at each other, sending the sound of clashing swords ringing through the air.

Mathers felt movement to his left and turned to find himself staring into Robert's sly grin. "Immortals heal very, very quickly," he whispered before pulling the dagger from his crotch and plunging it into Mathers' side. "Do you?"

"No!" Abbey screamed and jumped, slamming into Robert and sending them both rolling off the table and onto the ground. Mathers looked at the dagger sticking from his side and felt strong hands pulling him from the table. He looked into the eyes of Tomyris who blew him a kiss and winked. Then she mumbled something in a language he did not understand and darkness descended upon him.

EDNA HAD HER SIGHTS SET ON THE YOUNG MAN with the full head of red hair and thick beard. He reminded her of her first husband, God rest his soul, who said he couldn't take Edna's craziness anymore and disappeared in his Ford F-160. True, several weeks later they found him in a snow bank frozen to death, but Edna always carried a bit of guilt about killing him. If she wasn't insane, he wouldn't have left and then he would never have crashed into the snow bank and died. He always liked her buns and if she were able to get this cute guy to squeeze her buns, then she could make up for killing her first husband.

She heard a scream off in the distance and turned to see Mr. Graves chasing the Grim Reaper. Death was touching himself and Mr. Graves shouted obscenities. Everyone knew that Mr. Graves didn't swear. Mr. Graves didn't even talk. If Death got him to talk, this was a very, very serious thing.

"Edna!" Mr. Graves shouted, waving at her. "Death wants Abbey!"

Edna's blood ran cold. Death is after her little Abbey? "Well, he can't have her!" Edna screamed and ran towards Death and Mr. Graves.

Just then, a loud crash came from her right, near where the women were having the quilting demonstration. Mr. Chow appeared from behind the ale booth, both hands covering his crotch.

"People are coming out of the quilt!" he screamed in a shrill voice. "All kinds of crazy people are coming out of the Tapestry!"

"It's true!" Mrs. Bailey said, huffing and puffing from the opposite direction. "I seen 'em. They want Feng Shi!"

"They want my dick! Everyone wants my dick!" shouted Mr. Chow.

"Death is after Abbey!" Edna insisted.

"Stay away from my dick!" As if on cue, Boudicca and Zenobia erupted from the trees, swords clanking.

"They're coming to cut my dick off!" Mr. Chow kept yelling.

As the two Immortals struck swords, Edna handed a loaf of bread to Mr. Chow. "Hold this." The short man kept one hand clutching his groin and grabbed the loaf of bread in the other. With the deft of a major league pitcher, Edna weighed the bread in her hand, took aim and let the loaf fly with amazing force. It hit Zenobia directly in the back of the head and the woman stumbled as the blue woman's sword came down on her arm. The poor girl screamed in pain and fell to the ground, clutching her wound. With blinding speed, the blue woman grabbed Zenobia by the neck and hauled her off into the trees.

"And that," Edna said with a flourish, "is how hard stale bread can become."

A thundering sound exploded from behind her and a huge Frisian horse ran past and leapt into the clump of trees where the two warriors had disappeared. "This is a very busy place," Mr. Chow noted as he let go of his dick.

"Move!" Edna commanded. "Mr. Graves needs to stop Death!"

They set off at a run towards Mr. Graves and Death. As they ran, Edna could hear Mr. Chow yelling along the way, "The quilt! People come out of the quilt! It births people! Live births! Go see the live births!"

People shot them startled looks, but Edna didn't mind. Fuck 'em. At least they gave her a wide berth and didn't slow them down. Who knew how much damage Mr. Graves would suffer at the hands of Death. From somewhere she heard a woman scream, "There's a crazy, fat black lady beating people up for Feng Shi."

"Over here!" she heard Mr. Graves scream. Edna pushed Mr. Chow and Mrs. Bailey towards the voice and the trio rounded a tree to be greeted by Death at the edge of a clearing, holding a large knife toward Mr. Graves, who lay beneath him, pinned by Death's legs. Edna grabbed Mr. Chow's arm and pulled him to a stop.

"You take any steps closer, and we shall play with the knife, shant we?" Death chuckled at them and put the blade of the knife against Mr. Graves's throat.

"No!" Edna screamed. "Don't take him. Take me. I killed my husband."

"Just don't take my dick," Mr. Chow said.

"SHUT UP YOU IGNORANT PIECE OF SHIT, I'M TRYING TO SAVE A LIFE HERE!" Edna shouted at Mr. Chow.

Death smiled. "Let's see what he looks like inside, shall we?"

From out of the trees behind the Grim Reaper, Joan of Arc plowed through the low-hanging branches, sword in hand.

"You!" Death whispered. "Where's Robert? What have you done to him?"

The minute the knife was away from his body, Mr. Graves punched Death in the jaw. The knife went flying and Death fell backwards on the ground, out cold.

"I used to box," Mr. Graves said to nobody in particular.

"And Joan saves the day!" Mr. Rix screamed over the unconscious Death.

89

"**I** UNDERSTAND THAT SOME OF YOU ARE SURPRISED by what you saw here today, but that is one of our goals here at the Bastille—to reintroduce what has been forgotten into our modern society. Nudity: in the days gone by, nudity was a part of life and held little shame. Fierce fighting: in our time of distance killing via missiles and bullets, we often forget the horror of what hand-to-hand combat looked like. We at the Bastille hold onto our traditions, our history and our bond to the past. Thank you for your support and we look forward to seeing you all next year."

Livia smiled broadly and shook hands with the mayor as flashbulbs went off all around.

"Well," Eleanor said as Ruth clicked the remote and shut down the television, "you sure do know how to sell even the worst disaster."

"Yes," Livia said, brushing her hair back over her terry cloth robe. "I do."

"Well done, dear," Eleanor said, patting Livia's hand. "Well done."

The minute the crowd started to become unruly from the sword fights and naked people, Livia threw on her Louis Vuitton jacket, climbed atop the nearest stool, and called for attention. What followed was one of the most amazing media spins Eleanor had ever seen.

But even after Livia's impromptu speech, the Faire grounds remained a zoo with people rushing around unchecked, as all the security personnel had wandered off in search of more naked females. The women decreed to close the grounds early and began ushering people out. The evacuation took far less time than Eleanor had expected it to take, leaving the Ladies of the Bastille in peace long enough to imprison the Doctor within the Tapestry.

Zenobia put up no argument about being a part of the Great Ritual, as Eleanor expected. Regardless of her politics, everyone knew the work of the Guardians knows no political boundary. It is the one jurisdiction of all the Immortals.

As the women began the final Binding Spell chant, Merlin strode up to the small table and leaned on Abbey's shoulder. Abbey's one hand gripped Eleanor's, and the other clutched Ruth's while she leaned back into Merlin's strong shoulder. A shiver of pleasure ran through Eleanor then, as if a long tight muscle had been relaxed. With Abbey back in the fold, the Guardians functioned at full power and the sensation was exhilarating. Unlike the years during Abbey's amnesia stupor, the moment the circle began the Chant of Rejuvenation, an electric pulse radiated through their arms and shoulders. As the chant built to its crescendo, Abbey's strong voice rang out with the Spell of Closure. She had always sung those chords flawlessly and during her time away, Ruth was a close second. But Ruth's voice lacked Abbey's sweetness and range. Ruth's lungs lacked the force to send the ancient words through the air like Abbey could. And when the time came to repair the magics surrounding the Tapestry's borders and the knife was passed around the circle, it was Abbey who took the final cut. By the time Abbey's blood dripped onto the cloth, Eleanor could feel the air lying thick against her skin. She breathed in the scent of honeysuckle and rose, luxuriating in the quiver that ran through her.

As Abbey's blood ran down her wrist and dropped onto the Tapestry to join the blood of the other women, a burst of golden light shot out of the cloth and set the Immortal threads humming. Blue bolts of energy rippled over the surface of the Tapestry as the panel hovered in the air. The magical effect was almost instantaneous. The frayed ends of the embroidered pictures healed themselves, pulling themselves into tightly woven pieces of art. The tattered edges of the Tapestry grew longer and stronger around themselves, sending a white light across the surface of the fabric. The light grew larger until it encompassed the Immortals, the area around the wooden table and the entire stack of panels under the oak tree. Within minutes, the whole section of the Faire became a ball of light, spilling warm radiance onto the entire party of Immortals.

Then, quickly the effect faded; the light, the humming and the chanting wound down into silence.

Immediately, Merlin transformed back into his human form and, with a quick laugh and nod, he disappeared. Eleanor had no idea where he was nor when he would take his turn in the Guardians' circle. His full strength had returned and with it, his power to dematerialize. Men. They never stayed.

"I am proud of how you handled yourself," Eleanor said to Livia. "And how you saved face for all of us here at the Bastille." The compliment stunned Livia for a moment.

"Thank you, Eleanor," she responded softly. After a pause, Livia yawned and stretched. "I'm going to bed. Goodnight."

They all bade her goodnight as Ruth gathered the last of the dishes. "Well," she sighed, "that day certainly was interesting."

ABBEY DIDN'T PLAN TO ENTER HIS ROOM, but some undeniable force seemed to draw her to his door, move her hand to the doorknob, and turn it. She stood for a moment on the threshold, listening to him breathing. She tiptoed to his bed and sat next to him.

No evidence of the stabbing remained. His skin lay smooth and untouched.

She gasped when his hand reached out and grabbed her.

"I...I thought you were asleep."

"Self-defense," he grinned. "Have you ever had five women and four dogs hovering over you before?"

"Yes, actually," she laughed. "It can be...overwhelming."

He nodded. "To say the least."

For a moment they locked eyes and stared at each other in the dim moonlight shining in through the window.

"Detective—"

"Abbey," he sighed. "I've seen you naked. Can you at least call me Matt?"

"I shouldn't be here. I'm sorry to bother you." She stood up.

"You're not bothering me." He smiled. "I...I have a...concern."

"Only one?"

He nodded "Well...let's start with one...what does this," he gestured to his side, "mean?" She paused while she collected her thoughts. "It means that you...a part of you at least...is Immortal. You carry Immortal blood. You have never noticed it before?"

He shrugged. "I don't get sick. Never have."

"Then you have your answer." She looked down on him and smiled. "Thank you, Detective, for saving me."

"I asked you to call me Matt."

She looked at him for a moment then shook her head. "Detective," her voice carried a fierceness within it that Mathers had never heard. "I appreciate what you have done for my family, what you have done for me, and what you have done for the Bastille."

"I hear a 'but' coming on," Mathers said.

She nodded. "But...I have a place in this house. I have a role to play in the keeping of the Tapestry. I have...a life to return to." She paused and looked at him with an emotionless expression. "I am a witch and a member of the Guild of Immortal Women. Do you understand what I am saying to you?"

He nodded.

"Sleep well, Detective."

He watched her walk out of the room and close the door behind her. She never looked back.

WHEN THE DOORBELL SOUNDED, LYNN JUMPED, startled by the loudness of it. She had psyched herself into a frenzy about this visit, barely sleeping all weekend as she rehearsed her speech in her head.

"I'm sorry to call so early, but I need to talk to you," she blurted as soon as the door opened.

"Miss Swanson," Eleanor said, keeping the door partially closed. "It is rather early for a social call."

"Good morning, dear!" The familiar sound of Ruth floated from behind Eleanor. "Perhaps you can join us for pancakes?"

"It will only take a second," Lynn stammered.

"I have a WONDERFUL buttermilk recipe!"

"I could give you a call tomorrow morning at the office," Eleanor said, pushing the door shut.

"I saw everything, Eleanor," Lynn said. Her voice sounded more sinister than she had hoped, but desperate times called for desperate measures.

"Yesterday. At the Faire. I…I needed to check in with the patients… they all scattered around the Faire grounds, you know…so on a whim I climbed a tree. I love climbing trees; even as a girl, I could climb higher than my brother—"

"You had a point, Miss Swanson?" Eleanor snapped.

Lynn nodded. "I could see the whole area. I saw over the crowd of people surrounding the Tapestry. At first, I *thought* it was a crowd of people, but…then I saw…things…people…coming in and out of the

Tapestry. I realized that they weren't a crowd surrounding the Tapestry, but a guard set there to hide the Tapestry." She looked directly into Eleanor's eyes. "Hide it from the public while you did…did whatever it was you all did when you sang and…that blood, though, was gross."

For a moment, nobody spoke. Eleanor stared at Lynn through narrowed eyes. "What did we do, pray tell, Miss Swanson?"

It all spilled out of Lynn despite her attempt to stop it, "I don't want to cause trouble, really. It's just that I really hate my job, I mean I *like* my job, the social work part of it, but I really—and I mean *REALLY* —hate my annoying job with a bunch of Nazis who tell me to punch in and punch out and oh, jeez, this sounded so much better in my head when I was thinking about it last night."

"How is this related to me, please, Miss Swanson?" Eleanor said flatly.

"Well…" Lynn stammered, "I was thinking…can I have a job here?"

"That's what I thought you'd say," Eleanor said, swinging the door open and motioning for Lynn to enter. "Dear," Eleanor smiled, "I wasn't born yesterday. Nor the last century. This kind of thing has happened before."

Lynn stood frozen at the front door. "I figured Abbey…her dreams…she's Joan of Arc, isn't she? And the plane dreams…drowning… somehow she's connected to…"

Eleanor ignored Lynn and gestured for the girl to enter. "The last time some wayward girl happened to pry her way into the Bastille was…"

"1910!" Ruth said, jumping up and down. "That delightful young girl with the poodle. I loved that poodle. What happened to it again?"

"Tomyris' dogs ate it," Eleanor said, pulling the catatonic Lynn into the foyer. "My personal secretary was the last girl's job. You shall have that one."

Ruth jumped up and down in glee. "Do you like pancakes, dear? If you prefer, I can make eggs, instead; I have apples, and some oranges for a nice sauce—"

ABBEY STOOD STARING AT THE TAPESTRY outside Mathers' room when Eleanor rounded the corner. "Good morning, Abbey dear."

"I was just checking on the detective," Abbey said, nodding to the closed door.

"We must investigate further, my dear," Eleanor sighed. "I would like to know very much from which branch of the family—"

"I fear I am pregnant," Abbey said quickly.

"I know."

"The child is Robert's."

"I know."

"I had hoped he lied when he... but..."

Eleanor held Abbey close and kissed her hair. "I know."

"I want a child, Eleanor. But not like this...I have been denied the power to select the father of my child." She shook her head and pulled back to look Eleanor in the eyes. "Have you ever wanted a baby and hated the fetus at the same time?"

"Oh, my love, have you ever heard the story of my three sons? Come, let us eat Ruth's pancakes—or maybe eggs—and I shall tell you of another surprise we have had this morning as well. It seems the Bastille has a new secretary."

"Aunt Eleanor," Abbey said, pulling to a stop. "There is one thing I should like to discuss before we see Aunt Ruth." She waited for Eleanor to halt before continuing. "Robert. How did he escape? We rolled off the table together, but when I hit the ground, he was gone. Did no one see him escape?"

Eleanor hugged her again and continued to walk. "My dear, Robert de Beaudricourt is a slippery creature. He has been eluding us for hundreds of years. He said he had an escape plan, did he not?"

JOSHUA TURNED UP THE VOLUME OF "GIMME SHELTER" and shoved the last bit of the Bavarian Crème donut in his mouth. He pulled out the keys to the limo and unlocked the door. Hell, since the two freaks he worked for didn't show up at the pickup location last night, he may as well take this baby on a road trip. He threw the bag of junk food onto the front seat—chips, pretzels and red licorice—and plopped down into the driver's seat. He pushed the button for the sunroof and it slid open with a slight hiss.

"Please close that blasted thing, I'm trying to sleep," the voice erupted from the back seat.

Joshua jumped out of the car, spilling his chocolate milk onto the pavement of the 7-11. "What the—"

"Good morning to you, too, Joshua," Robert said from the rear seat of the limo. "Have a good night?"

"Where the hell did you come from?" Joshua said, stepping away from the car.

"I was…delayed," Robert said, throwing his hand over his eyes. "I had to make sure I wasn't followed."

"Followed?"

"Never mind, my boy." Robert yawned and looked at his watch. "Oh, dear," he said, sitting up. "We need to get a move on."

"Move…what…what are you talking about, boss?"

"We have to go retrieve the Doctor, my thin-brained young friend," Robert said, slipping his shoes on. "He has been…visited by an old friend and we are going to get him back." He motioned for Joshua to get into the car.

Joshua got into the limo and started the engine. So much for the road trip. He cranked up the stereo and "Honky Tonk Woman" blared from the speakers. He turned the music down quickly. "Okay, where to, boss?"

"Just drive," Robert said. "And don't call me Boss."

He chuckled and rolled up the piece of Tapestry lying next to him and shoved it into the crevice of the seats, where it had been since he devised his escape plan. One could never tell when a quick escape was going to be necessary.

THE END